The Blackness

Also by Patrick C. Walsh

The Mac Maguire detective mysteries

The Body in the Boot

The Dead Squirrel

The Weeping Women

23 Cold Cases

Two Dogs

The Match of the Day Murders

The Chancer

The Tiger's Back

The Eight Bench Walk

Stories of the supernatural

13 Ghosts of Winter

The Black Vaults Experiment

All available in Amazon Books

Patrick C. Walsh

The Blackness

The fourth Mac Maguire mystery

Garden City Ink

A Garden City Ink ebook
www.gardencityink.com

ISBN 9781985017382

Cover art © Patrick S. Walsh 2016
Garden City Design

"All I want is blackness. Blackness and silence"
Sylvia Plath

For Mick for a thousand kindnesses

The Night Before

She was still fizzing as she climbed into the taxi. She'd been so looking forward to her Saturday night out but it had turned out to be something of a disaster. She was absolutely, one hundred percent, certain that it was all Julie's fault. Why did she have to tell her that when she knew it would only upset her? In her anger she even started wondering if she should drop Julie and get another best friend.

She told the driver to drop her near the Millhouse pub. She'd been intending to meet up with some friends from college and, perhaps, one friend in particular. However, as she climbed out of the taxi, she realised that she wouldn't be good company that night. She decided that she might as well go home. However, she couldn't go back while she was still feeling this angry, one look at her face and her mother would know. Her mother always worried when she and Julie had a falling out and she decided that she'd probably upset enough people for one night.

The evening was relatively warm so she sat on a nearby wall and thought for a while. Thankfully there was no-one around and the solitude helped to calm her down. It didn't take long for her to come to the conclusion that tonight's mess was as much her fault as Julie's, probably more so. Once she got angry that was that, she was always one hundred percent right and everyone else just had to be wrong.

She sighed. Why did she always have to have such a short fuse? The only anger she felt now was directed solely at herself.

She'd known Julie since they were four years old. She loved her friend and the last thing in the world she wanted was for anything to come between them, least of all a stupid boy. She reckoned that some of her mum's hot chocolate and a hug would put her right. She set off towards home in anticipation.

As she walked home, she resolved to ring her friend as soon as she got back. Perhaps Julie would drop in before she went to bed and they could make it up properly.

Her head was full of these thoughts as she made her way back down the familiar dark and empty streets. She took the short cut as she wanted to get home as quickly as possible. Unthinkingly she almost bumped into someone and fear ran though her for a moment. Then she relaxed.

'Hello,' she smiled at the figure in front of her. 'What are you doing here?'

A bright pain in her jaw was followed by blackness.

When she awoke, she was in complete darkness. She was naked and lying on the floor. She felt her jaw, it was very tender, and her tongue told her the corner of one of her front teeth had gone. She felt extremely woozy as though she'd drunk too many shots or something. She sat up and heard the rattle of a chain. Something was around her neck, a metal collar. The chain was attached to the collar. She followed the chain with her hands. It was attached to a solid metal ring screwed into a wall. To her horror she found that was chained up like a dog.

The room felt strange, the floor and walls were smooth and sort of soft. The darkness was so complete that she wondered if she'd gone blind. She screwed her knuckles into her eyes and saw colours.

What had happened to her? She couldn't help feeling that this must be a weird dream. Perhaps someone had put something in one of her drinks? She thought back. She remembered her argument with Julie and then going home early. The last thing she remembered was walking home, looking forward to being with her mum and hot chocolate and after that? She couldn't remember.

A surge of panic rose in her.

She shouted. There was no echo, the walls seemed to soak up the sound of her voice.

She shouted again. Nothing.

Since she'd been a child, she'd been afraid of the dark and the terrors that it might conceal. It was always there somewhere in her worst dreams. She prayed with all her might that this might just be a nightmare and that she'd wake up soon. She followed a wall until she came to a corner. She sat down in the corner and hugged herself.

She cried as she called for her mother.

'Mum, mum help me. Help me please.'

No-one heard her. Her words were swallowed up by the blackness.

Chapter One

First day missing

Mac had been having problems sleeping. After a couple of hours of tossing and turning he finally gave up and got out of bed. He sat up carefully and stood up even more carefully. The pain levels were just about bearable.

So here he was at five thirty on a Sunday morning making coffee and toast. Not that the fact it was Sunday really meant that much to him anymore. When he was working the week had a definite structure. He would look forward to the weekends and holidays but now, when he worked so little, he found that it was the workdays that he appreciated the most. He just wished he could get more of them. Work was definitely the best pain killer for him.

His wishes were answered when he heard a knock on the door just before seven o'clock.

It was Detective Constable Tommy Nugent.

On seeing his face Mac felt a sudden stab of fear.

'Is Bridget alright?' he asked urgently.

Tommy was also his only child's boyfriend. He looked a bit puzzled.

'Yes, she's fine, at least she was when I saw her yesterday morning. No, Dan Carter's sent me. We've got a case and he wanted me to ask if you could help. He told me to apologise for the early call but he said that it couldn't be more urgent.'

A case! Mac's spirits immediately rose.

'Come in. There's coffee in the kitchen. Give me fifteen minutes and I'll be with you.'

He was washed, shaved and dressed in a little less. He was so excited that he almost left the house without his crutch.

'How's the back?' Tommy asked as they both walked towards his car.

'Oh, you know...' Mac replied with a smile.

The truth was that the pain had been quite bad recently and that's why he'd been having problems sleeping. However, with a real case now in the offing, he wasn't going to admit this to anyone.

Five minutes later they were entering Letchworth Police Station. There were few people around. The sound of Mac's crutch hitting the floor echoed down the hallway. The team had a large room near the rear of the station on the ground floor. Desks and chairs were still stacked high along one wall. A good third of the remaining floor space was covered in plastic and cardboard boxes. The team were crowded around a whiteboard in front of which stood Detective Superintendent Dan Carter. Dan, although newly promoted, still looked exactly the same as he had the last time Mac had seen him, in his late thirties, rumpled and gruff. He always looked as if he needed a shave.

'Mac!' he shouted, 'Come and meet the rest of the team.'

'The rest of the team' were words that made Mac smile. This meant he was a part of the team and that there was work to be done.

'Mac, you already know Adil,' Mac shook his hand firmly.

DS Adil Thakkar was a short and stocky man in his thirties and he'd been Dan's sergeant when Mac had worked with the Bedfordshire detectives on his first ever case as a private detective. Mac had found out later that he was a prop forward and one of the stars of the British Police Rugby team.

'...and Andy Reid of course...'

They both smiled as they shook hands. Andy Reid had worked for Mac's murder team in London as a Detective Constable some time ago. He was now a

Detective Inspector with Hertfordshire Police and he'd allowed Mac to help him out with a couple of recent cases.

'...and DC Leigh Marston...'

Leigh gave Mac a quick hug. They'd recently worked together on a case that had become known as 'The Letchworth Poisoning'. Mac noticed that she'd had her hair done a bit differently. It suited her.

'...also, from Hertfordshire is DS Jo Thibonais...'

A large woman in her early forties gave him a very wide smile and a very firm handshake.

'Now for the Cambridgeshire contingent. This is DI Chris Skorupski...'

A very tall serious looking man with a shaven head offered a very large hand. His handshake was surprisingly gentle.

'...and this is DS Martina McEwan...'

A blonde woman in her forties waved at him from the other side of the crowd.

'...and finally, DC Gerry Dugdale,' Dan concluded.

Gerry nodded at Mac. Mac reckoned that he was in his late forties, his face was starting to get lined and his hair was beginning to grey at the sides.

Mac smiled back. He'd had a couple of coppers on his team who'd looked just like Gerry. They were still Detective Constables after many years in the police and quite happy to be so. After all, Mac thought, every army needs its foot soldiers as well as its generals.

'For those of you who haven't met him before, this is Mac Maguire.' Dan looked around the team. 'He'll be acting as a consultant to the team. I take it you've all heard of Mac?'

All of the team nodded and looked at Mac in unison.

'Let's cut to the chase then,' Dan said. 'Yesterday evening, around nine fifteen, Natasha Barker, who is just eighteen years old, had an argument with her friend Julie Waddington. They were in the Hen and

Chickens pub in Hitchin town centre. During the argument Natasha walked out on her friend who assumed that she'd gone to a pub near where they both live called The Millhouse. When Julie popped in to see Natasha at her house around eleven thirty, she was surprised to find that she wasn't there. Julie knew that the pub shuts at eleven. When she got to the Millhouse they were closing up and, although some of the staff knew Natasha, none of them could remember seeing her that evening. As she walked back Julie rang Corinne Obiah, the friend that Natasha said she was going to see. She confirmed that Natasha hadn't turned up at the pub. Julie and Mrs. Barker then spent the next hour or so calling everyone that Natasha knew. No-one had seen her. Mrs. Barker called us at twelve fifty five this morning to report her daughter missing.'

'She's not been gone that long though, has she?' Gerry pointed out. 'It's just a matter of hours really.'

'I know but if Natasha has been abducted or murdered then, the quicker we act, the better chance we have. According to her mother Natasha has never spent a night away from home other than when she was on holiday with her mother or having a sleepover at her friend Julie's. Natasha's father died when she was young and it seems that she and her mother are very close. Mrs. Barker was adamant that there was no way that Natasha would have stayed out all night without letting her know. So, while I'm still hoping that she has a secret boyfriend and that they've run off to Paris or something, I think that we have to assume the worst.'

Gerry nodded in agreement.

Dan continued, 'So that we don't waste any time, I've already gotten the ball rolling with forensics. They'll be visiting Natasha's house this morning to have a look around and get some DNA samples just in case. Now, I know that we originally had some time pencilled in to move into our new office and start discussing how best

7

we can organise the team but I'm afraid that we're being thrown in at the deep end with this one. For the duration of the investigation we'll work together in teams of two. So, it will be Chris and Martina, Andy and Leigh, Jo and Gerry, Mac and Tommy and Adil and myself.'

Tommy gave Mac the thumbs up. They would be working together again. Mac smiled back.

'This arrangement is just for now,' Dan said. 'I've tried to ensure that you're working with someone you know so you can hit the ground running except for Jo and Gerry, of course. However, I'm sure that you two will get to know each other quickly enough.'

Jo gave Gerry a hugely sceptical look.

Dan turned to the blank whiteboard.

'I've already spoken to Mrs. Barker earlier this morning to see if there was any news and to get a photo of Natasha. However, we still need to do a proper interview with her and with Julie Waddington. As they already know me it would probably be best if Adil and I did that. Andy and Leigh, can you come with us as well? We'll hopefully be able to get the names of Natasha's other friends. You'll need to go around them all and see if they know anything. Chris and Martina, can you start looking at any known sex offenders living in the area and follow that line of enquiry up? This will be your main area of responsibility during the investigation.'

Chris and Martina nodded.

'Mac and Tommy, Natasha must have at least tried to get to the Millhouse or even home, so can you see if you can track down any taxi drivers who may have seen her or given her a lift? Also see if you can track down every-one working at the Hen and Chickens pub in the town centre and also the Millhouse last night. They might have seen or heard something.'

Mac and Tommy nodded.

'That leaves Jo and Gerry. I'm sorry but I'm afraid that you've drawn the short straw. Firstly, can you organise the Family Liaison Officer for Mrs. Barker. Andy here informs me that there's a uniformed officer called Stella Ajunwa who's highly thought of, so try her first. Next, I need you to get onto all the local estate agents and see if they have a shop or property free that we can use for a while as an incident room. Try and get somewhere in the town as close to the Hen and Chickens pub as possible. You'll also need to find a way of moving everything across that we might need. Also arrange for some uniforms to help us with the house to house enquiries. Ring me when they're ready and I'll let you know where I want them to go. I want to have a look at the area in daylight first.'

Jo and Gerry looked at each other and glumly nodded.

Dan continued, 'Everyone, before you go can you make sure that you pull out any boxes that you need to go to the incident room and Jo will arrange for someone to get them over later. Essential stuff only though. You'll find photos of Natasha and all the other information we've got so far on that table over in the corner. Make sure that Jo has all of your mobile numbers, everything goes through her for now. She'll call you all when we're ready for a debriefing, hopefully sometime early this afternoon.'

The team all nodded.

'Okay, what are you all looking at me for? Come on, let's get going!' Dan urged.

Tommy got a clip board and loaded it with a copy of each piece of information and two photos. He passed it to Mac as they walked to the car. Dan had managed to get the home phone number of the landlord of the Hen and Chickens from Julie Waddington. Before he started the car, Tommy gave him a call. From what Mac could hear he didn't seem all that happy at being woken up this early on a Sunday morning. However, he agreed to meet them at the pub as soon as he could get there.

As they drove towards Hitchin town centre Mac studied Natasha's photo. It was a good headshot. She was smiling and, in the background, there was a Christmas tree with bright shiny red balls. She had black hair, cut a couple of inches above the shoulder, and large expressive eyes. Mac wouldn't have used the word 'pretty' to describe her, she was much more attractive than that anodyne word might suggest. She looked out at him as though issuing a challenge. It was the look of a young independent woman who didn't seem to be suffering from any lack of confidence. He looked at the photo for some time. He was certain he'd never seen this girl before but there was something familiar about her. Now what was it?

'So, what do you think?' Tommy asked.

Mac looked over at Tommy.

'Sorry, think about what?'

'Has she run off to Paris or somewhere as Dan suggested?'

Mac frowned.

'I very much doubt it.'

'You're that sure?'

'I have a daughter who loved her mother. When Bridget was at home, she always made sure her mother knew what she was doing, even when she was going to be a couple of hours late back from college. She knew her mother would be worried otherwise. No, I agree with Dan. I think that something's happened to Natasha.'

The pub was on Bancroft, one of Hitchin's busiest shopping streets. It looked like it had been an old coaching inn in a previous life. It had black and white timbers and a covered entrance that was big enough for a carriage to pass through. A sign hanging at the front had a picture of a brown hen followed by a line of yellow chicks.

Tommy tried the front door. It was locked. A side door opened just beyond the carriage entrance and a bald head stuck out. It then disappeared inside again. They walked up into the beer garden and through the open door.

The pub was a bit gloomy and smelt strongly of the night before. There were several crates of alcopops stacked on the floor behind the bar. The bald-headed man had obviously been replenishing the shelves.

'Good morning,' Mac said showing the man his warrant card.

'So, what's this all about then?' the bald man said somewhat defensively. 'It's not them down the road complaining about the bloody noise again, is it?'

'No, it's nothing like that,' Mac said. 'I take it you're the manager?'

'Yes, Bob Souter's the name. Listen it's not even eight o'clock yet and it's a Sunday morning. I wasn't planning on working this early but as I'm here I've got lots to do...'

'Were you working here last night?' Mac asked interrupting him.

'Of course, I was here all night. Why?'

Mac showed him the picture.

'Did you see this girl?'

He showed Bob the photo. He didn't look at it long.

'Yes, she comes in here quite a bit. What's her name, now? Starts with an 'N' I think, Natalie, no Natasha I think it is. She comes in with Julie.'

'You know Julie Waddington?'

'Yes, she worked here for a few weeks last Christmas when we were desperate for staff. She was a good worker too. I was hoping that she'd want a permanent job but she said that she wanted to finish college first...'

A sudden thought seemed to occur to the pub manager.

'Has something happened to Natasha?' he said looking concerned.

'We hope not but she seems to have gone missing,' Mac replied. 'She was here last night and left just after nine but she never made it home. Did you see her or notice anything unusual yesterday evening?'

'Well, I couldn't help noticing to be honest. She and Julie had a right up and downer.'

'What was it about?'

The manager shrugged.

'No idea. I could hear that they were arguing but, with the music and all, I couldn't hear what they were saying. Kelly will know though. She was serving at that end of the bar and she's friends with both of them.'

'How many staff did you have on last night?' Mac asked.

Bob counted them on his fingers.

'Besides me, six in all.'

'Can you phone them all and get them to come here right away.'

'I'm not sure that they'll like me calling them this early on a Sunday...'

Bob's words petered out as Mac gave him a stern look.

'Okay, I'll do that right away.'

'We'll be back in half an hour,' Mac said.

Tommy followed him out of the pub.

'So, where to next?'

'That taxi rank over the road. It's my guess that's where Natasha went next when she left the pub last night.'

There were two taxis waiting at the rank. Two men were sitting on the wing of the car at the front of the rank. Mac flashed his warrant card.

'What firms might have used this rank last night?'

The two drivers looked at each other and shrugged.

'Why do you want to know?' the stockier, balder driver asked.

Mac showed them Natasha's photo.

12

'This girl disappeared last night. We're looking for her.'

They both stood up, their body shape and demeanour had totally changed.

'Sorry but we only do days,' the bald driver said looking to his companion, a younger bearded man who nodded in agreement.

'The question was what firms use this rank on Saturday evenings?' Mac re-iterated.

'Just the usual, there's six local firms who mainly use the rank. Technically if someone dropped off from outside the area, London for instance, they could use the rank too but that doesn't happen often,' the bald driver said.

'Give me the names of the firms,' Mac said.

Tommy noted down the names.

'Is there anyone else who might use the rank?' Mac asked.

'We occasionally get a few blaggers,' the bearded man said.

'Unlicensed drivers you mean?'

'That's right,' the bald-headed driver replied. 'Now and again we get the odd driver who wants to make a few quid on a Saturday night without having the bother of paying for a plate or insurance.'

'What do you do?' Tommy asked.

'If we catch them at it?' the bald driver asked. 'We take the license plate and report them to you lot. It doesn't happen that often around here though.'

Mac asked for their names. They gave them and Tommy noted them down. Mac thanked them.

'So where to now?' Tommy asked.

'Well, we've got a little time and there's a coffee shop just down the road. Let's give the pub staff a chance to turn up.'

While they sat and drank their coffee, they found the addresses of the taxi firms on the internet and worked out the best way to cover them all. They decided to visit the first one on their way to the Millhouse.

They walked back into the pub by the beer garden entrance again. Mac counted them. Five staff and the manager were waiting for them. One was missing.

'Kelly's on her way,' Bob explained. 'I had a bit of trouble contacting her.'

The staff consisted of three young men and two girls, all in their early twenties. They looked tired and more than a little uneasy. Mac showed them Natasha's photo. Four out of the five confirmed that she'd been in the pub the night before but couldn't add anything beyond that. They'd just have to wait for Kelly.

She turned up a few minutes later struggling to catch her breath. She'd obviously been running.

'I take it that you're Kelly?' Mac asked.

She nodded but she couldn't get a word out.

'Please sit down and get your breath back,' Mac said.

Mac looked at her closely. She was a short girl but quite pretty with auburn hair that cascaded around her shoulders. She definitely didn't look eighteen but Mac supposed that she must be if she was working in a pub.

'Sorry,' she said apologetically. 'I had to run. There aren't any buses on a Sunday.'

'That's alright,' Mac said. 'I believe that you know this girl?'

He showed her the photo.

Kelly's face went pale and her eyes went wide.

'That's Nat!' she said. 'Bob said it was about a missing girl. Is it Nat that's gone missing?'

'By Nat do you mean Natasha Barker?'

She nodded.

'Yes, sorry, it's what everyone calls her.'

'Bob said that you know Natasha. Is that right?' Mac asked.

'Well, I know Julie better I suppose but yes, I know Nat.'

14

'What's she like?'

Kelly shrugged her shoulders.

'Like Nat. She's not like anyone else I've ever met if I'm being honest. Julie's known her forever and she's absolutely mad about her. I think you'd need to be to put up with her.'

'Why, is she difficult to get on with?' Mac asked.

'Oh no, nothing like that, she's really good fun but she's just got so much energy and she's always coming up with new ideas. I honestly don't think I'd be able keep up with her.'

'Is she the sort of girl who likes to take chances?' Mac asked.

'In what way?'

'For instance, going somewhere with people she didn't know that well.'

Kelly shook her head.

'Oh God no! I mean all the boys are after her but she'd have to know someone for ages before she'd even consider going out with them. I mean it took Adam Oakley six months and then she dumped him four weeks later. That's what they were arguing about last night.'

'Bob here said that Julie and Natasha had a big argument. You're saying it was about this Adam Oakley?' Mac asked.

'Yes, Julie started seeing him two weeks ago but it took her a while to get up the courage to tell Nat. She knew what would happen and it did. Nat absolutely exploded!'

'Why was she unhappy with her friend going out with this Adam?'

'Because he was a total shit, that's what Nat said,' Kelly replied. 'She didn't say why but she really slagged Julie off for going out with him. She said that she was so much better than that.'

'Did she say anything else?' Mac asked.

15

'Not really, a bit more in the same vein and then she stormed off. Julie was really upset.'

'Have you any idea where Natasha might have gone next?'

'Well, I heard her telling Julie that she was going to see Corinne somebody at the Millhouse,' Kelly replied.

'I take it that she'd have had to use a taxi to get there?'

'Oh yes, the buses only run until eight o'clock.'

'Did she say why she was going to meet this Corinne?' Mac asked.

'To meet a proper friend, she said. Julie got even more upset when she said that. A little later, when she'd calmed down, Julie said she was going to pop in and see Nat on her way home. She said that Nat would be okay now that she'd got it out of the system and they could talk about it properly.'

Mac was thoughtful for a while.

'If you heard her saying that she was going to the Millhouse then other people in the pub must have heard too. Is that right?'

'God yes, she said it loudly enough,' Kelly replied.

'Was there anyone in here last night who was taking an especial interest in Natasha?'

'What do you mean?' Kelly asked looking even more concerned.

'Well, looking at her I suppose, listening to what she was saying.'

'Well, half the pub was full of men and most of those were looking at her. I don't know what they see in her unless it was that dress that she was wearing. It was black with black lace all across the front and it fitted her fantastically well. It must have been a designer, it was absolutely gorgeous.'

'So, no-one in particular was hovering around her?' Mac persisted.

'No, not that I can remember.'

Mac turned to the other staff.

'Did any of you see anyone taking an interest in Natasha last night?'

They all looked at each other and shook their heads.

'Okay, you're free to go but you'll need to give us your names, addresses and contact details before you go,' Mac said.

'So, not much joy there,' Tommy said as they walked back to the car.

'No, let's hope we can at least find the driver who took her home. We need to get some traction in this case and the sooner the better.'

Chapter Two

The first taxi firm they visited told them that none of their drivers had picked up at the rank between nine and ten. They said that all their drivers were busy from eight until well after eleven just trying to keep up with the phone bookings that came in. It had been a busy night.

The manager of the Millhouse was hard at work when they arrived. While they waited for the staff to arrive Mac asked Tommy to drive along the route that Natasha had taken from the pub. They turned right at the traffic lights and drove down a long road that bordered a field on the right-hand side. Mac was surprised to see a cow looking back at him from the field. They must have passed twenty or thirty of them before they finally turned left. Then they turned left again and went back on themselves for quite a distance. Tommy pulled up outside the small block of flats where Natasha lived.

Mac got out his tablet and opened up a map of the area. They'd basically driven around three sides of a long, thin rectangle. Mac had Tommy drive back slowly but he saw no obvious shortcut. He made a mental note for later.

They then spent a fruitless half hour at the Millhouse interviewing the staff. Some of them had seen Natasha before and two of them knew her from college. No-one had seen her last night. Mac asked the manager to send last night's CCTV footage from the car park just in case although he wasn't at all hopeful.

The second and third taxi firms confirmed that none of their drivers were near the Bancroft rank between nine and ten. They too had been busy keeping up with phone bookings.

The fourth firm didn't seem to have an office. The address was that of a semi-detached house just off St. Michaels Road. No-one was in.

They had more luck with the last two firms. They got the names and contact details of two drivers who had picked up a fare from the rank between nine and ten. Mac rang the driver who lived nearest.

The phone rang for some time before it was answered.

'Maureen, you'd better have a bloody good reason for waking me up this early,' a gruff voice said angrily.

'This isn't Maureen. This is the police and we need to speak with you,' Mac said. 'I've got your address and we'd like to come around right now if that's okay.'

'Why, what's all this about?'

'I'll tell you when we get there if that's okay.'

The line went silent for a moment.

'It's....it's not Maureen is it? She's alright, isn't she?'

'No, it's nothing to do with Maureen,' Mac replied. 'We'll see you in five minutes.'

The driver, John Davis, lived in a terraced house situated halfway down Verulam Road.

An unshaven, pot-bellied man in a dressing gown opened the door. He didn't say anything but gestured for them to follow him inside. They went into a living room that looked more like a storage space. It was half full of taped up boxes stacked unevenly on top of one another. The sofa looked like it was broken and the coffee table was dusty. The man reappeared with a pint-sized mug of tea in his hand.

'Sorry but I don't use this room much. Sit down.'

Mac looked at the broken sofa and thought of his back.

'I'd sooner stand up if you don't mind.'

'Suit yourself,' the taxi driver replied as he sat down on the only serviceable chair in the room.

'Have you just moved in?' Mac asked.

'Eighteen months ago. I just haven't got around to unpacking things yet.'

'A divorce was it?'

The man nodded glumly.

'She took me to the cleaners the cow did. It was her that opened her legs first too,' he said with real bitterness.

'Yet you still seemed concerned that something might have happened to her?' Mac pointed out.

'Well,' he said, rubbing his scalp hard with his free hand, 'I suppose I still feel something for her but God knows why. Anyway, if it isn't about Maureen what is it about?'

'You picked up a fare last night from the rank on Bancroft around nine thirty. Do you remember?'

His face crinkled with the mental effort it took.

'Oh yes, I remember. We were flying last night, one job after another, I love it when it's like that. Then around nine thirty we hit a bit of a dead spot for some reason. I'd just dropped in Bancroft so I thought I might as well call on the rank until something came up.'

He stopped to take a huge gulp of tea.

'I was only there for a few minutes when I got a fare. She was going to the Purwell.'

Mac showed him Natasha's photo.

'Was this your fare?'

He only needed a quick look.

'No,' he said with a confirmed shake of the head. 'The fare was in her fifties, ugly too. That one's a bit of a looker, I'd have remembered her.'

Mac wondered why any woman in her right mind would want to divorce such a man as this.

'Do you remember where you dropped her?'

'Yes, it was on Fairfield, one of those houses opposite the school.'

'Did you see any other driver pick up a fare that might have been Natasha?' Mac asked hopefully.

'Sorry, no. I was the only one on rank at the time.'

Mac thanked him and left. He was glad to leave the man and his house behind.

The door of the fourth house they tried on Fairfield Way was opened by a woman in her fifties. She confirmed that she got a taxi back from the rank on Bancroft the night before. She described the driver to a T.

'He was a fat slob. He'd have reminded me of Homer Simpson except Homer's much more handsome.'

'So that definitely rules Mr. Davis out then,' Tommy said as they walked back to the car.

'It would appear so. Let's try the other one then,' Mac said.

Tommy rang the number. The taxi driver, a Mr. Tony Hamilton, was up and was happy for them to visit him at home straight away.

Mr. Hamilton lived in a little bungalow on Whitehill Road. It was small, neat and freshly painted. The house inside was just as neat. A short man in his late fifties with his hair already greying led Mac and Tommy into the living room. A plump woman of around the same age was sitting in an armchair. She flashed them a smile.

'Please sit down,' Mr. Hamilton said as he gestured towards a new and comfortable looking sofa. 'I take it that you don't mind if my wife stays where she is.'

'No, no problem at all,' Mac replied sitting down with some gratitude. 'Your firm say that you picked up a fare from the rank in Bancroft last night around nine forty. Can you confirm that?'

'Oh yes, I remember him well. He'd had quite a lot to drink but he was happy with it. Not like some of them who get a bit fractious when they've had a few.'

The use of the word 'fractious' got Mac's attention. He looked around the room. In the corner there was a large bookcase. He could see some of the titles from where he sat, The Iliad, To Kill a Mockingbird, The Catcher in the Rye and quite a few by Dickens and Shakespeare.

'Where did you drop this man off?' Mac asked.

'On the Bedford Road, not far from the Rugby Club.'

He even remembered the number.

'Did you pick up anyone else after that?' Mac asked.

'No, that was my last job. I don't like working after ten, unless the firm's absolutely desperate that is.'

'How long were you on rank before you picked up this man?'

'I'm not sure if I'm honest. Five, ten minutes perhaps.'

Mac paused for a moment. That might mean that he arrived only ten minutes or so after Natasha left the pub.

'And you're sure that you never saw anyone when you pulled into the rank? There was no-one was hanging about nearby and no cars pulled off as you came in?'

Tony Hamilton shook his head.

'No, it was totally empty.'

It looked like Tony Hamilton only missed Natasha by a few minutes at most. Either that or he was lying.

'How long have you been working on the taxis?'

'Just over eighteen months now.'

'And what did you do before that?' Mac asked.

'I was an English teacher. I retired two years ago but I got fed up with it quite quickly. I only do the taxis part time, three or four hours a day during the week, and some Saturdays. They call me up when they're really busy. It keeps me going and the extra money doesn't hurt.'

He looked from Mac to Tommy.

'Can you tell me what this is about?'

Mac showed him Natasha's photo.

'This girl has gone missing. We think that she caught a taxi at the rank in Bancroft after having an argument with her friend. We're trying to find out where she went next.'

His eyes widened as he looked at the photo. He showed it to his wife. Her hand went to her mouth.

'That's Natasha Barker!' she exclaimed, sitting up.

'How do you know her?' Mac asked.

'We used to teach her,' the woman replied.

'And your name is?'

'Carol Hamilton, Tony and I both worked at the same school. Natasha was in both of our classes; he taught her English and I taught her Art and Design. She's missing you say?'

'Yes, she left her friend at around nine twenty last night and she hasn't been seen since,' Mac replied. 'Is there anything you can tell me that might help?'

The Hamiltons looked at each other.

'I'm not sure,' Carol said. 'When you said 'friend' was that Julie Waddington?'

'Yes, that's right. How did you guess?'

'It wasn't hard,' she replied, 'those two were always inseparable. Oh God, her poor mother! What must she be feeling?'

'What can you tell me about Natasha?' Mac asked.

'Not much from my side,' Tony Hamilton replied with a shake of his head. 'She clearly wasn't all that interested in English. She did just enough to scrape the necessary GCSE so she could go to college but that's as far as her interest went. Carol knew her better though, didn't you love?'

Carol nodded.

'She loved design, especially fashion design. She used to make her own clothes and everything. I thought she was really gifted. She was definitely the best student I've ever taught. I thought that she'd really go far and now this.'

'Is that what she was doing at college, design?'

'Yes, I remember looking at the brochure with her. She opted for Fashion and Textiles. I know one of the tutors there and she said she was head and shoulders above everyone else on the course. She used to joke about how we should get Natasha's autograph now as it would be worth money before very long.'

Mac asked Tony again if he'd seen any other drivers at the rank but, once again, he confirmed that he'd been the only one.

Outside Tommy said, 'It's strange that they should know Natasha. That's quite a bit of a coincidence isn't it?'

'Well, coincidences do happen but yes, I think we should keep the Hamiltons in mind none the less.'

They knocked on the door at the address on the Bedford Road that Mr. Hamilton had supplied. It took three or four minutes for the door to open. The man who opened the door was half asleep and was clearly suffering from a giant hangover. He clung on to the door for support. The door was green and matched his complexion.

Mac showed him his warrant card.

'Did you get a taxi home last night?' Mac asked.

The man shook his head.

'No idea,' he replied tersely.

He was falling back to sleep while still standing up.

'Do you remember what happened last night at all?'

The man opened his eyes and shrugged his shoulders.

'What day is it?' he asked.

'Sunday.'

The man thought on this for quite a while.

'So yesterday was Saturday?'

'That's right,' Mac confirmed.

The man looked really puzzled.

'Don't remember Saturday. Did we really have one?'

Mac decided to give up. He asked the man for his name. It took him quite a while to remember.

'Go on, get back to bed,' Mac said.

The man took him at his word and shut the door.

'We can always come back later,' Tommy said.

'I doubt he'll remember much even when he sobers up.'

'So, it looks like we've drawn a blank.'

'Possibly but we've still got one more to try,' Mac said. 'Let's go back to St. Michael's Road and see if anyone's in.'

They were lucky this time. The door was answered by a man in his late forties. He was unshaven, had long lank hair and jowls.

Mac showed him his warrant card.

'We called earlier but no-one was in.'

'I was in bed, I'm a deep sleeper. What's this about?' the man asked brusquely.

Mac thought that the man looked more than a little nervous. In fact, he was beginning to sweat a little. Mac was getting interested.

'And your name is?'

'It's Stuart...Ogilvy.'

Mac noticed a slight hesitation before he said his surname. The accent was northern, from Yorkshire Mac thought.

'Mr. Ogilvy, we think that a taxi driver picked this girl up at the Bancroft rank last night. We need to know where she went next.'

Tommy showed him Natasha's photo. The taxi driver gave it the briefest of glances.

'No, I've never seen her before,' he said with absolute certainty.

He'd recognised her though. Mac was sure of that.

'Are you sure?' Mac said giving him another chance.

'Yes, I'm sure. There's nothing wrong with my memory,' he replied testily.

'How many other drivers do you have?'

'Just me and one other. I work nights and he works days. Is that it now? I need to get back to bed.'

'So, what did you make of him?' Tommy asked as they walked back to the car.

'He's lying,' Mac said bluntly. 'He recognised Natasha and he's hiding something. Come on, we need to get back to the station as soon as possible.'

He went straight to where Chris and Martina were working.

'Have you found anything yet?' Mac asked.

They shook their heads in unison. Mac told them out his meeting with Mr. Ogilvy.

'Can you find out if there's anyone on the Sex Offender's Register who's absconded or who has an outstanding warrant? He'll be from Yorkshire, in his forties and his first name is probably Stuart. If you can get some photos then we should be able to identify him easily enough.'

'We'll have a look on the database. I'll let you know if we come up with anything,' Chris said.

Tommy brought him a coffee.

'Thanks,' Mac said as he gratefully accepted the steaming paper cup.

'So, you're sure that Ogilvy isn't his real name?' Tommy asked.

'Yes, fairly sure,' Mac replied. 'He said his first name quickly enough but there was that slight hesitation before he said 'Ogilvy'. He had to think about it.'

'So, what do we do now?' Tommy asked.

'We wait,' Mac replied. 'There's something wrong with our Mr. Ogilvy, I'm sure of it. I want to know what it is.'

Chapter Three

'Mac we've found something,' Martina shouted over at him.

A sharp pain hit him as he stood up but he ignored it. He was hobbling by the time he made Martina's desk some ten feet away.

'What have you got?' Mac asked excitedly.

'These three more or less fit the bill.'

She lay down three print offs. There was a summary of their offences and a photograph. Mac pointed at the middle one.

'That's him!' he said with certainty.

He handed the sheet to Tommy.

'That's definitely him alright.' Tommy read from the charge sheet. 'Stuart Braithewaite, he's been on the offender's register for fifteen years. He served eight years for indecent assault on two eight year old girls and there's a warrant out for him on a charge of making indecent images involving a nine year old girl in Driffield, Yorkshire.'

'I knew there was something!' Mac exclaimed.

'Do you think that he's got anything to do with Natasha's disappearance?' Tommy asked.

'Well, she's probably a bit old for him but who knows. We need to go have a look around his house and, as he has an outstanding warrant for his arrest, we won't even need to hang about for any paperwork.'

Mac turned to Chris and Martina.

'Chris, fancy a field trip? I hope so as you'll be the officer in charge.'

Chris and Martina didn't seem too heartbroken at being dragged away from their computers.

Less than half an hour later Mac and Tommy were once again standing outside Stuart Braithwaite's door except this time they were accompanied by Chris and

Martina and four uniforms belonging to the Support Unit. One of the Support Unit rang the bell and then banged loudly on the door.

'Police, Mr. Braithewaite. Please open the door,' Chris shouted several times.

When no-one answered Chris gave the nod and a member of the Unit battered it open with an Enforcer.

'Mr. Braithewaite, it's the police. Are you here?' Chris shouted.

There was no answer.

'Come on let's search the place,' Chris said. 'Martina and I will take two of the entry team and look upstairs. Mac and Tommy, can you look downstairs?' Chris asked. 'Oh, and be careful Mac and stay well behind the Support Unit, I don't want to get into any trouble with Dan.'

Mac nodded. Obviously, Dan had given instructions to the team about him. He hated being wrapped up in cotton wool but he knew Chris was right.

The hallway they were standing in was grubby and hadn't been decorated for quite a while. One of the entry team opened the door into a living room that was far worse. Stacks of flattened down cardboard boxes took up most of the room. In the space that was left a broken-down sofa sat in front of a coffee table that had seen much better days, in fact one of its legs was missing and four bricks served in its place. A small TV stood in the corner. It was old and dusty.

The kitchen was no better. The cupboards were a beige colour and the work surfaces were granite and had probably been quite expensive when they were first fitted. Now they were grimy and the stainless-steel sink was brown and discoloured and full of cups and plates, some of which were actually blue with mould.

'The upstairs stinks too!' Martina said with a grimace when she joined them.

'No luck then?' Mac asked.

'He's not upstairs but it might be worth checking out there,' Chris replied, pointing towards the overgrown garden. 'It's hard to see from here but from upstairs you can see that there's a brick building right down the bottom of the garden. It must be a garage or something. Come on, let's go and have a look.'

There was a visible path through the waist high grass. The Support Team went first followed by Chris, Tommy and then Martina. Mac went last and took it slowly, making sure he looked where he was walking. The building was bigger than Mac had expected and had probably been some sort of workshop in a former life rather than somewhere to park a car. It had a set of small windows all of which had been blacked out. They stood for a moment and listened.

It was still and silent for a minute or so but then they all distinctly heard a girl scream. No order was necessary. The Support Unit had the door open in seconds and they all flooded into the building.

A man sat in an armchair. He looked up at them in horror, his face turning a deathly white. It was Stuart Braithewaite. His trousers were around his ankles and they could all see his penis which was now rapidly shrinking. The scream had come from the biggest flat screen TV Mac had ever seen. Two naked men were doing unspeakable things to a young girl, a very young girl.

'Get that off now,' Chris said to one of the Support Team. He turned towards Braithewaite. 'I think we'd all feel more comfortable if you could get those trousers back into their normal position.'

Once he'd secured his trousers, which took some time as he nervously fumbled with the buttons and the zip, Chris informed him that he was under arrest.

Two of the Support Team took him away while the detectives had a look around the building. They were careful not to touch anything. There were racks and racks full of DVDs and even video cassettes. A work bench in the corner had a laptop and a stack of padded envelopes with names and addresses on.

'There's no need to wonder what they contain,' Tommy said.

'As it's your catch, do you and Tommy want to interview Braithewaite?'

'Yes, that would be great. Thanks Chris,' Mac said.

'No problem. Martina and I'll go and talk to Child Protection and let them know what we've found,' Chris replied. He turned and looked at the stacks of DVDs and addressed envelopes. 'I guess that we might just make their day.'

Chris asked two of the uniformed officers to stay and stand guard.

They'd left the taxi driver to stew in an interview room. He visibly jumped when Mac and Tommy entered the room. Mac sat and looked at Stuart Braithewaite for some time. He was scared and getting more scared by the minute.

'They're not mine, those DVDs they....they were there when I moved in. I was just looking that's all,' he said, desperation written large on his face.

He looked up at Mac and Tommy and only got stony stares in return.

'Honestly,' he added lamely.

'And I suppose the flat screen TV was handily left there as well,' Mac replied. 'Anyway, I'm not interested in that just now. Someone else will be coming along later to ask you some questions about your taste in videos.'

Mac showed him the photograph of Natasha again.

'Did you pick this girl up last night at the rank on Bancroft?'

He wearily nodded his head.

'Yes, around nine twenty. I didn't do anything with her though, I mean she's not...'

He stopped mid-sentence.

'She's not your type, I know,' Mac said. 'Now, if she'd been seven of eight years younger, I'd bet that you'd have definitely been interested. Where did you drop her?'

'Outside the Millhouse.'

'Are you sure?' Mac asked.

'Yes, I'm sure.'

'Where exactly did you drop her? Was it in the car park?'

'No, on the main road. There wasn't that much traffic.'

'Did you actually see her go into the pub?' Mac asked.

'No, I needed to get on to my next job so, as soon as she got out, I drove off.'

'How did she seem?'

The taxi driver shrugged.

'She looked a bit upset when she got in but she seemed okay when I dropped her off.'

'Did you see any other drivers at the rank when you picked up Natasha?'

Braithewaite shrugged.

'No idea, I wasn't really paying attention.'

Mac looked at Stuart Braithewaite for some time. He started to squirm.

'Why didn't you tell us this when we first asked you?'

He shrugged.

'I was afraid that you'd think I was responsible for her going missing and start poking about.'

Mac stood up.

'If you'd told us the truth straight away then we might have left it at that but no, you had to lie. Well I guess you'll have plenty of time to think that one over.'

Mac ended the interview.

In the hallway Tommy asked 'Do you think he's told us the truth?'

'Unfortunately, yes, but it's still a result, isn't it? Another monster off the streets and, if those addresses on the envelopes belong to other paedophiles then you never know, Child Protection might get a really nice haul.'

Mac's stomach clock had just gone off. He looked at his watch. It was already four o'clock.

'I desperately need some food,' Mac said. 'How about you?'

'Now that you mention it, I'm starving,' Tommy replied.

'Come on, I always think better on a full stomach.'

At the Magnets Mac opted for the large Sunday lunch. It seemed a long time since breakfast. Tommy had the double burger.

'So, what now?' Tommy asked while they waited for their food.

Mac put his coffee down and shrugged.

'We just keep chipping away at the case. That's all we can do, it's all we can ever do. We'll find that breakthrough sooner or later. I just hope it's sooner though.'

'Do you think that she's still alive?'

'Natasha?' Mac shook his head. 'Having seen too many cases like this I've learnt not to have too much hope. You always think that there might be a chance that the victim is being held prisoner or something but invariably it's always a body that we find.'

The food arrived and they both ate in silence.

Mac had just polished off his last Yorkshire pudding when his phone rang.

Tommy listened but all he heard Mac say was 'Thanks Jo, we'll be there.'

'They're getting the incident room set up in a shop that's up for sale on Bancroft. Dan wants us there in half an hour for a catch up.'

As they climbed into the car Mac suggested that they should go down the Stotfold Road as there would be less traffic.

'You'll have to show me,' Tommy said as they pulled off. 'I'm still finding my way around.'

'Have you had any luck with finding a flat yet?'

'No, I'm still looking unfortunately. I'm already getting fed up with having to come in from Luton every day.'

As they turned left at the Gardener's Arms Tommy heard Mac groan.

'Are you alright?' he asked with some concern.

'God, I hate this road now,' Mac exclaimed.

Tommy couldn't see anything untoward.

'Look at all the forty mile an hour signs and here's the hill...'

All of a sudden, they found that they were at the top of a steep hill. Hitchin was spread out below them to the right. Tommy had to brake hard on the way down to keep within the speed limit. At the bottom of the hill a set of traffic lights suddenly turned red.

'And these bloody lights, they always turn red when you get close but nothing ever comes out.'

Mac's last words were almost drowned out by the growl of three very large earth movers as they passed by carrying soil from the massive earthworks being carved into the hillside.

'Well, almost never,' he corrected himself.

He felt the need to explain.

'I used to love driving down that hill, just letting the car coast to seventy. It reminds me very much of a hill in Birmingham near where I used to live. When I was a kid, we used to freewheel our bikes down it. We nearly came a cropper quite a few times but it was so exciting. For some reason having to crawl down it at forty really annoys the hell out of me.' He glanced over at Tommy. 'It's silly I know...'

'What are they doing there?' Tommy asked as they passed a block of portacabins that was three storeys high.

'They're building a new rail link on the Cambridge line. Apparently, there was some sort of bottleneck at

Hitchin. They've been at it for quite a few months now and I don't think it's going to end anytime soon.'

They got stuck in the traffic on the Cambridge Road anyway. It was ten past five when they pulled up outside the shop. Mac could see Jo and Gerry filling the window full of 'Have you seen this girl?' flyers. Natasha's face looked out at him many times and again he had that little tickle at the back of his brain. What was it? Something like this had happened to him before and it had turned out to be from an old case of his. He made a mental note to send a copy of the photo to his old sergeant to check out just in case.

Dan and the rest of the team were all there when they entered the shop. Desks and phones had already been installed as well as copiers and other office necessities. Two men were working in the corner.

Dan saw Mac looking at the men.

'They're setting up the secure wireless router for the computers,' Dan explained. 'Okay now we're all here I want us all to present what we've found and Jo will write down any salient points on the white board. I'll start if that's okay. Adil and I interviewed Mrs. Barker first. She was obviously very upset and unfortunately couldn't add anything to what we already know. The Family Liaison Officer, Stella Ajunwa, confirmed that there's still been no contact from Natasha. We spent more time with Julie Waddington though. She and her mother are keeping Mrs. Barker company while she waits for news. Julie told us that the row in the pub was about a boy called Adam Oakley. He's an ex-boyfriend of Natasha's who Julie had started going out with and Natasha didn't take the news well. She also gave us a long list of people who she says are friends of Natasha's. Andy and Leigh have been working their way through them but they're going to need some help. I'll talk more about this when everyone's finished. Okay, Andy and Leigh.'

They both stood up and took their place by the white board which was still blank.

'Unfortunately, Natasha seemed to know quite a lot of people mostly through school and college,' Andy said. 'We managed to interview seven of them and, so far, we've drawn a total blank. We interviewed this Adam Oakley first and Natasha's disappearance was all news to him or so he said.'

'You sound a little doubtful,' Dan said.

'Yes, for some reason I thought he didn't quite ring true,' Andy replied. 'I think that we should definitely keep him in mind. However, everyone we spoke to confirmed that it would have been totally out of character for Natasha to disappear without informing her mother. One of them, a college friend called Wanda O'Leary, told us that she's been working hard on a fashion project that she's supposed to be presenting this week. She said that Natasha was very excited about it as some people were coming down from London to view her work, another reason for her not to go missing. Anyway, we've still got another thirty or so of her friends to interview so any help would be appreciated.'

'Okay, next up Mac and Tommy who I believe have had a busy day,' Dan said smiling.

Mac and Tommy stood up.

'We started at the Hen and Chickens where a barmaid called Kelly Harris confirmed the fact that Julie and Natasha had a row and that it was about Julie going out with this Adam Oakley. Most of the bar staff saw Natasha at the pub but couldn't remember anyone taking an especial interest in her. Unfortunately, Natasha told Julie in a very loud voice that she was going to the Millhouse, so anyone in the pub might have known where she was heading. The taxi driver confirmed that he dropped her at the Millhouse but he didn't see her actually go in. No-one at the Millhouse remembers seeing her and some of the bar staff there knew her from college. There was also something of a coincidence, if that's what it was. One of the taxi drivers who also picked up at the rank in Bancroft is called Tony Hamilton. The punter he claimed he picked up there was severely hungover when we saw him so it's unlikely that he'll be able to confirm Mr. Hamilton's story. Mr. Hamilton also said that it was his last job of the night so he's not got much of an alibi. Now, he's a retired teacher and he knew Natasha, in fact he taught her English. We also spoke to his wife Carol, who is another retired teacher, and she taught Natasha Art and Design at the same school. They both appeared to be above board but it's still a bit of a coincidence.'

Mac and Tommy sat down.

'Yes, and one worth following up,' Dan said. 'Now I'm sure that you're all aware that Mac and Tommy, ably assisted by Chris and Martina, have also been responsible for taking a major weirdo off the streets. I had a very nice message from Child Protection an hour ago and they were very pleased indeed. As well as a ton of evidence found in the outbuilding, they've got a load of names from a laptop found there. Luckily, Mr. Braithewaite wasn't too hot on computer security and he just kept them on a Word document. So well done all of you. You haven't done the reputation of this unit any harm, believe me. Okay, Chris and Martina.'

Chris stood up.

'We've been going through the Sex Offenders Register for any likely suspects but we've found nothing definite as yet. We're just looking at the Three Counties area at the moment but, if we don't get anything soon, we'll expand the search to include London, Essex and Buckinghamshire too.'

Chris sat down.

'Jo and Gerry, have you got anything to add?' Dan asked.

'I'll just be glad to start doing some proper police work,' Gerry muttered grumpily.

'Me too,' Jo chimed in.

'You'll get your chance starting in about ten minutes. Thanks though for helping to get everything set up here. You've done a good job.' Dan's face turned serious. 'I'm going to ask you to carry on for another few hours and I don't need to tell you how important an early lead can be. However, we may be in this for the long run so pace yourself, make sure you get enough sleep and eat regularly. We may be at this for a while.'

He thinks she's dead too, Mac thought.

'Okay, if you see Andy, he'll supply you with the names and addresses of some of Natasha's friends. He'll give you four each. Do the interviews and then go home and get some sleep. I want you back here at seven o'clock sharp. Coffee and Danishes will be available here every morning so we can get on with it straight away. Any questions?'

'What about her phone?' Jo asked. 'Has there been any activity?'

Dan shook his head.

'I've got an expert monitoring it but the phone appears to be dead. We'd be able to get a location if it was live so we suspect that her phone may have been destroyed. By the way, the expert I mentioned will be joining us on attachment for this case tomorrow and I'll introduce him then. Right, I think that Andy and Leigh have been good enough to split the names and addresses and put them on separate sheets of paper. If you find anything ring Jo immediately and she'll ensure that everyone else gets the message too. Otherwise I'll see you all here tomorrow morning. Best of luck everyone.'

Leigh gave Mac a sheet with four names and addresses.

'We've given you Corinne Obiah as you've already interviewed the staff at the Millhouse.'

'Thanks.'

37

He thought that this was very bright of Andy and Leigh, otherwise he'd have had to ask.

'Come on Tommy, let's try Corinne first and see what she has to say.'

Chapter Four

They drove back to the Purwell estate and stopped outside a house in Bradley's Corner. Like all the others it was a small brick sixties ex-council house and, like all the others, it was quite neat and tidy.

A young girl with huge dark eyes partially opened the door. They could only see her head peeking around the edge.

'Is Corinne in?' Mac asked.

The girl just gave them a solemn look.

Mac showed her his warrant card.

'Can you tell her that it's the police. We need to speak to her.'

She gave them another solemn look and then shut the door.

A few minutes later a teenaged version of the girl opened it again. She looked no less solemn though.

'I'm Corinne Obiah. I take it that it's me you want to talk to?' she said.

'Is there somewhere we can talk?' Mac asked.

'The living room.'

She led them into a small room that contained two two-seater sofas and a large TV. A box of tissues was open on the coffee table and a number of them lay crumpled up on the table top.

'There's still no word?' she asked once they'd all sat down.

'I'm sorry no,' Mac replied. 'Do you want anyone to join us, your mother or father?'

'Dad left years ago and Mum's at work, she's a nurse. There's just me and my little sister here.'

'Okay. What can you tell us about Natasha?'

'I met her when we both joined the course...'

'That's the Fashion and Textiles course at the college?'

Corinne nodded.

'We got on straight away. God she was so much fun...'

She stopped herself mid-sentence and gave Mac a bleak look.

'She is so much fun I meant, I mean she's not dead or anything...is she?' she said, looking fearfully at Mac and Tommy's faces for confirmation.

'I'm afraid we can't say anything for certain at the moment,' Mac said.

Corinne's bottom lip started trembling. Mac knew he'd need to move fast or she'd be in tears.

'How do Natasha and Julie usually get on?'

'Great mostly but, when they fight, you'd better watch out. They're like sisters really, I mean Nat and me are good friends but Julie and her are just so close. They even finish each other's sentences, it's like they're telepathic or something.'

'Why did Natasha say that she might meet you in the Millhouse when she was with Julie in town?'

'She said that if it was a bit slow in town she might try and persuade Julie to go back to the Millhouse around ten o'clock,' she said as she removed a tissue from the box and blew her nose.

'Were you there by yourself?'

'Oh no. There was a gang of us, about eight I think, all from the college.'

'Is it possible that she could have come in without you noticing?' Mac asked.

She shook her head with certainty.

'Jonny Aldis was with us and, believe me, he'd have noticed if she'd have come in. He was looking out for her all night.'

'Why is that?' Mac asked.

'Because he's mad about her that's why,' Corinne replied. 'He's a bit shy but he's been helping Nat with her project and anyone can see that he fancies her. I felt that she was warming to him a bit too. I thought that might have been the real reason why she wanted to drop by the pub last night.'

'What time did Jonny leave the Millhouse?'

'He was still there when I left, it must have been well gone eleven. He was still hanging around in case Nat turned up, I'd guess.'

'Do you know where he lives?' Mac asked.

'Yes, he lives not far from here on Purwell Lane,' she said before giving him the house number.

'That's the road with the field on one side?'

'Yes, that's right,' she confirmed.

'Tell me, how do you know his address?'

'We've been around to his house a couple of times during the college lunch break. His mum's quite nice and she does us all sandwiches.'

'Why would she do that?' Mac asked.

Corinne thought for a while.

'Well, Jonny's a bit shy as I said. I guess that his mum was just happy that he'd made some friends.'

Mac thought on this, a boy who was a bit of a loner who had a fixation on a girl. It was sometimes a recipe for tragedy.

'Would you say that Jonny's liking for Natasha was, well, normal shall we say?'

Corinne looked puzzled for a moment until Mac's meaning dawned on her.

'You don't think that Jonny had anything to do with Nat's disappearance, do you?' She thought about it for a moment and then shook her head vigorously. 'No, I can't believe that. Jonny's one of the sweetest boys I've ever met. I wished he fancied me to be honest, he wouldn't have had to chase so hard. No not Jonny, I can't believe that he'd ever harm Nat.'

Despite her protestations Jonny's house was definitely going to be Mac's next call.

'Is there anything else you can tell us that might help?' Mac asked at the end.

'I'm sorry, I really wish there was,' she replied as a single tear drop ran down her face.

Mac got Tommy to give her a card, just in case.

They'd all stood up when Mac remembered something, the three sides of the rectangle.

Mac let her wipe her face with a tissue before he asked, 'By the way is there some sort of short cut that you can take to Natasha's block of flats from Purwell Lane?'

'Yes, there's an entryway just a couple of doors up from Jonny's house. It takes you in between the houses and into the car park that belongs to the old people's home. You walk up the path past the home and it brings you straight to where Natasha lives.'

The address Corinne had given him proved to be that of a very large bungalow. Mrs. Aldis opened the door a split second after Mac rang the bell.

'Jonny where... Oh! Who are you?' a woman in her late thirties asked with some surprise.

Mac showed her his warrant card.

'Is this about Natasha?' she asked.

'Yes, we'd like to speak to your son Jonny if that's alright?'

'Well, it would be alright but he's not here I'm afraid.'

'Can we come in?' Mac asked.

She showed them into a tastefully furnished living room with a very comfortable looking sofa. He was glad to take the weight off his feet for a while.

'Would you like some tea or coffee?' she asked.

They both asked for coffee.

'So, what do you think? Are we looking at this Jonny?' Tommy asked in a near whisper.

'God yes, a shy loner hankering after the most popular girl in the class. He gets rebuffed and takes his revenge. A bit of a cliché but unfortunately it has been known to happen. There was a case...'

Mac had to stop talking as Mrs. Aldis returned sooner than he'd expected. She carried in a tray with a large cafetiere, a milk jug and three cups.

'I hope no-one takes sugar,' she said. 'We don't use it normally.'

Mac and Tommy assured her that it was okay as it was.

'So, still no word about where she is?' she asked as she handed the coffee cups around.

Mac shook his head.

'Her poor mother, what must she be going through?' Mrs. Aldis said as she gave Mac a sorrowful look.

'When did Jonny hear that Natasha was missing?' Mac asked.

'Last night. We'd both just gone to bed when I heard Jonny's phone ring. He told me later that it was Julie Waddington asking him if he'd seen Natasha.'

'How did Jonny take it?'

'Not well I think but I can't always be sure. He doesn't let his feelings show that much if you know what I mean.'

'What did he do last night?' Mac asked.

'He just sat in the living room all night,' Mrs. Aldis replied. 'I found him asleep in the armchair this morning with his phone on the table next to him. I guess that he'd been hoping that Julie would ring during the night and tell him that Natasha was okay. Anyway, he rang Julie straight away when he woke up and, when she said there was no news, he drank some orange juice and went straight out. He didn't come back until this evening when he grabbed a sandwich and went out again.'

'Have you any idea where he's gone?' Mac asked.

'God knows, he never really tells me anything if I'm honest.'

She shook her head and her eyes brimmed with tears. Mac guessed that she was worried about her son. Was it simply because he'd gone missing though or was there something else?

'When was the last time that Natasha was here?' he asked.

She thought for a moment.

'Yes, it was about a week ago. She and Jonny are working on this fashion project together but he persuaded her to take some time out and sit for him.'

'Sit for him?' Mac asked wondering if she meant what he thought she meant.

'Yes, he wanted to sketch her.'

'He's an artist then?'

'He could be if he ever took it seriously. You know I think he quite likes Natasha because he could have always sketched her from memory. He only needs to see something once and he can sketch it, even days later.'

'Can we have a look?' Mac asked.

She led then down the hallway and into one of the back rooms.

'We gave this to Jonny as a sort of studio. It gets a lot of light during the day you see.'

There wasn't any easel or canvasses but there was a stack of large sketch pages. Mac leafed through them. A lot of them were abstract designs, some quite good and others quite unsettling for some reason. Then he came across Natasha.

It was just a pencil drawing but there was some magic there. Mac had never met Natasha but looking at the sketch felt like a sort of introduction. It was a profile drawing but the eyes were glancing to her right and they looked straight out of the drawing. She had a playful and knowing sort of smile on her face. If the look was meant for the artist Mac reckoned that he was definitely on the inside track. There was real subtlety in the drawing but something else as well. Mac could only think it was love.

'You said 'we' gave Jonny the room. I take it that there's a Mr. Aldis around?'

'Oh yes but I'm afraid that he's not here. God knows but I could do with him. He's an electrician, he works on one of the North Sea oil rigs. He won't be home for another ten days or so.'

'Have you contacted your husband yet?' Mac asked.

She shook her head.

'His job is dangerous enough without having him worrying about Jonny. Anyway, he'd can't exactly jump on a bus, can he? He'd need to arrange for a helicopter to pick him up and I don't want him to go to all that trouble. Anyway, Jonny's probably just out looking for her, isn't he?'

She smiled as she said this but her smile looked anything but confident.

'Okay, when you see Jonny tell him to stay at home until we call again. We need to speak to him,' Mac said.

Mrs. Aldis showed them out. Once outside Mac asked her where the entry was that led towards the flats. She pointed it out to them.

Mac walked down the entry which was narrow and had two high wooden fences on either side. This led into a small car park which was more or less empty at this time of night. It was well lit and visible from the upper floors of the two-storied houses on Purwell Lane. On the opposite side of the car park there was a pathway. On either side of the path there were high brick walls which curved to the left and then to the right before it ran alongside the old people's home.

Tommy walked on ahead and fifty yards or so later he came out onto the road opposite the flats where Natasha lived. He looked behind him but Mac was nowhere to be seen. He was worried and so he backtracked and saw Mac standing like a statue in the path with the curving brick walls on either side.

45

'Are you alright Mac?' Tommy asked with some concern.

He got no answer. Mac stood stock still.

'Shall I get you some help…?'

Tommy's words were interrupted.

'It happened right here,' Mac stated.

Tommy looked around him.

'What happened here?'

Mac turned and looked at Tommy.

'This is where she was taken.'

Tommy looked around him again. He wondered what Mac was seeing that he couldn't.

'How could you possibly know that?' he asked.

Mac looked straight at him. His eyes were luminous with excitement.

'Because it's perfect.'

Chapter Five

At Mac's insistence Tommy called Dan and requested a forensics team.

'You did tell him that it was urgent?' Mac asked.

'Yes, I told him,' Tommy replied.

'It hasn't rained since Natasha went missing so that's good.'

Tommy hadn't seen Mac like this before. It was as though he wasn't quite there and his eyes were focussed on some invisible event that was happening right in front of them.

'Are you sure you're not in pain?' Tommy asked again.

Mac didn't answer. He turned around and looked at the high walls.

'It's perfect,' he whispered to himself.

They hadn't been waiting long when three men in white coveralls approached them from the flats.

'What have we got?' one of them asked.

'Natasha Barker was abducted and I think it was from this very spot, right here in between the two curves,' Mac said. 'I'm hoping that you can verify that.'

'Okay,' the forensics man said. He turned to his colleagues, 'Get the tapes up there and there. I'm sorry but I'm going to have to ask you to step back a bit.'

Mac and Tommy backed off and stood behind the scene of crime tape watching the team do their work. They were joined by Dan and Adil shortly afterwards.

'What makes you think she was taken from here?' Dan asked getting straight to the point.

Mac shook his head as though trying to clear it. Tommy thought that he now looked like the old Mac once again. The Mac with the far-away eyes had been a little scary.

'It's a short cut that the kids from the college use and, if I was a girl walking home at night, I'd definitely go this way in order to get home as quickly as possible. The car park is overlooked by the houses on Purwell Lane so it wouldn't be a good idea to do it there but this is perfect. Anyone standing at that spot would be invisible from either end of the path. Natasha wouldn't have seen him until the last second.'

'Camera here!' one of the forensics team shouted.

Another member of the team put a small right-angled ruler on the ground and took multiple photos of something. Whatever it was it was too small for Mac and Dan to see. The forensics man who had called out now picked something up using tweezers and looked at it closely before placing it carefully in a small evidence bag. He then put the bag in his kit box. He then took a swab from the box and took a sample of something from the floor.

Dan's curiosity got the better of him.

'What is it?' he asked. 'What have you found?'

The technician took his time resealing the swab and putting it away before he strolled over to the tape.

'We can't be positive but it looks like a bit of a tooth, the corner of an incisor I'd say, and it looks like there's some blood there too.'

'Is there enough for DNA?' Adil asked.

'Oh God yes but we'll need to match it against the samples we took from the girl's house earlier.'

'How long before we get the results?' Dan asked.

'I'll give it top priority,' the forensics technician replied. 'You should have the results sometime tomorrow morning.'

It was clear from Dan's face that the next five minutes would have been much more preferable.

'Okay, I suppose we'll just have to wait then,' Dan said. 'Come on Adil, let's visit Mrs. Barker and see if she can confirm whether or not Natasha was likely to have used the shortcut.'

'Do you mind if we come along?' Mac asked. 'I'd just like to have a look at where Natasha lives.'

'Sure, come on.'

PC Stella Ajunwa opened the door. She was very smartly dressed in a crisp white police blouse and skirt. She was a tall woman in her early thirties and she had a beautifully coiffured Afro hairdo which surprised Mac a bit. He hadn't seen one for decades which he supposed meant that they were well overdue a comeback.

'Any news?' she asked anxiously.

'We might have found where Natasha was abducted from but we won't know for sure until tomorrow,' Dan said. 'How's she holding up?'

Before she could answer Mrs. Barker opened the door at the end of the hallway. She looked at the four officers and her face showed that she feared the worst.

'We've no news as yet I'm afraid, Mrs. Barker,' Dan said quickly.

She almost looked relieved at Dan's words.

Dan continued, 'We need to ask a few more questions, if that's alright?'

'Yes, yes of course. Please come in and sit down.'

Mrs. Barker, a woman in her fifties, had a face that had known troubled times. She was wearing a pink dressing gown and fluffy slippers.

'Would you mind if I have a look at your daughter's bedroom?' Mac asked.

She led Mac and Tommy back down the hallway and opened the door for them. She didn't go in or even look inside.

While Dan and Adil were asking Mrs. Barker about the shortcut, Mac looked about the room. It could have been any eighteen year old girl's bedroom. It was painted pink with posters covering the walls except that the posters weren't those of boy bands but fashion models. Some were quite old, in fact, one announced the new 'A Line dress from Dior'. It looked like it was from the fifties.

In the corner of the room there was a little work bench on which there was a sewing machine. Underneath the bench was a plastic box which seemed to be full of odds and ends of material. On the wall above the bench hand drawn sketches of clothes were tacked. Mac couldn't comment on the designs but the sketches looked professional enough. To the left of the bench there was a bookshelf. All of the books were about fashion designers; Chanel, Gaultier, Balenciaga, Cardin and more.

It looked like Natasha was serious about her course.

'Well you were right about the shortcut,' Dan said from the hallway. 'Mrs. Barker actually encouraged her to use it as not many people know about it.'

'Unfortunately for Natasha, it looks as if her abductor did.'

Mac stood still for a moment. There was something somebody said. Looking at the small flat it was obvious that the Barkers weren't rich but somebody said something...

Yes, he had it!

'Is Julie still here?' Mac asked.

'Yes, she's sitting with Mrs. Barker,' Dan replied.

Julie, a thin pretty girl with long fair hair, sat holding Mrs. Barker's hand. She was pale and tense. Mac could see the fear in her eyes when she looked up at him.

He introduced himself.

'I believe that Kelly Harris who works at the Hen and Chickens is a friend of yours?'

Julie nodded.

'She said that Natasha was wearing a special dress last night, she thought it might have been a designer. Was it?'

Julie shook her head.

'Nat got the dress for fifteen pounds from a chain store but then she unpicked some of the seams and re-sewed them so it fitted her better. She also put a panel of black lace over the... oh the boob area, if you know

50

what I mean. The lace cost nearly as much as the dress did.'

'Kelly said it looked gorgeous.'

'It did, it looked absolutely gorgeous on her,' Julie confirmed.

A tear ran down one cheek.

'Have you any photos of the dress?' Mac asked.

'No, she'd only just finished it before we went out. I was going to take some photos later but then we had the argument.'

Mac thought for a moment.

'Why did you have the argument at that specific time?'

'I wasn't going to tell her until we were on our way home,' Julie replied. 'I knew that she wouldn't be happy about it but then she'd have had all night to calm down and we could have spoken about it properly today. Then last night, just before nine, Adam texted me saying he was going to be in the pub in fifteen minutes. I told him to stay away as I was with Nat but he wouldn't have it. So, I had to tell her then and, of course, she exploded and then stormed off. The best of it was that Adam never turned up after all. Natasha was right, he is a shit.'

'Why didn't you mention this before?' Dan asked.

'Mention what?' she asked, looking puzzled.

'About Adam not turning up.'

'I don't know,' she said. 'It's not important, is it?'

Dan looked at Mac. They both knew it could be more than important.

'Just one last question, did Natasha make any sketches of the dress?' Mac asked.

Julie thought for a moment.

'Yes, I'm sure she did.'

They followed her into Natasha's bedroom. Julie riffled through a pile of sketches.

'Here,' she said handing Mac a sheet of sketch paper. The sketch was rough and only showed the outline of the dress. It had two thin straps, a panel of lace in the front and it was tight around the waist and legs. For some reason Mac thought of Audrey Hepburn.

'Is there any of the lace left that she used for the... the boob area?' Mac asked.

Julie went through the scrap box and pulled out a thin strip of material.

'That's all there is I'm afraid. As I said it was expensive so she must have measured it up very carefully.'

Tommy pulled an evidence bag out of his pocket and placed the sketch and piece of material inside.

Outside Dan rang Andy and asked him about his earlier interview with Adam Oakley.

'Did he say anything about texting Julie?'

'No,' Andy replied. 'I asked if he'd contacted Natasha or Julie yesterday. He said that he hadn't.'

'Thanks,' Dan said and ended the call.

'Well, either Julie Waddington or Adam Oakley is being less than truthful. I know who I'd put my money on. Come on, let's see this Adam Oakley for ourselves.'

Dan told everyone what he wanted them to do when they got there.

Tommy and Mac followed Dan's car to a side street just off the Cambridge Road. It was a small estate of semi-detached private houses with some bungalows mixed in. Dan's car pulled up outside a house that had a large black BMW four-by-four parked outside.

A shaven headed man with tattoos opened the door.

'God, not you lot again!' he said, pulling a face. 'You do know that we've already had the police visit us once today?'

'Yes, we know that. I take it that you're Mr. Oakley, Adam's father?' Dan asked as he showed him his warrant card.

'Yes, come in then. The neighbours will have their eyes out on stalks otherwise.'

The house inside was thickly carpeted and had some nice furniture but it was all slightly over the top, Mac thought.

'He's upstairs,' Mr. Oakley said. He then shouted at the top of his lungs. 'Adam, down here now!'

A few seconds later a young man appeared. He was dressed in a black T shirt and loose track bottoms.

'Dad, why do you have to do that when you know I've got someone...'

He stopped dead when he saw the four policemen.

'Adam Oakley?' Dan asked.

The young man nodded. His complexion had turned pale.

'I've already spoken to the police,' he said nervously.

'And you'll speak to us again,' Dan said.

'What if I don't want to?' he said with a touch of defiance.

'Then we'll arrest you, put some handcuffs on and take you to the station,' Dan replied. He looked straight at Mr. Oakley as he said, 'I'm sure that the neighbours will get some nice photos, it might even make the local papers, who knows?'

Mr. Oakley started to look exasperated by the whole thing.

'Oh, just talk to them and get it over with,' he ordered.

His son came meekly down the stairs and sat on the settee.

'Can we have a look around while we're here?' Dan asked.

'That's no problem as far as I'm concerned,' Mr. Oakley replied. He stressed the 'I'm' and looked straight at his son while he said it.

Adam didn't say anything but he didn't look very comfortable.

Adil took himself upstairs while Tommy started looking around the back of the house.

'Where were you last night?' Dan asked.

'I was with some friends,' Adam said.

Mac noticed that he was avoiding any eye contact. Dan took a notebook and pen out.

'What were their names?'

Adam thought for too long in Mac's opinion.

'Joey Damon and Aaron McEnery,' he eventually replied.

'Do you know their addresses?'

'Why would you need them?' Adam asked nervously.

'You weren't with them at all, were you?' Mac stated, looking at Adam's face intently as he replied.

'I was. I was...' he looked up and saw the two policemen staring at him. He sighed. 'I was with them but earlier on. They left about eight to go watch a match at a friend of ours. I didn't fancy it.'

'What match was that?' Dan asked.

'It was a Barcelona game. A friend of ours called Robby records them and we all make a date to watch it at his flat and have a few beers. We usually go to a club afterwards.'

'So, if you didn't watch the match then what did you do?' Dan asked.

'I walked around for a bit. I just couldn't make my mind up what to do. Then I went into the Vic and had a drink.'

'That's the Victoria pub?'

Adam nodded.

'Is that where you texted Julie from?' Dan asked.

'I was at a loose end and fancied meeting her. So, I texted her and said that I was coming down to the Hen and Chickens.'

'So, what stopped you then?' Dan asked.

'Well I met someone, someone I used to go to school with.'

'A female someone I take it?' Dan asked.

'Yes,' Adam replied. 'We hadn't seen each other for a while and we kind of hit it off.'

54

'So, what happened then?'

'We had a few drinks and a curry and then I took her here.'

'She spent the whole night here?' Dan asked.

'She spent more than a bloody night,' Mr. Oakley said with some disdain. 'She's still upstairs!'

'Adam, can you go and get her?' Dan asked.

Before he could move a young woman dressed in a man's dressing gown was being escorted down the stairs by Adil.

She told them that her name was Janie Bartlett and she confirmed Adam's story. She also told them that she'd never met Natasha.

Shortly afterwards Tommy appeared. He shook his head. He'd found nothing.

Dan put on his best stern face. Mac thought it was very good.

'Why didn't you tell the police officer who was here before about this?'

Adam shrugged his shoulders. He looked very uncomfortable.

'Have you told me the truth now, leaving absolutely nothing out?'

Now both Dan and Mr. Oakley were giving him stern looks.

'Yes, yes I have,' he replied nervously.

Dan stood up.

'Okay, but, if I find that you've been lying or forgetting to tell me something, I'll be back with the handcuffs and we'll be talking down at the station. Is that clear?'

Adam nodded meekly.

'Pity, I thought he might have been good for it,' Dan said as they walked back to their cars.

'Yes, ex-boyfriends usually make good suspects,' Mac replied. 'I'd still bear him in mind though. Get someone to thoroughly check out the girl. It's only her word after all.'

'I'll do it myself tomorrow and we'll visit the Victoria and the curry house too. Let's see if they can confirm what he says.' He looked at his watch. He was surprised to see that it was not far off ten o'clock. 'Let's knock it on the head for tonight. I'll see you all at seven tomorrow.'

Tommy drove Mac home. They got caught at the lights at the bottom of the hill again. They waited patiently as absolutely no lorries went out of the site.

'Have we got anywhere today?' Tommy asked. 'It doesn't feel like it.'

'It's often like this at the beginning,' Mac replied. 'I think it's a bit like looking at something in a microscope. You have to twiddle the knob and bit by bit you bring it all into focus. We're still twiddling at the moment.'

'Do you think that she's still alive?'

Mac made no answer.

Tommy took that as answer enough.

Chapter Six

Second day missing

Mac surprised himself by sleeping right through the night for once. He was relieved as he would need all the energy he could muster to get through the day. He performed his morning ritual. He sat up and then stood up and assessed his back pain. It was bearable and he was thankful for that too.

Tommy rang the bell at six forty five exactly. Mac had showered and shaved and felt as ready as he could for the day ahead. As they went down the hill Mac asked Tommy to slow down as they passed by the site entrance. For once the lights were actually on green. He read the 'due to be completed' date as they drove by. He still had another two months to go before he could have his hill back to himself.

The smell of coffee hit Mac as he walked into the incident room. Everyone seemed to be there except for Jo and Chris who came in within seconds of each other a few minutes later. There were three new faces, a burly uniformed sergeant, a very young-looking constable and a young man seated in the corner oblivious to everything except the laptop screen in front of him. Mac smiled as he recognised the straight-up hair style.

Mac and Tommy just had time to help themselves to a cup of a coffee and a Danish pastry before Dan started speaking.

'Okay, we all seem to be here so let's get on with it. Before we start, I'd like to introduce Sergeant Colin Willis who's leading the team doing the door to doors in the area around where Natasha lives. He'll give us an update of what they've found so far. I'd also like to introduce PC Amanda Lingard who'll be looking after the incident room and liaising with any members of the public who might wander in and who may want to give us some information. Also, in the corner there, you'll see Martin Selby hard at work.'

Martin turned, looked at the team and gave an almost imperceptible nod.

Dan continued, 'Martin's been attached to the unit for the duration of the case and he's our computer expert. If you need anything from the police databases or have any queries even slightly related to computers, phones or information held on the internet please ask Martin. You'll be glad you did.'

Martin gave them the slightest of waves and went back to his screen.

'So, Chris and Martina, can you make sure that you liaise with Martin? I'm sure that he'll be able to take on a lot of the database related work which should hopefully free up some of your time for investigative work.'

Chris and Martina didn't seem at all unhappy about Dan's suggestion.

'Okay then. Jo, as we can all read your writing, if you want to take up the marker pen then we'll begin. If each team can give us the bullet points of what they found yesterday so we all know where we're up to and then I'll quickly assign tasks for today. Right, first up its Mac and Tommy.'

Each team of two got up in turn and quickly gave the high points of what they'd found the day before. When they'd all finished Mac looked down the list –

David Hamilton – taxi driver, former teacher, knew Natasha, was in the vicinity of the rank on Bancroft. No alibi?

Jonathan Aldis – was in the Millhouse, a loner who had a crush on Natasha. Need to check if he was there all night.

Adam Oakley – ex-boyfriend, has an alibi, needs checking

ViSOR threw up four possible candidates so far, nothing compelling as yet but all worth following up

One of Natasha's friends reported that, after an argument, a fellow student called Micky Morgan, said she'd hurt Natasha. Worth following up plus still eleven names on Julie's list to follow up.

Mac looked at the white board. There wasn't really that much to go on as yet, he thought.

'Finally, a piece of technology,' Dan announced as he turned on a large flat screen TV newly hung on the wall. 'Martin, can you get a map of the Purwell up?'

A few seconds later a map appeared on the screen.

'Colin, can you show us what areas you've covered on the door to doors so far?'

The uniformed sergeant stood in front of the screen.

'We've interviewed everyone in the small block of flats where Natasha lives, except for two residents who were out, and we've also interviewed just about everyone in the street on either side up to here and here.' He pointed at the map with his finger. 'There's nothing as yet, no-one saw or heard Natasha on Saturday evening. A few of them knew her by name and quite a lot more by sight. In all we've got six re-visits to do so you never know.'

The sergeant moved away from the TV screen.

'There may be a good reason why no-one in that area would have seen Natasha. We think that she might not have made it that far.' Dan said. 'Martin can you focus in on the short cut and show us the 'Earth' view?'

The screen zoomed in and then turned into an aerial photograph.

'When Mac was interviewing Corinne Obiah, she told him that there was a short cut from Purwell Lane to the flats where Natasha lived. From Purwell Lane the entryway looks like all the others. However, whereas all the others only lead to the back entrances of the houses, this one leads into the car park here situated behind the houses. From there this path takes you by the retirement home and then straight to the block of flats where

Natasha lives. We've confirmed with Mrs. Barker that Natasha would almost definitely have taken this route home from the Millhouse. Mac is firmly of the opinion that Natasha was abducted right here.' Dan pointed to the middle of the curved section. 'At this point on the path there are high brick walls on either side and, if you stand in the middle of this curved section, you'd be invisible from both ends of the path. Forensics found what they think is a chip from an incisor tooth and a small amount of blood. We're waiting for the DNA results to see if they came from Natasha.'

Dan looked at the team to see how they took the news.

'I can see from your reaction that most of you think that this might be good news. If we do get DNA confirmation then it will be the first hard evidence we'll have found. We'll at least know that she was abducted, where she was taken from and that violence was used. However, knowing this won't make any difference to what we need to do today. Colin, can you get your men doing door to doors all along Purwell Lane? Especially concentrate on those houses nearest the entryway or which overlook the car park. Someone must have seen or heard something. Andy and Leigh there's still a lot of people on Julie's list and we could do with getting through them as soon as possible. Jo and Gerry, can you assist them with this?'

Jo and Gerry nodded and looked a little happier at the prospect of some real work.

'Chris and Martina, can you follow up on the candidates from the Sex Offender's Register?' Dan said. 'Mac and Tommy, can you question everyone at the retirement home? Mrs. Barker said that the short cut was only known by the locals so whoever took Natasha might be from the estate. However, it's also possible that our man's been stalking her. If that is the case then someone in the home might have seen something over the last few days or weeks.'

Mac was grateful, covering the retirement home would hopefully mean less walking.

'Sure, we could also try Jonny Aldis again while we're there,' Mac suggested.

'That sounds good,' Dan said. 'Okay then, that just leaves checking out Tony Hamilton's and Adam Oakley's alibis for me and Adil to do. Before you go please make sure that you have Martin's phone number. Everything will now go through him. If you find something important by all means let me know straight away but phone Martin next. He can join up the dots between all the different bits of information we'll hopefully be finding. We've also had some keys made for the incident room in case you need to access it late at night. Please make sure you pick one up from Amanda on your way out. Okay, what are you waiting for?'

The team had started queueing at Amanda's desk when Dan's phone rang. Everyone stopped and turned.

In a very short conversation Dan only said 'Yes' twice and finished with 'Thanks'.

He turned to the team.

'The tooth chip and blood definitely belong to Natasha. Now let's go and catch this bastard!'

Tommy parked the car as near to the entrance of the retirement home as he could. He opened a set of double doors for Mac only to be confronted with another. These were locked. Mac pressed the button of the nearby entry phone.

'Yes, can I help you?' a woman's tinny voice replied.

'I hope so. We're the police and we'd like to ask a few questions,' Mac said.

The buzzer sounded and Mac opened the door. The smell of urine and air freshener hit him. He saw an incredibly old-looking woman spryly traverse the lobby. She was dancing a waltz with an invisible partner. She was very light on her feet but, on seeing Mac, she veered towards him and the open door. He ushered Tommy and then quickly shut the door behind him. He tested it to make sure that it was properly shut. The woman stopped dancing and stood in front of the two men staring at them expectantly as a small child might.

'Alright Victoria, your room is that way,' a woman said pointing towards a corridor.

The woman started dancing again and whirled off in the direction indicated.

'How can I help er...' Mac handed the woman his warrant card. She examined it carefully. '...Mr. Maguire. My name is Mrs. Collins and I run this home,' she said handing him back the card.

Mrs. Collins was in her early forties, well upholstered and used to being in charge. She reminded Mac of a headmistress that he'd had in primary school.

'I was just wondering if you heard that we were working outside last night?' Mac asked.

'Yes, I did. I finish at six but one of the night staff told me that some men in plastic suits were crawling around on the floor and taking photographs near the back entrance. Is this about the missing girl?'

He nodded.

'We've established that she was abducted from the entry way just outside the home.'

Mrs. Collins put her hand to her mouth in shock.

'She was abducted right outside the home? God help us all,' she said making the sign of the cross.

'Tell me, do you have any CCTV cameras in the car park?'

'I wish I had the budget to be able to afford CCTV cameras,' she said. 'Even if I did, I'd spend it on something else. Anyway, there's been no need, I laid down the law regarding parking with all the neighbours and I must admit that so far they've been very good.'

'I see. I was just wondering if there's any chance that anyone here might have noticed something out of the ordinary the night that Natasha Barker disappeared?' Mac asked.

'I'll wish you luck with that,' Mrs. Collins replied. 'Most of our residents suffer from one sort of dementia or another. Believe it or not but you've just met one of our more high-functioning guests. However, there is someone who might be able to help you. But, before you see her, perhaps it might be best if you see the three night ladies first.'

'Were they on Saturday night as well?' Mac asked.

'Oh yes. They always do the whole weekend and you're lucky, they're still here having a cup of tea and handing over before they go home.'

He followed Mrs. Collins down corridor after corridor, all lined with doors upon which cheery signs said, 'Martha's Room', 'Ethel's Room', 'Barbara's Room' and so on. There didn't seem to be many men in the home. They eventually came to the canteen, a large open space containing tables and chairs and a serving hatch which was now closed. Six members of staff were sitting at a long table, drinking tea and talking. They stopped talking when they drew near.

'Margaret, Donna and Sylvia, these two men are from the police. They'd like a word with you all,' Mrs. Collins said.

They all glanced nervously up at Mac and Tommy.

'Where would you like them, Mr. Maguire?' Mrs. Collins asked.

He pointed to a table at the opposite side of the room.

'We'll take them one at a time, if that's okay. Perhaps Margaret first?'

Margaret made her way over to the table. She was taller than Mac, in her mid-forties and a little shambling in her movements but she looked a pleasant and good-natured woman.

He explained why he was there. When he mentioned that Natasha had been abducted right outside the home her reaction was pretty much like her boss's.

'I'm really shocked,' Margaret said. 'I live locally and I used to see Natasha sometimes with her mum. I still can't believe that someone could do such a thing and in Hitchin too.'

'Did you see or hear anything the night Natasha disappeared?' Mac asked. 'That's the night before last.'

She gave it some thought then shook her head.

'Unfortunately, the staff area that's used as a hub at night is right in the centre of the building, so the windows don't look outside.'

'And I take it that none of the…er…guests,' he'd nearly said 'inmates' but guessed that it wouldn't be appreciated, 'reported anything unusual to you, especially around ten o'clock?'

She shook her head.

'Most of the guests are asleep well before then, except possibly for Emily, but no-one reported anything as far as I'm aware.'

'Have you ever seen anyone suspicious hanging around the home?' Mac asked.

She gave this some deep thought. Mac mentally crossed his fingers.

'No, I don't think I have if I'm honest,' Margaret replied. 'Just the usual people I see.'

He thanked her and moved on to night lady number two. Donna was the youngest of the three. She worked three nights a week and was doing a Sociology degree as well. She wasn't from the estate and she said that she'd never seen Natasha before. Mac asked her if she'd seen anyone hanging around the home.

'There was someone, I saw her a few nights running out in the car park last week as I came to work.'

'A woman?'

'Yes, she was a woman, perhaps in her late thirties and she was quite slim. She was probably just waiting for her husband, I'd guess.'

A woman? Mac didn't think it had any bearing on the case but mentally filed it anyway.

Sylvia, the third night lady, was thin, around forty and somewhat nervous. She kept fidgeting and touching her face throughout the interview. Unfortunately, she seemed to know even less than the other two.

When he'd finished with the night ladies, he asked Mrs. Collins who Emily was.

'She's the guest I was going to take you to see,' she replied. 'You'll see why when you meet her.'

'Can we have a word with the day staff first just in case they noticed something?' Mac asked. 'You know, anyone strange hanging around, that type of thing.'

All in all, Mac and Tommy interviewed eleven members of staff. Almost all of them had seen Natasha at one time or another but none of them had noticed anything strange over the last few weeks or anything else that might have been of help.

Mac had to hope that this Emily might be a bit more forthcoming.

Mrs. Collins led them down another long corridor and stopped outside a door right at the very end. A sign proclaimed it to be 'Emily's Room'.

She knocked on the door and a thin voice said, 'Come in.'

Mrs. Collins led them into the room.

'Emily, this is Mr. Maguire from the police. He has a few questions to ask you.' Mrs. Collins turned to him and Tommy and said, 'I'll leave you to it. Please come and see me on your way out.'

He turned to Emily who was gesturing for him and Tommy to sit down on a small sofa. She was seated in a black office swivel chair. She was tiny and probably well into her seventies, Mac thought. Her wide smile made her look like the stereotypical nice granny. The room had a single bed, a desk with an open laptop on it, an office chair and the two-seater sofa they were sitting on. A large window covered most of one wall, screened by a venetian blind.

'Emily, I take it you've heard of the disappearance of Natasha Barker?' Mac asked.

'Of course, I have, it's been all over the news. Such a shame, she seemed such a nice girl.'

He was surprised by her answer.

'Did you know Natasha then?'

'No, not by name anyway, but I used to see her walking by with some of the young people from the college at lunchtimes and in the evenings,' she said pointing to the window.

He went and had a look. The slats of the venetian blinds were turned so they were horizontal and you could clearly see the car park and the end of the entry way that led from Purwell Lane.

'What did you make of her?' Mac asked.

'Oh, I so love looking at all the young people,' Emily replied with a smile. 'They're so full of life, so passionate about things. Natasha seemed as passionate as any of them. She always had a cloud of friends around her, all vying to get a word in edgewise as young people do.'

'Two nights ago, Natasha was abducted from the entry way that runs beside the home, just a few yards from your window. It happened at around ten in the evening,' he stated.

Emily's face clearly showed her surprise and then something else, a sort of dark thoughtful look.

'From here? Oh, that poor girl! So that's what all those men in plastic suits were doing last night. I thought it was quite exciting, like something from CSI. The thought had crossed my mind though that it might be connected to Natasha somehow but it still comes as something of a shock.'

'Did you see or hear anything?'

She put a finger to her lips.

'Let me think, ten o'clock, two nights ago? Yes, I'd just started watching the news while waiting for Match of the Day to come on.'

'Match of the Day?' Mac asked surprised that she might be into football.

'Oh, I never miss a programme, Mr. Maguire,' Emily said. 'I love my football, why me and my late husband Alfie were season ticket holders at Brentford for over thirty years. Even when we moved to Hertfordshire, we used to get the train into London for every home game. Now, last Saturday it was the big match, the title more or less depended on it, and so I couldn't miss that. Now, did I see or hear anything?'

She gave this some serious thought.

'Oh yes, there was something. It was unusual but it has happened once or twice before.'

'What was that?' Mac asked.

'I saw someone walking from the car park, they were going into the entryway towards the flats.'

'Could you see what they looked like?' Mac asked hopefully.

'Oh no dear, the blinds were drawn so I couldn't see out.'

She could see a look of puzzlement on Mac's face.

'It's the light, dearie,' she said pointing to the window.

Mac went and looked out of the window again. A tall lamp post stood in the centre of the car park and, on seeing it, Mac knew what she meant.

'You mean that you saw their shadow on the blind as they walked between the light from the lamp post and your window.'

'That's it, dearie. You can't miss it when that happens as the whole room goes darker. I like to watch telly with the lights down you see. They let the neighbours use the car park so long as they get their cars out before nine in

67

the morning. She's very strict on that is Mrs. Collins. When they started leaving their cars there all day, she had a few cars clamped and after that they didn't do it anymore. It's mostly the people who live on Purwell Lane who use the car park but occasionally people from the flats might use it if all the parking spaces are full up there.'

'How can you be sure it was around ten?' Mac asked.

'Oh, it was a bit earlier than that. I remember looking at the clock, it was just five to ten.'

'Are you sure you can be that accurate?'

'Oh yes dear,' Emily said pointing to a little alarm clock on a table next to her chair. 'It's Japanese and it's very good. I check it against the clock on the telly and it doesn't lose much time.'

'Did you hear anything?' Mac asked.

'No dear, sorry but the old hearing isn't what it used to be and so I use those things when I listen to the telly,' she said pointing to a set of headphones. 'I don't want to wake up any of the old dears you see.'

Mac glanced over at the laptop. It was a very expensive make.

'Is that yours?'

'Oh yes, I wouldn't know what to do without my laptop,' Emily said with a smile. 'My son works and lives in London and he comes up to see me most weekends but every evening we have a little video chat on Skype, the grandkids too and it's so lovely. My son got it for me a year or so ago and since then I've learnt so much. I'm doing a course on JavaScript at the moment.'

'JavaScript?' Mac asked.

'It's a sort of programming language dear. I'm hoping to start writing my own programmes soon,' she said excitedly.

Mac was impressed. He paused and thought about Emily's reaction to the news of Natasha's abduction.

'When I first told you about Natasha being abducted from right outside the home you were surprised but there was something else, wasn't there? If you know anything or have any suspicions, no matter how slight, you must tell me.'

Emily considered this for a moment and then nodded her head.

'I think that you might want to speak to Sylvia.'

'Why?' Mac asked.

'She showed…oh how can I put it? She showed an interest in some of the college girls, especially Natasha I think.'

'But I thought that she only works nights?' Mac asked.

'She does nights at the weekend and three days a week as well; Tuesdays, Wednesdays and Thursdays,' Emily replied. 'My window is the only one that looks out into the shortcut that the girls use and a couple of times I caught her looking out at them as they walked by. She had such an expression of, I don't know, longing is the best way I can put it. I can only think that she was attracted to them in some way.'

Mac raised his eyebrows. This was not what he'd expected at all.

'How do you know that she was especially attracted to Natasha?'

'I caught her once as she came out of my room and she was checking some photos on her phone. They were all of Natasha. I really don't like telling you this because Sylvia's such a nice person. You don't really think that she could have anything to do with Natasha's disappearance, do you?'

'I don't know Emily but we'll need to find out why she was so interested. Before I go, can you confirm it was just the one shadow you saw?' Mac asked.

'Yes, I could see the shape quite clearly, there was just the one person.'

'Did you see a shadow going back the other way say ten to fifteen minutes afterwards?'

'I'm sorry Mr. Maguire, but, once the news had started, I'm sure that I wouldn't have noticed.'

Mac thanked her and asked her to contact the police if she had any more information.

He sought out Mrs. Collins.

'Is Sylvia still around?' he asked.

'I'm afraid that you've just missed her. She's gone home.'

'I'll need her address and phone number then.'

'You don't think she's got anything to do with Natasha's disappearance, do you?' Mrs. Collins said with apparent concern.

'Mrs. Collins, I'm afraid that I can't say anything at the moment but I do need that information as soon as possible.'

Three minutes later she gave him a slip of paper.

'Please, Mr. Maguire, go easy on her. She's very fragile.'

As Mrs. Collins didn't seek to explain further he gave her his thanks and left.

Sylvia lived no more than five minutes walk away from the home. Even so Mac made straight for the car.

'She's really something that Emily, isn't she?' Tommy said with a smile.

'God, I wish I had her marbles. It took me quite a while to learn my way around a computer and after a year she's learning advanced computer programming. Believe me, she's as sharp as they come. Okay, let's go and talk to this Sylvia. I want to know why she was so interested in Natasha.'

Chapter Seven

Sylvia lived in the ground floor half of a council flat just a few streets away from the retirement home. The paint on the front door was peeling and the flat had a neglected look about it.

'Tommy, I think you might like to have a little look around while I talk to Sylvia. Say you need the loo or something,' Mac suggested.

'Good idea,' Tommy replied.

Mac rapped on the door and it eventually opened a few inches. A surprised looking Sylvia peeked out of the narrow gap.

'I was just going to bed,' she said her voice quivering with nervousness.

From her face alone Mac knew she had something to hide.

'Do you mind if we come in?' Mac asked.

Sylvia hesitated and then reluctantly held the door open for them.

She led them down the flat's single corridor into a small, dingy living room that hadn't been decorated for some years. He sat down next to her on a dilapidated sofa. Tommy stood behind him.

'Do you live alone?' Mac asked.

'Yes, my husband, he…he left me six years ago. I've lived alone since then,' Sylvia replied.

'When I spoke to you earlier you said that you knew nothing about Natasha and that you and she had never met. I'd just like to be sure that I heard you right.'

'Everything I said was true. I've never met the girl or said a word to her.'

'But you have seen her, haven't you?' Mac persevered.

'Yes, I've seen her around, you see everyone on the estate sooner or later,' Sylvia said.

'So, you've just seen her around, is that it?'

Sylvia nodded. She started to fidget nervously again. She was hiding something and not making a particularly good job of it. Tommy asked to be excused and Sylvia gave him the directions to the toilet.

'Sylvia, do you have a phone with a camera on it?' Mac asked.

Sylvia kept glancing towards the door that Tommy had just walked out of.

'Yes, doesn't everyone?'

At that point they both heard a door open in the corridor outside.

'What's he doing out there? That's not the toilet door,' she exclaimed.

Sylvia jumped up and ran out of the room.

He followed her down the corridor and then into a bedroom. Tommy was staring at a mass of photos that nearly covered one wall.

Sylvia started shouting at them.

'Get out! Get out! You shouldn't be in here. This is my life, my life!'

She was on the verge of becoming hysterical so Mac held her and tried to calm her down. As he did this he glanced over her shoulder at the wall of photographs. Almost all of them were of Natasha. He walked her back to the living room and sat beside her on the sofa while Tommy got her a glass of water. He gave her the time she needed to calm down.

'I wasn't doing anything wrong, was I, in taking those photos?' she asked in a low voice.

'It depends. Why did you take them? Were you attracted to her?' he asked gently.

'I was, I was attracted to her and now she's gone too. I feel like killing myself, there's no goodness in this world, no goodness at all.'

'What do you mean she's gone too?' he asked, stressing the word 'too'.

Sylvia got up without saying a word and led them to another room at the end of the corridor. She opened the door but wouldn't go inside. Mac went in and looked around the room. It was a young girl's bedroom but it was all wrong, it was too tidy. Everything was laid out too exactly, the dress on the bed, the hair brushes on the small dressing table, the shoes in a neat row along the wall. The posters of pop stars were yellowing around the edges and there was a musty smell that told him that this room hadn't been occupied for some time. He sighed.

It wasn't a bedroom, it was a shrine.

He picked up a framed photo that stood next to the hair brushes. It showed a younger Sylvia, a Sylvia who was alive, with a girl who was around eleven years old. The young girl had black hair and features not unlike Natasha's. He went out into the hallway. Sylvia was leaning against the wall. She looked as if she needed its support.

'When did you lose your daughter, Sylvia?' he asked as gently as he could.

'Just over seven years ago now. She was walking home from school, keeping on the pavement like I always told her to do and a driver ran her over. He was in a van and he lost control, it mounted the pavement and it killed her. She was with three friends and not one of them had a scratch, can you believe that? They only gave him a slap on the wrist, he smiled when they sentenced him while I'm still...'

She couldn't finish the sentence.

'Is that why you were interested in Natasha? Was it because she looked a little like your daughter?'

'I wasn't doing anything wrong, was I? Believe me I wouldn't have hurt a hair on that girl's head. My Sally would have been around Natasha's age now, going to college and having boyfriends and all that. I just used to pretend a bit that Natasha was my Sally all grown up, just for a while, just to ease the pain a bit. I'd look at the photos and pretend we were having conversations. Crazy, isn't it? But now Natasha's gone too and I feel like I've brought it on her somehow. I've brought my bad luck down on her. It's like...oh God, it's like I'm losing my Sally all over again.'

Sylvia broke down into huge convulsive sobs and started sliding down the wall. She would have fallen to the floor if Tommy hadn't caught her. They did their best to console her but she was beyond any consolation they could give.

Tommy picked her up and carried her to the sofa.

'Tommy, call the home and ask for Mrs. Collins. Get her to call a doctor and see if Sylvia has a friend or someone who can come and sit with her.'

Tommy did as he was asked while Mac tried to comfort Sylvia.

'Mrs. Collins says the doctor is on his way and she's also called Margaret who should be around in a few minutes.'

She never stopped crying the whole time that they were there. It was more than crying though, Mac thought. It was despair and she gave herself over to it totally, her body convulsing with each sob.

Margaret arrived five minutes later and looked at Mac and Tommy as if they were children who'd done something very naughty indeed. Nevertheless, Mac was immensely grateful when she took over. As he made his way out into the fresh air he felt as if he'd just emerged out of a black cave full of utter hopelessness.

'Christ, Mac! The things some people have to live with,' Tommy said.

He looked quite shaken too.

Mac couldn't say anything at that moment, a dark shiver ran down his spine. Sylvia's plight reminded him that he'd suffered his own bereavement. In his darkest moments he always consoled himself that, although he knew that the pain would never go away, it might at least lessen with time. Sylvia's hadn't and that scared him. He and Tommy walked back towards the car in silence.

'We'll need to go back to the home,' Mac said before getting in the car. 'I've got a few more questions that I'd like to ask'.

He pressed the button of the entry phone again and Mrs. Collins let them in. She led them into a small office and shut the door behind her.

'Why didn't you tell me?' Mac asked.

'I'm sorry, I couldn't. I promised Sylvia that I wouldn't repeat her story to anyone. She was afraid of people being overly nice to her and she said that it would just keep reminding her of her loss. How is she?'

'She's very upset. We left her with Margaret. Tell me about Sylvia,' Mac asked.

'She started working here a couple of years or so after her daughter died. She told me all about herself before I gave her the job, she's a very honest person. In the years she's been working here, she's proved to be a good worker and, unlike some I've had, very caring towards our guests. It's just so unfair that so much misery should be heaped on one person, to lose a daughter and a husband like that.'

'Her husband? She said he'd left her.'

'He did, in a way. He committed suicide, Mr. Maguire. He loved his daughter so much that he just couldn't stand living without her, especially when the person responsible got such a light sentence. Sylvia said the man who killed her daughter left the dock smiling and that's what she sees in her worse nightmares.'

'I wish that there was something I could do to help her,' Mac said.

'I feel like that too but what can you do? I've tried to support her as best I can and I thought that she was doing so well recently,' Mrs. Collins said with a sigh.

'She thinks that it's her fault that Natasha's gone,' Mac said gloomily, 'that she's somehow given Natasha her bad luck.'

'Poor woman. I'll drop around and see her on my way home.'

'I'd like another word with Emily before I go, if that's okay?' Mac asked.

Mrs. Collins led them once more to Emily's room. She was busy on her laptop, inputting strings of symbols that made no sense to Mac.

'Oh, it's you again Mr. Maguire. Twice in one day, people will start talking about us,' she said with a twinkle in her eye.

He couldn't help smiling too.

'Emily, there was just one more question I wanted to ask. The shadow that you saw on the blind, is there any way that you could tell if they were a man or a woman or if they were wearing a hat? Anything at all really.'

She screwed up her face as she thought.

'I don't think they were wearing a hat as I could see the head quite clearly, apart from that...' she shrugged her shoulders.

'Thanks, Emily. I just thought I'd ask while I was here,' he said as he stood up.

As he went towards the door he looked back and saw her deep in thought.

'What is it Emily?' he asked.

'There was something I've just remembered, it's probably not important though.'

'Please tell us anyway,' Mac said sitting down again.

'Well, I think that the shadow had something below its right hand unless it was a trick of the light. It looked like a stick with a rectangle below it. I'm afraid that's all I could make out.'

'Are you sure that it was the right hand?'

'Of course, Mr. Maguire, I'm not quite gaga yet. It was on the same side as my left hand as I looked at the window and so, if the shadow was coming towards me then it must be the shadow's right hand.'

Mac was impressed again. He was also curious.

'Emily, you're as bright as a pin, how come you ended up in here?'

'It was my Alfie,' she replied. 'He started forgetting small things and then big things and I just couldn't manage him anymore. So, we sold the house and we both moved in here. I lost him two years ago but we were quite happy here so, when he went, I didn't want to move. It's like a bit of Alfie's still hanging around if you know what I mean.'

'Believe me Emily I do. Thank you.'

'Just one more thing, Mr. Maguire. I wasn't sure if I was seeing things, perhaps my eyes aren't so good these days but I think that the stick turned into two sticks just before the shadow disappeared.'

'Into two you say?' Mac said. 'Thanks Emily, you've been a real help.'

Outside the home Mac stood still. Tommy waited patiently, not wanting to break Mac's train of thought.

'I think I know how our man got Natasha out without being seen,' Mac eventually said.

'Really?' Tommy said with some surprise.

'Yes, I think that Emily's just given us the answer.'

Tommy tried to rewind the interview in his head but came up with nothing.

'What did she say then?'

'The one stick turning into two,' Mac replied. 'How tall was Natasha?'

'Five feet five if I remember right,' Tommy replied.

'So not very tall then. Yes, I'd bet that she was taken out of here in a suitcase.'

'A suitcase? How can you be so sure?'

'They do suitcases in all sizes and I've seen some truly massive ones on the luggage carousel at the airport,' Mac said. 'All our man needed to do was have it by him, unzipped. After knocking Natasha down and stunning her, he tapes up her hands and feet and simply rolls her into the case, legs and neck bent. He zips her up and rolls her away. If anyone had seen our man all they'd have seen was someone wheeling a heavy suitcase to a car. Nothing suspicious about that, is there?'

'Let me think for a minute,' Tommy said.

Mac allowed him slightly more. He knew Tommy had it when a big grin spread across his face.

'I get it now, one stick then the two. Most suitcases with wheels have a handle with two metal rods that you use to pull the case along. If he had a case with four wheels then the case was probably side on when Emily saw the shadow first, so just one stick, but then the man must have turned to go into the entryway and Emily was now seeing the case at an angle so she now saw two sticks.'

'Well done,' Mac said with sincerity. 'I knew that you'd get it.'

'It's really clever though, isn't it? Stun her with a punch, tape her up and then roll her into a suitcase. It wouldn't take more than a few seconds, would it?'

Mac scowled.

'Yes, all very simple and also very effective which is why it's making me think some very uncomfortable thoughts.'

'What do you mean?' Tommy asked.

'I'm wondering if our man hasn't had some practice. Perhaps Natasha isn't the first girl he's abducted.'

Mac's next call was at the Aldis house. The door opened even quicker that on their previous call.

'Oh!' Mrs. Aldis said with some surprise, 'I thought it was...'

Her face was pale and her hand went up to her mouth. Mac noticed that her hand was shaking.

'I take it that we've missed Jonny again?' Mac asked.

She nodded but said nothing further.

'Can we come in?'

She turned and they followed her into the living room.

Once they were sat down Mac said, 'Something's happened hasn't it?'

She nodded. She wrapped her arms around her body as if she were hugging herself.

'Tell us,' Mac said softly.

'Well, Jonny came back late last night. I woke up and heard him in his bedroom. He told me that the police had been asking some of his friends about him. He started unpacking some boxes and, when I asked him what he was doing, all he said was that he needed some things for the morning.'

'And then what?'

She didn't answer. Both her hands went to her mouth and she started rocking.

'Mrs. Aldis, a girl is missing and probably in great danger. You need to tell us what you know,' Mac said a little more sharply.

She removed her hands from her mouth and wrung them together.

'He's gone. I woke up early this morning and caught him just before he went out of the door. He had his rucksack on his back. He said he was going to be gone for a while and he didn't know when he'd be back.'

Her face was bleak with worry.

'Gone where?'

'I don't know but he took all his gear with him.'

'What gear?' Mac asked.

'His camping gear, the tent, his sleeping bag, the stove, the rations, they've all gone.'

'Does Jonny do a lot of camping?'

Mrs. Aldis nodded.

'Yes, he and his dad go off for a week at a time. They don't bother with camp sites, they go hiking and camp out wherever they find themselves. My husband says he likes the space and to be surrounded by land for a change. Jonny just loves being with his dad.'

'So, he could camp out anywhere really,' Mac said. 'What about these rations? How long might they last him?'

'The box is empty so I guess that he'd have enough for at least a week, if not longer.'

Mac thought on this.

'Tell me again what Jonny said and please give us the exact words if you can remember them.'

'When he was going out of the door he said 'I'll be gone for a while and I won't call but don't worry, I'll be alright'. He won't be able to call anyway as he forgot and left his phone here.'

Mac immediately wondered if the real reason Jonny had left his phone was because he knew his location could be traced if he'd taken it with him.

'Did he say anything else before he went out of the door?' Mac persisted.

'Yes, he started walking away then he came back and gave me a hug and said 'I have to go, something bad has happened to Nat'.'

Mac frowned.

'You're sure that's exactly what he said?'

'Yes, I'm sure,' she replied.

Mac could see that she didn't seem to be aware of the possible implication of what she'd just told them.

Something bad has happened to Nat.

The obvious question was how could he know that for sure?

Mac sighed. Jonny Aldis had just put himself right in the middle of the frame.

Chapter Eight

Mac phoned Dan immediately with the news. He said that he'd be there in fifteen minutes and that he'd arrange for a forensics team to visit as soon as possible.

'Is it serious?' Mrs. Aldis asked her hands shaking even more.

Mac's expression told her all she needed to know.

'Is there a relative or a friend that you can call?' he asked.

'Yes, my sister lives just on the other side of Hitchin.'

'Then I'd give her a ring if I were you, you'll need some company. What about Jonny's dad?' Mac asked.

'He told me to only call him if it was something serious...'

She stopped and looked at Mac.

'You don't want him hearing about this on the news, do you?' Mac asked.

'The news? Oh God no, I'll call him right away.'

The two policemen took themselves off into the hallway while Mrs. Aldis made her call.

'I don't suppose it will take long for the press to find out, will it?' Tommy said.

'As soon as the men in white suits and the crime scene tape goes up outside, they'll put two and two together and make five whatever we tell them.'

Mac looked at his watch. It had just gone one thirty. Nine minutes later Dan and Adil arrived. Mac told them what they'd found.

'Do you fancy him for it, Mac?' Dan asked.

Trust Dan to ask him the one question he couldn't answer.

'If I'm being absolutely honest, I don't know. He's a big lad and could easily overpower someone as small as Natasha. He might even have had a motive, shy loner and most popular girl, it's almost a cliché, isn't it? But what about opportunity, did he have that? Would you mind if Tommy and me go and interview Corinne and her friends again? If they can confirm that he never left the pub then it might help us to rule him out.'

'Good idea, Mac. I'll let you know if we turn anything up here,' Dan replied.

As Mac walked to the car, he surprised himself by saying a little prayer that it wasn't Jonny. In his mind's eye he could see Natasha looking out at him from his drawing. He was convinced that the person who drew that could never have done Natasha any harm. However, he had his duty to do and, if that meant finding that Jonny was guilty, then so be it.

Seated in the car Tommy asked, 'Where to?'

'Let's try Corinne again first. Hopefully she'll be able to give us the names of everyone who was there.'

'She'll be at college, won't she?'

'Try her home first,' Mac suggested. 'I don't think she'll be in the mood for college somehow.'

Mac was right. It was Corinne who opened the door to them. She didn't look at all surprised to see Mac and Tommy again.

'Is your mother at home?' Mac asked as she let them in.

'She's at work but I've got some friends with me.'

She led them into the living room again. The small room was packed with young people, four on the small sofas the rest sitting on the floor.

'Were any of these in the pub last Saturday?' Mac asked in hope.

Corinne looked around the room.

'Yes, we're all here I think...'

Mac said a silent hallelujah.

Corinne was interrupted by one of the girls.

'Jonny isn't here,' she pointed out.

'Yes, that's right. Has anyone seen Jonny?' she asked.

They all shook their heads.

'It's Jonny I need to ask you about. You've certainly saved us some time by all turning up here together.'

'I didn't want to go to college, not while Nat's still missing,' a young man with pimples and gelled hair said. 'I just didn't know where else to go.'

They all nodded sombrely at this.

'Now this is important,' Mac said. 'I need to know if Jonny was with you at all times last Saturday or if he left the pub or even went outside for a few minutes. Did he?'

They all looked at each other. Most shook their heads, most but not all. A young man with long hair tied up in a black bandana with a skull motif looked thoughtful.

'What's your name?' Mac asked him.

He looked startled at the question.

'Matty,' he replied, sounding as if he wasn't quite sure that he'd answered the question correctly.

'You know something. Tell me what it is, Matty,' Mac said softly.

He looked at the rest of the young people before he answered.

'I went outside for a bit, for a smoke,' he glanced up at Mac as he said this and his face reddened slightly.

Mac didn't need to ask what it was he was smoking.

'Anyway, we were having a chat but Jonny kept looking up and down the road. I guess he was looking to see if Nat was coming, Corinne said that she might drop in later. Then I went inside.'

'He didn't go back in with you?' Mac asked.

The young man shook his head.

'What time was this?' Mac asked.

'About quarter to ten I think.'

Mac looked at the young faces in front of him.

'When was the next time that any of you saw Jonny after this?'

They all looked at each other. A few of them shrugged.

'He was there when he got his round in,' a young girl piped up.

'Yes, that's right,' Corinne confirmed.

'And what time was that?' Mac asked.

'Around ten thirty, I think,' she replied. 'We only had one more after that.'

'So, can any of you say, with certainty, that you saw Jonny between nine forty five and ten thirty? Think hard, this could be important.'

A young girl who hadn't spoken before tentatively put her hand up.

'I think I saw him outside. He was sitting on one of the benches.'

'Can you be absolutely sure that this was between nine forty five and ten thirty?' Mac asked.

She gave this some thought, then shrugged.

'No, I'm sorry I don't think I can. We had some shooters just before that and they always go to my head.'

Mac was almost disappointed. It seemed as if Jonny might have had the opportunity after all but was he really the type of person who could abduct someone and then calmly go back to his friends in the pub and buy a round of drinks?

'What was Jonny like when he bought his round? Was he excited, worried, was there anything out of the ordinary about him?' Mac asked.

They all looked at each other. Corinne spoke for them.

'No, he was just Jonny. He never shows much emotion if I'm honest and it can be hard to know what he's thinking sometimes but he really cared for Nat that much I do know. It wasn't Jonny, Mr. Maguire, he would never hurt Nat.'

'And do the rest of you think that too?' Mac asked.

They all nodded in unison. Mac hoped to God they were right.

'Well, that doesn't help his case much, does it?' Tommy said as they walked back to the car.

'No, it doesn't,' Mac replied. 'We now know that he might have had the opportunity, the means and maybe the motive too. What do you think?'

'I think he looks good for it. If that girl was right and Jonny was sitting outside the pub, he must have seen Natasha get out of the taxi. Perhaps Jonny offered to walk her home and then tried to kiss her or something and she wouldn't let him. Then they had a row and he hit her, he's a big lad, perhaps he even killed her when he punched her. He could have hidden the body some-where close by and then went back to the pub for an alibi.'

Mac had already considered this possibility and he found it depressed him for some reason. Mainly, perhaps, because it could just be the truth.

Dan and Adil were standing outside the house when they returned. The crime scene tape was up and a small crowd of gawkers were standing the street side of it. A couple of them had very professional looking cameras.

God, it didn't take them long, Mac thought.

'You're policemen, aren't you? Did Jonny Aldis kill Natasha, did he?' a young sharp-featured blonde girl shouted as Mac pulled the tape up over his head. She then took some pictures of him and Tommy before shouting, 'Have you found where he buried her yet?'

Mac didn't reply. They not only had Jonny murdering Natasha but burying the body too. Experience had taught him that, while the press had their uses, they were often more trouble than they were worth.

'Let's go inside,' Mac suggested to Dan as he glanced back towards the pressmen.

He could hear the cameras whir as they went into the house. They stood in the hallway while Mac told Dan what they'd found.

'So, that still leaves him as our best suspect by a mile,' Dan said. 'It's unlikely that he could be keeping her somewhere so I think we have to go on the assumption that, if it was him, then he killed her and hid her body.'

'Tommy here thinks they might have had a row,' Mac said trying to be as even handed as he could.

'Well, if it did come to anything physical, she wouldn't have stood a chance,' Adil said. 'Apparently, Jonny Aldis has a black belt at Tae Kwon Do.'

Things seemed to just keep on stacking up against him, Mac thought.

'Does he drive or have access to a car?' Mac asked.

Dan shook his head.

'He hasn't even started taking lessons yet according to his mum and she said that he couldn't have used her car anyway. It's got a flat and she hasn't had it fixed yet.'

'He only had forty-five minutes at most so, if he did do it, she must be somewhere nearby,' Tommy said.

'There's a bloody great field right opposite the pub,' Dan said. 'We'll start the search there. I'll need to get on and organise that straight away.'

'What do you want us to do in the meantime?' Mac asked.

'We've checked out Adam Oakley and it looks like he was telling us the truth for once,' Dan said. 'Can you carry on with Tony Hamilton? Martin will give you all the information we have on him.'

As they drove back towards the incident room Tommy asked, 'Do you think they'll find her?'

What could he say? That he hoped that a suspect was innocent and based on what? A drawing he'd seen for a few seconds. It all sounded a bit daft, even to himself.

'Who knows?' he answered non-committedly.

'What about your theory about the suitcase and that?'

'That could have just been someone coming back off holiday, I suppose,' Mac replied a little grumpily.

Mac thought about what he'd said as they drove back and found that he didn't believe his own words. Jonny wasn't a killer and Natasha *was* taken away in a suitcase. He knew this to be true but how could he be so certain?

Again, that little tickle came at the back of his brain. Yet it was still so totally non-specific that it was starting to really annoy him now. On the way back Mac sent the photo of Natasha to his old sergeant Peter Harper and asked him if he could check out their case files just in case.

Martin had the file on Tony Hamilton ready for them when they arrived. There was only Martin and Amanda Lingard manning the incident room. It somehow felt forlorn and annoyed Mac even more than the tickle did.

'I need to eat,' Mac said his grumpiness growing.

He could feel his blood sugar dropping like a stone.

'Come on, let's read this while we get some food.'

Tommy followed Mac to the Hen and Chickens. They ordered two burgers and coffees. The landlord served them himself. Mac asked him if he'd thought of anything else since they last met. He drew a blank.

Mac split the slim case file in two and they ate in silence as they read. Mac wolfed down his meal, he was even hungrier than he'd realised.

He wiped his mouth with a serviette.

'Anything?' he asked.

Tommy looked up.

'No, he looks squeaky clean from everything I've read so far.'

'Same here, there's not even a speeding conviction. He did supply a witness statement some years ago though. He gave evidence that helped to put an ASBO on a serial offender.'

'What was the offence?' Tommy asked.

'Threatening behaviour towards a supermarket check-out lady,' Mac replied. 'Well, it shows that he's public spirited if nothing else. I can't believe that there haven't been a few bumps along the way though.'

'So, where do we start?' Tommy asked.

Mac decided to let Tommy take the lead.

"Where do you think we should start?' he asked.

Tommy gave it some thought.

'His last headmistress perhaps, she's still at the school apparently.'

Mac smiled.

'That's as good a place to start as anywhere. Let's get going then.'

He checked his phone but there were no messages from Dan. Mac found that he was quite relieved.

Chapter Nine

The school was just a short drive up the hill from the town centre. Mac was quite surprised when he saw a very large Edwardian building standing proudly in its own grounds. If he hadn't known better, he'd have assumed that it was a grand hotel or something along those lines.

The headmistress was a Mrs. Hilary Meredith. Tommy asked for her at reception. They only had to wait a few minutes before a tall thin woman in her late forties strode towards them. She was dressed in a black skirt, a crisp white blouse and a black jacket. She looked very business-like. She had a quick word with the receptionist before turning to face Mac and Tommy.

'Can I see your cards, please?' she asked with the sure air of someone used to being obeyed.

Mac and Tommy duly showed their cards as ordered.

'Very well, follow me,' she said striding off down another corridor. Mac couldn't keep up. She opened a classroom door and waited, tapping her toe, until he arrived. She ushered them both inside.

'This is free for the next half hour which is all I can spare at the moment. What can I do for the police?' she asked as she sat on one of the desks.

'We're enquiring about a former teacher, a Mr. Anthony Hamilton,' Mac said.

'Tony?' she asked with some surprise. 'What's he supposed to have done?'

'Nothing as far as we know. You'll have heard the phrase 'eliminating a person from our enquiries' before. Well, that's exactly what we're doing now.'

Her sceptical expression told Mac that she didn't quite believe him.

'Is this something to do with Natasha Barker?' she asked with some suspicion.

Mac decided that there was no point beating around the bush with Mrs. Meredith, she was far too sharp.

'Yes, Mr. Hamilton now drives a taxi part-time and he was in the area around the time Natasha disappeared. As I said we're just trying to eliminate him from our enquiries.'

'Well, I suppose you have to check these things out but I can guarantee that Tony had nothing to do with Natasha's disappearance.'

'What makes you so sure?' Mac asked.

'He was a good teacher, not as inspirational as some perhaps, but he was a solid dependable teacher. I'd give a lot to have a few more like him on my staff right now.'

'I'm sorry but I have to ask this question. This is a girl's only school. I have to know if there were ever any problems reported related to Mr. Hamilton's conduct with the girls?'

She stood up and paced up and down before answering.

'Yes, there was, just the one. Around seven years ago I'd guess,' she replied.

'Was Natasha here at the time?'

'She'd have probably just started with us around the time this happened.'

'Tell me,' Mac said sitting on a desk himself.

'We had the misfortune to have a girl called Joy Ackley join us a couple of years or so before Natasha did,' the headmistress said with obvious distaste. 'Even after all this time her name still makes me feel a little nauseous. She was bad news right from the start; disrupting classes, stealing and then, a little later on, she was accused of threatening behaviour towards her fellow pupils and even teachers. She played truant a lot and, if I'm honest, I was quite glad when she did as the school always ran that little bit smoother when she was away. Let's see, she'd have been thirteen when she made the accusation against Tony.'

90

'Tell me exactly what she accused Mr. Hamilton of,' Mac said.

She gave an audible sigh.

'She claimed that Tony had cornered her in the book store and that he'd put his hand down her knickers. She said that he'd sexually assaulted her.'

'In what way?'

The headmistress looked up to the ceiling.

'Joy said that Tony had 'fingered her'. Her words not mine.'

'And had he?' Mac asked.

She looked offended.

'No, of course not. I'd have had him out of the school in a second if I thought there was even the slightest possibility that he had. I took the matter seriously, of course, but I also had the school's reputation to think of as well. I investigated the matter thoroughly and I even got an independent investigator involved in the case. We both reached the same conclusion. She was telling us a pack of lies.'

'Who was the independent investigator?'

'An ex-policeman, he used to be a Detective Superintendent,' the headmistress replied.

'A friend of yours?' Mac asked.

'Yes, he was but that didn't mean that he wasn't thorough. Bob was a good investigator and I told him to leave no stones unturned. I trusted Tony but I needed to be absolutely sure that Joy was lying.'

'And he was able to confirm that?'

'Yes. He interviewed a number of the girls in her class and they stated that Joy had been talking about getting her own back on Tony for some weeks before she claimed the assault took place.'

'Her own back for what?' Mac asked.

'Tony had caught her smoking on school premises for about the umpteenth time,' the headmistress said. 'A lot of teachers would look the other way where Joy was concerned but not Tony. Joy told some of her class that she was going to get Tony alone somewhere and then claim that he 'touched her up'. Her words again.'

'How did she take the findings?'

'She went mad, cursed us with some words even I hadn't heard before and said she'd get even with the school if it killed her.'

'And did she?'

The headmistress shook her head.

'We said that she or her parents could go to the police and formally report the matter but she never did.'

'Her parents never reported it?' he asked with some surprise.

'No, and if you want me to tell you what they're like I'm afraid that I can't, except for the fact that they obviously never cared that much for their daughter.'

'If you never met them then how can you be so sure?' Mac asked.

'Because in all the time she was here they never visited the school once, not for the open day, not for sports day, not any day,' the headmistress replied. 'I was wondering if it was Joy putting them off somehow until I had a word with the truant officer. He'd had meetings with them after he'd issued them with some penalty notices for non-attendance. He said that it was quite obvious that they couldn't have cared less whether Joy attended school or not.'

'What happened to her?'

'She got expelled a year later and I breathed a huge sigh of relief when it happened.'

'What exactly did she get expelled for?' Mac asked.

Another large sigh.

'For bringing men on to school property and trying to entice younger girls to have sex with them for money,' she said through gritted teeth.

'She wasn't exactly sugar and spice then?' Mac said.

'No, I honestly believe that she's the most malicious, manipulative, evil creature that I've ever come across in well over twenty-five years as a teacher.'

'And that was it? That was the only problem that you ever had with Tony Hamilton?' Mac asked.

'Yes, he was a model teacher in most respects. He even gave up a lot of his own time to produce school dramas and the like.'

Mac thought through what he'd just heard. He knew he'd have to follow it up just in case but couldn't help wondering if this might be a stone best left unturned.

'What was the name of the Police Detective Superintendent?'

'Bob, Bob Waters,' she replied. 'Unfortunately, he died last year.'

A bit of bad luck there, Mac thought.

'Where did he work out of?'

'Stevenage Police Station,' she replied.

He could always ask around the station and find out what he could about Bob Waters.

'Do you still have copies of yours and DS Waters' investigation reports?' Mac asked.

'Yes, they're still on file somewhere but it might take me a while to find them.'

'Can you send them here when you do?' he said writing down Martin's email address. 'I'd appreciate it if you made this a priority. Oh, and we'll also need an address for Joy or her parents, if you have one that is?'

'I've no idea where Joy is or what she's doing and I don't want to either,' the headmistress said with a scowl. 'There'll be an old address for her parents somewhere in the records. I can probably let you have that quite quickly. If you wait in reception then I'll have someone bring it to you.'

She held the door open for them. The audience was at an end.

'God she's a bit scary, isn't she? We should employ her to interrogate suspects,' Tommy said as they walked back to the reception area. 'I'm sure that she'd get more out of them that we ever would.'

Mac laughed out loud. He knew exactly what Tommy meant.

They only had to wait a few minutes before a young woman brought them the Ackley's address. It was on one of the estates on the other side of Hitchin. Mac had never visited there before but it looked much the same as many in the area, brick-built in the sixties, most of the houses being neat and tidy and with a reasonably new car parked outside. Except for one that was, the one they pulled up outside.

The paint was badly peeling and there was a small patch of garden that hadn't seen a spade for decades. Mac rang the bell. There was no sound. He rang again and again there was no sound. He knocked the door, hard.

There was the sound of shuffling from the other side of the door as a figure, blurred by the patterned glass in the door, approached.

The door opened a few inches and a face appeared. It somehow didn't look that much different that it had in the patterned glass. It was puffy and blurry and topped with long, lank greasy hair of an indeterminate colour. Looking at the woman gave Mac the sudden urge to clean his glasses. He could smell alcohol on her breath and it wasn't cooking sherry.

'What do you want?' she said aggressively the words slurring into each other.

'Mrs. Ackley, we're the police,' Mac said showing her his warrant card.

She peered at it, her head going backwards and forwards in an attempt to focus. She eventually gave up.

'What do you want with me then?' she asked.

'Can we come in? I'm sure that you don't want the neighbours to hear,' Mac asked in a conciliatory manner.

'Sod the neighbours, they can all die as far as I'm concerned,' she said sharply.

'Okay, we're trying to find your daughter Joy. Is she still living at home?' Mac asked.

'No, I kicked the bitch out years ago after I caught her stealing from my purse.'

'Do you have any idea where she's living now?'

She shrugged her shoulders.

'Don't know, don't care.'

'You've no idea at all?' Mac asked.

'On the game in Luton last time I heard. Is that it?'

Before Mac could answer she slammed the door shut. Another audience over.

'With a mother like that then it's no wonder Joy turned out like she did,' Tommy said.

'Well, I'm sure it didn't help any,' Mac said. 'Come on let's go to Luton Police Station. If she's been on the streets for any length of time she's bound to have been arrested at some point or at least cautioned.'

Tommy knew the way well enough. He'd been working there only a few weeks before. As they walked into the office Tommy had to shake hands and bear the brunt of something that might have been called wit had it been a bit funnier. Mac saw DC Mary Sullivan seated at a desk in the corner and made a beeline for her.

'Hello Mary, how did the exams go?' he asked.

She looked up from her computer in some surprise.

'So, it's yourself then. What brings you back to the beautiful town of Luton, doing a bit of sightseeing?' she asked with a wide smile on her face. 'By the way the exams went great. I'll officially be Detective Sergeant Mary Sullivan in a few weeks.'

'I had every faith that you'd do it.'

'I found what you said really helped,' she said.

95

Mac thought but couldn't remember any sage bits of advice that he might have given her.

'What did I say exactly?'

'About how you failed the exam first time around. I thought that if the great Mac Maguire could fail one exam then it was okay if I did too. That kind of took the pressure off a bit. I ended up in the top ten per cent, so they told me.'

'Good for you, really well done,' Mac said. 'However, I'm not here sightseeing, I'm helping out with the Natasha Barker case.'

Mary's face took on a serious expression.

'How can I help?' she asked.

Tommy came over and joined them. After he and Mary had exchanged greetings Mac got back to business.

'We're looking for a woman called Joy Ackley. She'd be around twenty now and we think that she's been on the streets for a couple of years or so. Can you check to see if she has any sort of a record? We need to speak to her so an address would be nice.'

'No problem,' Mary replied.

A few minutes later she had an answer.

'Joy Ackley, she been cautioned but not charged. She gave the same address the last two times so you might be in luck.'

Mac had Tommy write it down.

'Thanks,' Mac said. 'Oh, and good luck with being a sergeant, although personally I don't think you'll need it.'

Mac turned to go and Tommy followed for a few yards.

'She made sergeant?' Tommy asked the penny having finally dropped.

Mac nodded. Tommy ran back to congratulate Mary while Mac made his way to the car park. A step later Mac came to a sudden stop. His left leg had gone almost totally numb from the knee down, numb except for a blinding pain that shot down it from his lower back. It really shook him. Even after all this time pain could still come as a complete surprise.

No, not now, he said to himself. He could hear Tommy running to catch up with him. He quickly wiped a tear away from his eye.

'Are you okay, Mac?' Tommy asked.

'Just waiting for a certain slowcoach that's all,' Mac said trying to keep his voice even. 'Come on, let's see if Miss Ackley's at home.'

Mac managed to sit down in the car without making a sound, something that took all the willpower he had.

'It's not exactly the nicest part of Luton,' Tommy said as he looked at the address.

He was right. It all looked very familiar to Mac. He'd been here before when he'd helped Dan Carter with the Hart-Tolliver case. They drove down streets lined with Victorian terraced houses, some of which were well looked after having had fresh paint jobs and new white plastic windows. However, the street that they pulled up in looked shabby and neglected. The house they were looking for had black plastic bin bags rather than flowers in the tiny front garden. Many had been chewed at by animals and the contents were leaking.

Finding no bell Mac rapped at the door. Getting no answer, he rapped again.

The door was eventually opened by a young woman wearing a torn pink dressing gown and little on under-neath. She was as pudgy and indeterminate as her mother.

'Look, I told you I'd have the money tonight...' she said as she opened the door. 'Oh, who are you?'

Mac showed her his warrant card.

'Alright, what the bloody hell have I done now?' she asked as she went back inside the house.

Mac and Tommy followed her in. She led them into a bare living room and sat down on the only seat, an old stained chaise longue as big as a single bed. He guessed that it was used for quick sex sessions and that explained the stains. Mac didn't want to sit down on it and so had no choice but to stand. It did his pain no good.

'We're here to ask you some questions about allegations you made against a teacher some time ago, a Mr. Anthony Hamilton.'

She looked at them suspiciously.

'Why? Why now? It's been at least seven years, hasn't it? Is this one of those, oh, what did they call it? You know, sort of abuse cases?'

'Historic abuse cases, you mean?' Mac suggested.

'Yes, that's it, like for that old perve Savile. I heard some of them he abused came into some money, compensation like.'

'This is nothing like the Jimmy Savile case,' Mac said. 'We're just checking the facts around your allegation of sexual abuse by Mr. Hamilton. The headmistress investigated the matter and came to the conclusion that you were lying. Did you lie?'

She pulled a pack of cigarettes from the pocket of her dressing gown and took her time lighting one up. While she did this Mac could see the cogs going around in her head. She finally reached a decision.

'No, I wasn't lying. That skinny bitch covered up like they always do. They always protect their own, don't they?'

'You mean the headmistress, Hilary Meredith?'

'Yes, the cow had me expelled, fitted me up she did.'

'So, you're saying that you were sexually assaulted and that it was covered up?' Mac said his stomach starting to churn.

'Yes, that's exactly what I'm saying,' she said drawing her dressing gown tightly around and exposing even more of herself. 'I think I'd like to make it legal. How can I do that?'

'You mean you want to press charges against Mr. Hamilton for sexual assault?' Mac clarified.

'Yes, that's it. What you just said.'

Mac had been afraid of something like this. However, if she wanted her day in court, he couldn't deny it to her, especially in light of the fact that so many genuine allegations of child abuse had been swept under the carpet in the recent past. Mac had serious doubts about Joy Ackley being a genuine victim though. He hadn't liked the way her eyes had lit up when she said the word 'compensation'. However, as he often had to remind himself, it wasn't up to him.

'Well, what do I do?' she said standing up.

'If you want to get dressed and come with us to the station then we'll take your statement there,' Mac said.

She glanced over at the clock.

'I've only got an hour and a half. Will that be time enough?' she asked.

'We'll take your statement at Luton Police Station and then you'll be free to go,' Mac replied.

They waited in the car and ten minutes later she wobbled out on some red high-heeled shoes. Her skimpy dress was definitely a pint pot holding a quart and a bit. Mac presumed that she was going to work straight away after making her statement.

No-one said a word the whole way to the station. Once there, Mac did his duty and warned her that giving a false statement was a criminal offence but she didn't appear to be listening.

She repeated her story for the tape but added in something new.

'So now you're saying that Mr. Hamilton had sex with you?' Mac said. 'That wasn't mentioned in the original investigation.'

'That's because it didn't happen until later, until after the cover up. He was free to do what he wanted then, wasn't he?' she said.

'And how many times did sex take place?' Mac asked. She had to think for a while.

'Six times.'

'Where?'

'The same place where he touched me up, the book store. It was his little sex room, wasn't it?'

'That's the book store in the classroom where he used to teach?' Mac asked.

'That's right. It wasn't just me either. I saw other girls too, that Natalie was one. I saw her coming out of the book store once and she didn't look very happy.'

'Natalie?'

'That girl who's missing, you know Natalie,' she confirmed.

'You mean Natasha Barker,' Mac replied.

'Yes, that's her,' she replied. 'I knew it started with an 'N'. Well, not long before they got rid of me, I saw old Hamilton giving her the eye. I'll bet that the next thing he did was to ask her to help him with the books just like he did with me. Once in there he locks the door and then does what he likes.'

'Are you absolutely sure?' Mac asked.

'Of course, I'm sure. That Natalie was different looking, wasn't she? It was definitely her.'

Mac gave this some thought and then looked up at Joy Ackley.

'If you wait here someone will write up your statement and then you can sign it and go,' Mac told her.

'Will I get a lift back?' she asked anxiously. 'I've got to be somewhere.'

'Don't worry,' Mac said. 'We'll make sure that you get to work on time.'

They left her in the interview room. He slowly walked to the car park while Tommy arranged for someone to process her statement. His pain wasn't getting any better. He looked at his watch. It was nearly six. He asked Tommy to drive him straight home.

'Of course, I can see that you're not looking so well,' Tommy replied.

'Can you update Dan before you go home?' Mac asked.

'No problem. Do you think that there's anything to what she's saying?'

'I'm not sure but we have to give her allegations due weight and investigate them thoroughly,' Mac replied. 'If they'd have done that years ago then a lot of children who suffered terrible abuse might had been spared.'

Mac wouldn't say it but he was still highly sceptical of Miss Ackley's motives. He felt as if he'd just over-turned a stone and found a scorpion.

Chapter Ten

Third day missing

Mac woke up in stages. He was nearly there anyway when the alarm went off. He turned it off and lay back for a couple of minutes trying to summon the courage to sit up. He did. It wasn't as bad as he feared. The really hard part was next though. He stood up and waited for the pain to hit him. It didn't. He tried a few steps. His back was sore but just about bearable which was far better than he'd expected.

He smiled as he shaved. He'd been so sure that today would be a bed day and he was so grateful that it wasn't.

He had coffee and toast and even managed to fill the bird feeders before Tommy arrived. He looked concerned as he watched Mac limping towards the car.

'Are you sure you're okay, Mac?'

'Well, it's not great but it's not terrible either. Don't worry though, sometimes the pain goes away a bit as I get through the day.'

Mac said a little prayer that he might be right.

As they drove down the hill Mac could see the traffic light turn to red. They pulled up as once again no traffic came out of the site. It still annoyed the hell out of him for some reason. He was going to ask Tommy what Dan had said the previous evening but Tommy beat him to it.

'You...er...haven't heard from Bridget, have you?' he asked.

Mac looked over at him. Tommy seemed to be a little worried and he wanted to know why.

'No, I went straight to bed last night. Why? Has something happened between the two of you?'

'No, no...well, perhaps sort of. I was due to meet her to look at a flat last night and, if I'm honest, I got talking to Dan about the case and nearly forgot all about it. By the time I remembered and drove to the flat, there was no-one around. I've tried calling her but her phone must be switched off.'

'And you think that she might be mad at you?' Mac said.

Tommy shrugged, 'Well, yes. I think she really liked this flat.'

'Have you two decided to move in together?'

'Well yes…hasn't she told you?' Tommy asked, looking more than a little sheepish.

'No, she didn't,' Mac said as he tried to keep a serious expression on his face.

Tommy looked even more concerned as he quickly glanced over at Mac.

'Well, it's alright with you, isn't it?'

The 'isn't it?' ended on a tremulous upward inflection. Mac couldn't hold it any longer and burst out laughing.

'Oh, it's fine with me and I know that it's more than fine with her. She told me at Easter that she hoped you'd ask her to move in with you, especially now she's going to be working locally.'

'She did?' Tommy grinned. 'I only got the courage up to ask her a few weeks ago. I was surprised when she said yes. I mean she's so…well, perfect.'

'She's many things but I wouldn't count perfection as being one of them,' Mac said. 'Don't worry though, she might have been mad at you last night but it won't last. I'm really glad you've both come to the sensible decision. I take it that you've been having problems finding somewhere suitable?'

Tommy nodded.

'We've not got much time left either, I'm already well into the notice period for my flat. It's such a shame, this one looked so good too.'

'Don't worry, something will turn up,' Mac said.

They pulled up outside the incident room. The smell of coffee welcomed Mac once again as he opened the door. Another cup would be just fine.

A few minutes later and they were all assembled around the white board.

'Okay, we'll very quickly go through where everyone is up to,' Dan said. 'Chris, Martina do you want to start?'

Chris stood up.

'We had four candidates from the Sex Offenders Register who live locally. We've checked them all out but nothing's come of it so far. Martin's come up with three more that look a bit more likely plus we had someone walk in with some information. Amanda?'

Amanda stood up and looked quite nervously out at the team.

'A Mrs. Evelyn Tarbot walked in just after four o'clock yesterday afternoon. She's a retired lady who lives just opposite the rugby club. She reported that a neighbour of hers was 'acting suspiciously', her words. She'd seen him taking food and other things into a big shed that he has in his garden, one that he keeps permanently locked. She thought that perhaps he was holding Natasha there. Apparently, this neighbour is not 'the right type', her words again.'

Amanda sat down.

'Apparently, Amanda managed to winkle out of Mrs. Tarbot how she managed to witness all these comings and goings,' Chris said with a smile. 'She lives in the top part of a house in a dormer conversion and uses a stool and a pair of high-powered binoculars.'

'Well, she'll be worth talking to then,' Dan said. 'I'll bet she knows everything that happens around that area. Okay, Andy and Leigh.'

Andy let Leigh speak.

'We've gotten around all but two on the list of Natasha's friends. There's at least one possible lead to follow up. The last of Natasha's friends we spoke to said that two boys at the college were spreading it about that Jonny Aldis had murdered Natasha and that they knew something about it.'

'Really? What about this Mickey Morgan?' Dan asked.

'We checked her out and, while it's true that she said some threatening things about Natasha, it just appears to be a normal case of teenage friends falling out with each other. Anyway, she was away with her family in London the night that Natasha went missing and she looked as upset about it as anyone if I'm honest.'

'Thanks, Mac and Tommy?'

'We've been looking at the teacher, Anthony Hamilton, and investigating an incident from his past. A Miss Joy Ackley has now formally accused Mr. Hamilton of rape and sexual assault which she says happened when she was thirteen. She's also stated that Mr. Hamilton showed quite an interest in Natasha and that she once saw Natasha coming out of the book store in his classroom. That's the place that she says that Mr. Hamilton used to have sex with pupils.'

'Is there anything in it?' Dan asked.

Mac shrugged.

'I'm not sure if I'm honest.'

'Well, we have to follow it up,' Dan said. 'I always thought it was a bit of a coincidence him being so close by when she picked up the taxi. Colin anything from the door to doors yet?'

The burly sergeant stood up.

'Nothing much I'm afraid. A man in one of the houses on Purwell Lane reported that he saw headlights in the car park around the time Natasha disappeared. I'm afraid that's about it. We also managed to catch up with all of those who weren't in when we first did the door to doors but nothing there either.'

'I'm afraid that the search of the field opposite the pub has also turned up nothing so far,' Dan said, 'but we've still got some way to go with that. It's a lot bigger than you'd think. Okay, before I start dishing out tasks for the day has anyone got any ideas that they'd like to share?'

They all looked at each other. Gerry stuck his hand up.

'How are we getting on with finding Jonny Aldis?' he asked.

'We've done all the usual things but nothing so far. To be honest I was hoping that you might have found some leads through talking to his friends.'

'He seems to be the secretive type,' Gerry replied. 'Do you mind if I have a go at looking for him?'

'What's your idea?' Dan asked.

'I used to be in the Army before I joined the force and I did a lot of camping too. I'm just wondering if that might help in identifying places he might use.'

'He could be anywhere though. What are your assumptions?' Dan asked.

'If he did kill Natasha then yes, he could be miles away by now, but what if he didn't?' Gerry said. 'Natasha's friends are all insistent that it wasn't him. Perhaps he's looking for her himself. In that case he might be very close by on some bit of parkland perhaps, there's a lot of that in and around Hitchin.'

Dan gave that some thought.

'And if he didn't kill her then why would we want to find him?' he asked.

'He might know something, something he doesn't know he knows, if you know what I mean,' Gerry replied. 'He was with her a lot just before she disappeared, so perhaps he saw something or she said something to him that might be important.'

Dan gave it some more thought.

'Okay, I'm sold. Gerry and Jo, start searching for Jonny Aldis. Pull in some uniforms if you have to.'

Gerry looked really pleased at this but Mac couldn't help noticing that Jo looked exactly the opposite. She gave her partner a sour look.

'Okay, Andy and Leigh, carry on with Natasha's friends and also have a look at these two boys who are saying that Jonny Aldis murdered Natasha. In fact, bring them in. I want to see them whether you think they're telling the truth or not. Chris and Martina, carry on with the sex offenders and Mrs. Tarbot. If you have any time free after that then meet me in the field. Mac and Tommy, can you interview Anthony Hamilton and see if there's any substance in Miss Ackley's accusations. Adil and me will get our wellies on and go back to that great bloody sticky mess of a field. If we find anything, I'll let you all know. Right, let's get on with it then.'

As Mac headed to the door, he heard Gerry say to Jo, 'Talking about wellies I hope you've got some.'

She looked horrified.

'Wellies? If I can't wear high heels then I don't want to know.'

'Well, you're going to need them, especially as there's a forecast for rain today,' he said with a big smile.

'Rain? I joined this unit because I was fed up doing a desk job. Please God let me go back!'

Gerry seemed to be actually enjoying Jo's discomfort.

They're like chalk and cheese those two, Mac thought. He could see Jo giving Gerry daggers when he turned his back. A thought occurred to him.

'Jo, you were stationed at Stevenage, weren't you?'

'Yes, and I wish to God that I was back there right now,' she replied.

'Did you know a Bob Waters who worked there?'

'Yes, sure I did, he died not long ago.'

'What was he like?' Mac asked.

'Can I ask why you're asking?'

Mac told Jo about the report that he'd done for the school.

'Well, Bob was straight up and down, a good investigator too. He didn't do any favours if you know what I mean. He'd have given his wife a speeding ticket if he had to.'

'So, you'd trust his report?' Mac asked.

'Absolutely,' Jo replied.

'Thanks, that's all I needed to know.'

As they walked towards the car Tommy's phone rang. He had a message. He looked at it and smiled broadly.

'I dodged a bullet there,' he said passing the phone to Mac.

It was a text from Bridget.

'Sorry Tommy but couldn't make it, last minute emergency at work and then phone battery went dead on me. I've rang the flat and we can view tonight. I'll see you at seven and I'll make it up to you x B'

Mac laughed.

'Yes, you did. Anyway, the best of luck with the viewing. Where is it?'

'Just down the road from where you live actually.'

'Really?' Mac said as he tried to hide a smile.

Having Bridget so close by would be wonderful. He'd missed her dreadfully when she first left home for university but even more so since his Nora died. The thought also occurred to him that, with both Bridget and Tommy being good cooks, a nice hot home-cooked meal every now and then might be a distinct possibility. Things were definitely looking up.

As they pulled up outside Tony Hamilton's house his good mood evaporated. He really wasn't looking forward to this.

Mrs. Hamilton opened the door.

'Oh, it's you,' she said managing a smile. 'Please come in.'

'Is your husband around?' Mac asked.

'He's in the garden,' she said brightly. 'Shall I go and get him?'

Mac could hear the sound of a lawnmower outside. It stopped and a minute later Mr. Hamilton came into the room.

He smiled at Mac and Tommy.

'How can I help you?' he asked.

'I'm sorry,' Mac said, 'but there's no easy way to say this. I'm going to have to ask you to come to the station with me. We need you to make a formal statement.'

He looked mystified.

'A statement? A statement about what?'

'A Miss Joy Ackley has alleged that seven years ago you sexually assaulted and raped her.'

The shock was evident on Mr. Hamilton's face. It was his wife who spoke first.

'That bitch! We've already been through hell because of her once. How can you believe a word she says?' she said angrily.

'I'm not saying that we do but she's alleged that a crime has taken place and we have to investigate,' Mac said as evenly as he could.

'It's alright dear, they're just doing their job,' Mr. Hamilton said. Turning to Mac he continued, 'I'll just have a quick wash and then I'll be ready to go with you.'

While Mr. Hamilton was gone Mac noticed that Mrs. Hamilton's expression had turned from anger to one of fear.

'Oh God, she's going to do it to us again, isn't she? I wish I'd never...'

'You wished you'd never what, Mrs. Hamilton? Mrs. Meredith said that Joy Ackley had it in for your husband because he caught her smoking or is there more to it than that?'

Mrs. Hamilton sat down.

'While that's true, I think it might be more to do with me, with something I did,' she said her face readying itself for tears.

'What did you do?'

'I caught her bullying one of the younger girls,' she replied. 'Joy was banging her head off the wall. The poor girl was so frightened that she'd wet herself. I sent her home and then had a word with Joy or rather she had a word with me, several words actually and most of them beginning with the letters 'f' and 'c'. It was most unlike me but I'd had a very hard day. Anyway, I totally lost it and I smacked her in the face, twice. She hardly flinched when I did it. She just looked at me with those evil eyes of hers and she told me that she'd get her own back. I thought that she'd report me to Mrs. Meredith, as she had a right to of course, but she didn't. Then, a few weeks later, when she alleged that Tony had assaulted her, I knew it was aimed at me.'

'I see. So, she had a reason to get back at the both of you,' Mac observed.

'Why now though, Mr. Maguire? Why now after all these years? We've been so happy and now...' the tears finally came.

Mr. Hamilton came into the room and went straight to his wife and comforted her.

'Is it okay if I ring a friend to come and sit with her?' he asked.

Mac nodded.

Once seated in the interview room in the police station Mac asked him if he wanted a solicitor.

'No, why should I? I've got nothing to hide. I'm an innocent man and I'm quite happy to answer your questions,' he replied.

Mac read Joy Ackley's statement to him. Mr. Hamilton's face showed his shock, especially at Joy's allegations about him and Natasha.

'Is there any truth in Miss Ackley's allegations?'

'No, none whatsoever,' he protested, 'and as for her saying that there was something between me and Natasha that's absolutely unbelievable. I'm sorry but I can't get my head around any of this.'

'Did you have any sort of sexual encounters with Natasha, Joy or any other pupil?' Mac asked.

'No, never. I could never understand what some men saw in young girls, I mean they're just children, aren't they? I really don't know what to say or how I can prove it to you though.'

'If you didn't sexually assault Joy Ackley why do you think she's making these allegations?' Mac asked.

'I've no idea. She definitely had an axe to grind with me after I caught her smoking but that was years ago. I'd have thought she'd have forgotten all about that by now though.'

Mac looked closely at the teacher. He seemed lost and confused. As far as Mac was concerned, he was ticking all the right boxes so far.

'Okay I'll get someone to take your formal statement and then you'll be free to go home.'

'What happens next?' Tony Hamilton asked with some nervousness.

'We'll investigate further and then I'll give my findings to my superior. If we find anything then he'll consult with the Crown Prosecution Service about possible charges.'

'You're thinking of charging me with something?' he asked his face showing his total bewilderment.

'I didn't say that. A serious allegation has been made against you. If we find evidence of your guilt you will be charged. However, if we find that Miss Ackley has knowingly made a false allegation then we'll be charging her,' Mac explained.

'Oh, I see,' he said, looking a little calmer. 'Why do people do these things? Why do they wilfully hurt each other so?'

'I really wish I knew,' Mac said with deep sincerity. 'I'll get someone to drop you home.'

'So, what do we do now?' Tommy asked as they stood in the hallway.

'Let's go back to the incident room and see if those reports have arrived from the school. If this DS Waters was as good an investigator as the headmistress and Jo claim then we might as well use his report as the starting point.'

When they got back Martin had not only received the reports but had produced a nice pile of printed paper for Mac and Tommy to read.

Mac read DS Waters' report first and then swapped with Tommy and read the headmistress's report.

'They cover pretty much the same ground, don't they?' Tommy said.

'Yes, and they both mention the same four witnesses,' Mac said. 'I think that our first move should be to interview them again and see if they stick to their stories. You never know...'

Mac was interrupted by Martin who had a phone to one ear and was waving his free hand around.

'It's Dan, they've found a body,' he said.

Chapter Eleven

Mac never said a word the whole way there. Tommy, sensing his mood, thought he might be best left alone.

He supposed that he should have been excited at the news that a body was found but he wasn't. He knew that it confirmed that Natasha was dead but they'd all thought that after the first twenty-four hours anyway. If someone's been murdered then the best piece of evidence you can find is the body. Mac wasn't excited about it though. If Natasha was buried in the field then it meant that it was probably Jonny Aldis who had put her there.

Yet he had been so absolutely certain in his mind that Jonny wasn't the murderer. Was it just the drawing or something else? He had the feeling it was something else but what on earth could it be?

The thought crossed Mac's mind that perhaps the real explanation might be that he was just losing it.

Following the instructions that Martin had given them, they drove a good way down Purwell Lane before pulling up. Only ten yards or so on the other side of the fence a white tent had been erected. Mac looked down the road. He could see the front of Jonny's house just a couple of hundred yards away. A section of the fence had been removed and Mac made his way onto the field. It was uneven and full of thick tussocks of grass so Mac knew that he had to take care. He gingerly picked his way towards the tent as though he was walking through a minefield.

Dan and Adil were standing outside the tent talking.

'What have we got?' Mac asked as he drew near.

'Have a look,' Dan said.

Mac went through the open flap of the tent. Two men in white suits were working around a rectangular hole some four feet deep. A body were exposed. Mac had

113

seen enough exhumations to know that this body had been there for some time.

It wasn't Natasha then!

'Any ideas yet?' Mac asked one of the forensic technicians.

He didn't look up or even stop working as he replied.

'Well, it's a female, quite old I'd say, past fifty anyway. No signs of violence as far as we can see. She's been here for a while I'd say but she's very well preserved. The ground's a bit peaty here so that might explain it.'

'Thanks,' Mac said.

Tommy noticed that the news that it wasn't Natasha had elevated his mood somewhat.

'How did you find the grave?' Mac asked.

'Something called ground penetrating radar,' Adil answered. 'We borrowed the rig and the guy who owns it from an archaeological dig a couple of miles away.'

'Now that was a good idea. Do we know who she is yet?' Mac asked Dan.

'Not yet,' Dan replied, 'but I'm hoping that the detailed forensics examination will give us a better idea. If we can't solve it quickly then we'll be handing it over to someone else. We've got enough to be getting on with. What are you doing?'

'We've had the reports into the allegation of sexual assault from the headmistress. In both reports four witnesses stated that Joy Ackley had been talking about getting revenge on Tony Hamilton by faking a sexual assault for some weeks before it actually happened. We need to make sure that they stick by what they said seven years ago.'

'Okay, the best of luck then,' Dan said as he looked over the huge extent of the field that was still left to be searched. 'I think we'll be stuck here for a while yet.'

They said their goodbyes and Mac started making his way back to the street and back to a thankfully even surface. He was only a few feet away from the pavement when his left foot went into a hole. It was only a few inches deep but it was enough. He felt his back twang and the pain speared him.

He would have fallen if Tommy hadn't been quick enough to catch him.

'Mac are you alright?' Tommy asked even though he could clearly see that he wasn't.

'Don't let Dan see. Help me back to the car,' Mac said breathlessly.

Sitting down in the car brought the blinding pain on again. Mac tried to stop it but a loud grunt left his lips.

'What do you want me to do?' Tommy said as he drove back up the hill.

'Help me get in the house then get my medication,' Mac said through gritted teeth. 'That's all you can do for now. I need to dose up and then try and sleep through it. It's the only way.'

Mac felt every little bump in the road on the way back.

Tommy very carefully drove the car up the kerb and drove over the grass verge to get as close to the front door as he could. He helped Mac to the bedroom and then took off his shoes and trousers. Mac yelled as he lay flat on the bed. His face was white and etched with pain.

'Where's your medication?' Tommy asked.

'Kitchen cupboard on the left. Just bring it all in. Bring a glass and a big bottle of water too.'

Tommy found the packets in the cupboard, all in neat little rows. He opened some other cupboards and found a big plastic tub. He took the lid off and placed all of the packets inside. He found a glass, took a large bottle of sparkling water from the fridge and went back to Mac. He could hear him grunting from the kitchen. He said a little prayer that what had happened to Mac would never happen to him and then felt immediately guilty about it.

'Here,' Tommy said. 'What should I give you?'

'Fentanyl, I need to put another patch on. I only changed the other one last night but I'll leave that on too. I'm going to need all the help I can get. You'll need some scissors though.'

Tommy ran back into the kitchen and ran back with some scissors.

'Okay, just cut it where the arrow's pointing, not below it though, you'll cut into the patch.'

Tommy carefully cut the packet as he'd been instructed.

'Inside you'll see a small clear square of plastic. Get it out.'

Tommy fiddled around inside the packet and pulled out what looked like a clear plaster except that this was square and had blue text printed on it. He was surprised that it was so small.

'Good,' Mac said. 'There are two plastic wings that need to be removed. Watch out as the surface will be very sticky so don't fold the patch or you'll have to start all over again with a new one.'

Tommy carefully removed one wing and then the other.

'Now, place it on my shoulder here,' Mac said pointing to the top of his shoulder blade.

Once on Mac patted it down and rubbed it gently to get it warm.

'What else?' Tommy asked.

'I'll need one of the Diclofenac tablets and two of the little blue ones from the purple pack.'

He handed the tablets to Mac who washed them down with the water.

'What can I do now?' Tommy asked.

'Nothing, except to wash your hands. You'll have got some of the glue on your fingers and it's powerful stuff,' Mac replied as he lay back. 'There's nothing else you can do now Tommy. Just pull the curtains on your way out. Don't come around tomorrow unless I call you.'

'Shall I tell Bridget?'

'No, please don't!' Mac ordered. 'She will only come over when she should be working. There's nothing she can do Tommy, there's nothing anyone can do. Thanks for all you've done for me though and for not letting Dan see me like that. Oh, can you tell Tim I won't be around tonight but don't tell him why. Say it's work or something.'

Tommy didn't like it but he did as he was ordered.

He rang Dan and said that Mac was a little unwell. It was nothing much, he lied, just precautionary.

'Better not take any chances, I suppose. You've got some interviews to do, haven't you?' Dan asked.

'Yes, four classmates of Joy Ackley.'

'Do me a favour and take Adil here with you. He's bored stiff and he's driving me right up the wall.'

Tommy promised Dan he'd pick Adil up at the field.

As he drove down the hill again, he couldn't help wondering if Mac would be up to carrying on with the investigation. He wasn't that religious but he still found himself saying a little prayer that he'd be alright. He liked working with Mac but the main reason he'd said the prayer was because he knew that the investigation really needed him.

Mac lay there as the day waned and the room gradually got darker. He tried turning on his side to find a better position but it only hurt him more. The drugs were starting to kick in now. While they'd help lessen the pain, he also knew that he'd be in for a weird and wonderful ride, a night full of strange lucid dreams and disassociated thoughts. It was like having your arms and legs tightly strapped so you couldn't move as you sat on a rollercoaster that swooped high and low through the cobwebs of your memories and into the darkest recesses of your mind.

Mac almost dreaded it more than the pain. He yearned for the blackness of deep sleep and non-existence.

He feared that it might be a long time coming.

Chapter Twelve

Four days missing

After many hours of tossing and turning he eventually went back down into the blackness of sleep. It was only black for a while though; disjointed images, thoughts, even smells went past his mind's eye in a chaotic parade. He was just a spectator at some mad cinema show that was going on inside his head.

It finally faded away and most of his memories of it thankfully faded away too. He opened his eyes. It was light.

'She wouldn't do that!' a woman's voice said in his head.

Mac vaguely remembered a dream where someone was saying this. But who was she and what did it mean?

He lay there for a while thinking about this. For some reason he knew that it was important but he hadn't the vaguest idea why. He decided to creep up on it.

He sat up and found that this wasn't too hard to accomplish. Then, after he'd said a prayer and girded his loins, he stood up and he winced as the pain hit him again.

It wasn't as bad as it had been but it was still there. He looked at the clock. It was eight o'clock. From the fact that the sun was shining brightly outside he concluded that it must be morning.

He limped into the kitchen and made himself some coffee and toast, all the while trying not to think about his dream. Even before he'd finished eating his toast, the fatigue claimed him once again and he had to go back to his bed. Before he went, he took two more little blue pills. His only option when the pain was this bad was to try and sleep through it.

He lay down and sleep quickly overcame him once again. It was thankfully a deep, normal sleep, only interspersed with vague dreams.

Mac slept on until the next morning.

Chapter Thirteen

Five days missing
He turned the alarm off and lay there for a while, right on the borderline between sleep and waking. Without being bidden the answer came straight into his mind. He was in someone's living room and a blonde woman in her forties was saying with absolute conviction, 'My Jessie, she wouldn't do that!'

He sat up. He knew that this was what he'd been searching his brain for, although exactly what it meant he wasn't quite sure as yet. He braced himself and then stood up, smiling when he found that his back was once again within normal levels. It would hurt but it wouldn't stop him doing things. Today he needed to be able to do things. Before he did anything else, he took off the older pain patch and said a little prayer that he might have a clear head today.

While he was brushing his teeth, a name popped into his head. Charlie Booker.

He looked into the mirror for some time. Of course, Charlie Booker! At the time Charlie been a DI at Barnet police station. Mac knew that it all tied in. He looked at the clock. It was now just past seven. He called Tommy who, to his surprise, had obviously been asleep.

'What, what?' Tommy said still not quite sure where he was.

'It's Mac here, can you pick me up? We need to go to Barnet Police Station.'

There was a pause.

'It's not even six yet,' Tommy lamented.

'Six? Is it really?' Mac said as he checked his clock. It said ten past seven. He must have inadvertently changed the time somehow.

'It doesn't matter. This is important Tommy.'

There was a short pause.

'Okay, give me half an hour,' Tommy said.

Mac dressed and got himself some coffee and toast. He was excited, in fact he was buzzing. He knew this meant something. He knew it. While he waited, he made some phone calls.

There was a message from Peter Harper, now DI Peter Harper Mac observed with a smile. He hadn't come up with anything. Mac now knew why. It had been a case alright but not one of his.

Tommy kept to his word. A half an hour later the bell rang. He saw a totally different Mac to the one who had been ravaged by pain. This one looked energetic and eager to get on with it.

'How are you Mac?' Tommy asked. 'I must admit you're looking a lot better than you did the day before yesterday.'

The day before yesterday, Mac thought. A whole day was missing from his life. Mac hated those days when the pain won and not just because it hurt. He was getting older and more conscious of time. It was a day that he'd never get back again.

'I'm okay Tommy, honestly. A day's rest has done me good.'

'So, what's this all about?' Tommy asked as they walked towards the car.

'I'll tell you on the way if that's okay.'

As they drove down the motorway Mac told Tommy what he knew.

'I've had a sort of itch in my head, if you know what I mean, ever since I first saw Natasha's photo. I knew I'd never seen her before but there was something that was familiar about her. I've been thinking and thinking and I've finally come up with the reason why. I'm pretty sure that Natasha's disappearance is somehow tied into a case that I reviewed some fourteen years ago. Exactly how, I'm not sure but hopefully we're going to find out soon.'

'Fourteen years ago?' Tommy exclaimed giving Mac a sceptical look. 'And you really think that this case has got something to do with Natasha?'

'I do but let's talk about it when we get there,' Mac said. 'By the way what happened yesterday?'

Tommy gave it some thought.

'Well, we managed to interview the four girls whose statements were in the school reports and they're still absolutely adamant that Joy Ackley discussed how she was going to frame Mr. Hamilton weeks before the allegations were actually made. Not only that but one of the girls put us onto another witness. She'd been one of Joy's gang at school. She also confirmed what the others had said.'

'Why would she though, if she'd been one of Joy's friends?' Mac asked.

'Well, apparently one of the twelve year old girls that Joy was trying to recruit as a prostitute was this friend's younger sister. She didn't take it well.'

'Well, that might break a friendship up alright,' Mac conceded.

'Then Dan had the two kids from the college brought in,' Tommy said. 'You know, the ones who were spreading it around that Jonny Aldis had murdered Natasha.'

'Did they know anything?' Mac asked.

'Nothing at all as it turned out, they were just being malicious little toe-rags. That's Dan's description by the way minus the swear words. So, Dan let me be the good cop and he was the bad cop. He was really good too, he frightened the hell out of them.'

'Is he going to charge them?'

Tommy shook his head.

'They're not worth the trouble Dan said but he didn't tell them that. Just before he let them go, he told them charges would be prepared and they'd know in six to eight weeks.'

'So, he's going to let them stew for a while. Good for him,' Mac said.

'Then there was the suspect that Mrs. Tarbot had some doubts about.'

'That's the lady with the binoculars?' Mac asked.

'Yes, that's her. Anyway, she wasn't too far off as it turned out. Dan raided the shed and found four Romanians inside. They were basically being used as slaves by a gang master picking fruit in the area. We've passed it over to a team from Cambridgeshire who are looking into this type of crime.'

'So, we've uncovered a paedophile, two malicious slanderers and a slave master so far but I take it that we're really no nearer finding Natasha?' Mac asked.

'That's about it,' Tommy confirmed.

'Okay, well I'm hoping that our little outing might help with that.'

Tommy slowed down and drove down the side of Barnet Police Station. He stopped at the gates to the car park and spoke to someone via the intercom. They took pity on him and the gates opened.

'Over there,' Mac said pointing towards a grey-haired man who was smoking a cigarette outside the main building.

Tommy parked right in front of the man. He smiled as he watched Mac climb out of the car.

'Charlie, how are you?' Mac asked.

The two men shook hands warmly. Mac introduced Tommy.

'You might not believe it,' Mac said as he turned towards Tommy, 'but this man here was my sergeant when I first joined the Met. You don't look old enough though, Charlie.'

'Oh, stop joshing Mac,' Charlie protested with a smile. The smile then instantly left his face. 'It's Jessica Watson you're here about then?'

'Yes, yes that was her name Jessica. Her mother called her Jessie, didn't she? When I rang you about the missing girl you knew exactly who I meant, didn't you?' Mac said.

'Yes, it was a sad case and one that I never forgot. I was really surprised to get your call after all these years though. Come on, follow me.'

Charlie took them down a couple of corridors and into an interview room. A thick manila folder sat on the table.

'Is that it?' Mac asked.

'Yes, that's the case file. They still did everything on paper in those days,' Charlie replied.

Mac was almost hesitant to open it but he forced himself.

'Tell me what you remember,' Mac asked as he started looking through the file.

'I remember pretty much all of it for some reason, even though it was all those years ago. A young girl disappears without a trace, it's not right, is it? It would have been better if she'd turned up dead, at least her poor mother could have buried her and grieved for her properly.'

Yes, that was it. The blonde woman had been Jessica's mother.

'What happened to her?' Mac asked.

'The mother? She died a few years later,' Charlie replied. 'From what I heard she more or less drank herself to death.'

Mac looked through the file and then stopped dead. He'd found a photo of Jessica. He sat down and looked at it closely.

So that's what this is all about, he said to himself.

Without a word he passed the photo to Tommy. He could see the effect it had.

'God, she and Natasha could almost be sisters!' Tommy said.

He also saw the dawning in Tommy's eyes as to what this implied.

'Fourteen years ago!' Tommy said with some wonder.

'What?' Charlie asked. 'Who's this Natasha?'

Tommy got his phone out and found the news story on the BBC. It had a photo of Natasha.

'Yes, I can see the resemblance. This girl's gone missing too then?' Charlie asked.

'Yes, it's been all over the news,' Mac replied.

'I heard about the disappearance from the wife but I don't have time to watch the news these days. I don't spend much time indoors now I'm retired.'

'Oh, that's right, you breed roses these days, don't you Charlie? I remember now.'

'Two seconds and a third this year but I'm still waiting for a first prize though. Mac, do you honestly think that these two cases are connected, even though there's fourteen years between them?' Charlie asked

'I do,' Mac said with complete certainty.

Charlie thought about this for a moment and then nodded his head.

'Okay, what do you want to do?'

'Can you take us to her house?' Mac asked. 'I'd just like to have another look around the area that she disappeared from.'

'Sure,' Charlie replied.

Charlie climbed into the back seat and directed Tommy towards a small estate on the outskirts of Barnet. To get to it they drove down a stretch of road that had houses on one side and a high fence on the other. Beyond the fence several railway lines glinted in the morning sun.

At the end of the road they turned left and then left again before they pulled up outside a semi-detached house.

Mac got out and looked at number ninety-three. He remembered it all now.

'How come you were on this case in the first place?' Tommy asked. 'Barnet wouldn't have been in your normal operational area, would it?'

'I was doing Charlie a favour,' Mac replied, 'or, I should say, returning one, or several if I'm being honest.'

'Yes, I must admit that this one got under my skin for some reason,' Charlie said. 'I kept going over and over it in my head and it was driving me right up the wall. I was so sure that I must have missed something that I asked Mac to come in and do a case review. I was really hoping that he'd find something that we hadn't, something that would give us a clue.'

'It must have been about three weeks after Jessica had disappeared that I came down,' Mac explained. 'I did a thorough review and couldn't find a single thing that had been overlooked. Charlie's team had, in my opinion, done everything they could do and more. Before I went back to London we came here and we interviewed Jessica's mother again. That's what I remembered this morning, Jessica's mother. She said 'My Jessie, she wouldn't do that'.'

'Yes, I remember,' Charlie said. 'You asked if it was possible that she might have gone off with a boyfriend.'

'Who lives here now?' Mac asked, looking at the house.

Charlie shrugged.

'I've no idea.'

'Let's find out then,' Mac said.

He looked at his watch. It was now just before eight. He rang the bell and waited. A woman in her late twenties opened the door, a woman who bore quite a resemblance to Jessica. Mac showed her his warrant card.

'We're looking again at the Jessica Watson case. She lived here fourteen years ago. Did you know her or her family?' Mac asked.

The woman showed some surprise at his question. She didn't reply, she just gestured at the three men to follow her inside into the living room. She stood by the fireplace and pointed at a picture.

'That's Jessie,' she said.

Mac picked up the framed photo. It showed two young girls, one about fifteen the other around ten or eleven.

'Is that you?' Mac asked, pointing to the younger girl. She nodded.

'Yes, that's me. We used to play a lot together when we were kids. She was older than me but we still got on really well.'

'And your name is?' Mac asked.

'Gemma, Gemma Greenwood. Jessie was my cousin.'

'How come you're living here then?'

'Auntie Brenda left the house to me when she died,' Gemma explained. 'She didn't last all that long after Jessie disappeared. It broke her heart, she just didn't want to live without her. I had some great times in this house when I was a kid but now it just seems a bit sad.'

'Did you talk to the police around the time Jessica disappeared?' Mac asked.

'Yes, to this man here if I remember right,' she replied waving towards Charlie.

'If you don't mind, could you tell us again what happened the evening Jessica disappeared?' Mac asked.

'Sure,' she said sitting down on an armchair. She pointed to the sofa which was a tight squeeze for the three of them but they managed it.

'I was in this house the evening she disappeared. I watched her while she got herself dressed and she let me help her a bit with her make-up. She was going into London for an all-nighter she said. Auntie Brenda was dead set against it and they had a big row. There was nothing unusual in that, they were always arguing about something or other. She called for a taxi and then walked me home. She left me outside my door and gave me a kiss on the cheek. She never came back.'

Gemma's face puckered up as she fought to keep the tears back.

'That's right, she didn't catch the taxi outside her house, did she? Why was that?' Mac asked.

'It saves some money if you catch the taxi on the main road. People still do it now. Otherwise the taxis have to go a good bit up the road to get onto the estate and then turn back on themselves.'

'I take it that there's some sort of shortcut?' Mac asked getting more interested.

'Yes, it's about a hundred yards or so down the road on the opposite side. My mum's house is almost opposite.'

'Show us.'

Gemma took them outside and pointed to some houses just down the street.

'That's it there, just between those two houses. Can I ask you a question?'

'Of course,' Mac said.

'Why are you asking me about Jessica after all this time? Are you re-opening the case or something?'

Mac looked at Tommy and Charlie and thought of what to say.

'I'm sorry but I can't be too specific at the moment. It just might be that Jessica's disappearance could have some connection to a case we're currently investigating.'

'He's done it again, hasn't he?' Gemma said. It wasn't a question. 'Is it that girl from Hitchin?'

'What makes you ask that?'

'I couldn't help noticing that she looks very like Jessie and she's near enough the same age too,' she replied.

'Why did you say 'he's done it again'?' Mac asked.

'I always knew that she'd been taken by someone. Jessica and Auntie Brenda fought a lot but they really loved each other. There's no way she would have left, especially not without saying a single word to anyone. Someone took her, someone killed her. I just know it.'

She looked bleakly towards the entryway.

'I watched her as she walked down there. She looked back at me and smiled. That was the very last time I saw her.'

A tear ran down her cheek.

'I'm glad you're investigating her case again,' Gemma said. 'Just do me a big favour and find the bastard who took our Jessie away from us.'

As they walked towards the entryway Tommy asked, 'Do you really think that the same man who abducted Natasha also abducted Jessica Watson fourteen years ago?'

'Yes,' Mac said, 'that's exactly what I'm thinking.'

They turned left and into the short cut. The brick end walls of the houses on either side made the entryway dark until they came to some head high wooden fences on the other side of which Mac presumed were the back gardens belonging to the houses. They came to a sort of junction as another walkway cut across at ninety degrees. To the right the walkway was narrow and all along it at regular intervals were the back entrances to the houses on either side. It was overgrown and didn't look like it was used much. To the left the walkway was also narrow but it opened out after fifty yards or so. Mac walked down that way.

The reason it opened out was because there was a row of six garages and a driveway that looked like it curved right back onto the main road. Mac stood there for a while.

'What do you think?' Tommy asked eventually.

'Remember when I said that our man had had some practice?' Mac replied. 'I think that this was part of that practice. It was dark out when Jessica disappeared and the lighting here looks pretty scant even now. So, she walks down this way and perhaps our man is hiding around the corner here. He hits her then tapes her up and rolls her quickly into the suitcase. He could have parked his car there by the garages so he only has to wheel her a short distance, roll the case into the boot and then drive off.'

Tommy looked about him.

'That makes sense to me,' he said.

'What do you think Charlie?' Mac asked.

'It makes sense to me too now that I think about it,' Charlie said. 'The driver who'd been given the job of picking her up was over five minutes late so we always thought that she might have been picked up by someone she knew or even by an illegal taxi driver. We never got anywhere with that line of enquiry though. If you're right then she never even made it to the main road.'

'Is that taxi driver still around?' Mac asked.

'Yes, yes he is. As a matter of fact, I saw him the other day in the garden centre and it immediately brought Jessica back into my mind. Coincidence or what?' Charlie said. 'Anyway, his name's Gwyn Davies. He's still with the same firm he was working for fourteen years ago.'

'Think you could ring him and get him to meet us on the main road?' Mac asked.

While Charlie was ringing the taxi firm Tommy asked, 'What do you think we can learn from the taxi driver?'

Mac shrugged.

'I've no idea really. I just thought that, as he arrived only five minutes or so after Jessica was taken, then he might be worth talking to. Not only that but taxi drivers really know their patches. I'm just wondering if he saw something that might be relevant and, perhaps, he doesn't even realise it.'

They strolled down to the main road and a few minutes later a car with a taxi sign on the roof pulled up. A short stocky man with black hair going grey at the sides climbed out of the driver's seat. He slowly walked towards the three policemen, all the time looking at them closely, as though he might be able to make out what it was all about just from their expressions.

'You wanted to see me?' he asked in the sing-song accent of the Welsh valleys.

He looked a little anxious.

'It's Gwyn, isn't it?' Mac said. 'Look don't worry, we're not here because of you. We're reviewing the Jessica Watson case. Do you remember her?'

The taxi driver visibly relaxed. He sat on the bonnet of his car and crossed his arms.

'Good God, how could I ever forget that? I've thought about her a lot over the years. Girls never go missing around here, never. Only her.'

'I believe that you were a few minutes late?'

Gwyn scowled.

'The missus asked me to pick up some milk and I nearly forgot. There's a little shop on the way here and I thought it wouldn't take a second to pop in and buy a bottle. When I got in there was some guy having a row with the shopkeeper and it took me ages to get served. I wasn't helped either by those bloody lights they had just up there by where the site entrance was. Even so, I was surprised when she wasn't here when I arrived. I waited for nearly ten minutes and then I guessed that someone else must have picked her up or maybe she'd changed her mind. I never thought much of it until I heard the news the day after.'

He looked up at the three men.

'Are you opening the case up again or something?'

'We're not sure yet,' Mac replied. 'As I've said we're just reviewing it. Is there anything that you might have remembered later that you might have forgotten to tell us at the time?'

132

'No, I told Mr. Booker here everything I knew. I wanted you lot to find Jessica, I really did. I often wondered if my being late…well you know.'

He gave the policeman a sad look.

'Well, if it's any consolation we think it's possible that Jessica might never have even made it this far. We think that she might have been abducted where the walk-ways cross up there,' Mac said pointing up the entryway.

'You're not just saying that are you?' he asked as he unfolded his arms and stood up.

'No, we really think that's what might have happened,' Mac replied.

The taxi driver turned away and looked up the entryway.

'You know for fourteen years I've wondered whether me stopping for that sodding bottle of milk might have been the difference between that little girl disappearing or being alive today. Fourteen bloody years!'

He turned around and Mac could see tears in his eyes. They somehow looked out of place on the man's face. For a second he got a glimpse of the burden the taxi driver had been carrying for all that time.

He wiped his eyes with the back of his hand.

'Big baby, aren't I?' he said, trying to smile.

'No, no you're not,' Mac stated. 'If you do remember anything else please ring me.'

He gave the taxi driver his number who then climbed into his car. He was just about to shut his door when Mac shouted.

'Stop! Gwyn, stop!'

'What is it?' the taxi driver asked as he got out of his car again.

'You said something about traffic lights and a site entrance. What did you mean by that?' Mac asked with some urgency.

'It was just down there,' he replied pointing down the road. 'About four lamp posts down if I remember right.'

133

'What was?'

'The entrance to the site,' Gwyn replied. 'God the amount of earth they moved out of there was amazing! The only problem was I used to have to get the car washed regularly as they seemed to drop most of it on the road.'

Mac thought he had it now. He just needed one answer more.

'What were they doing on the site?'

'They were putting an extra set of tracks in, weren't they?' Gwyn said. 'Massive job it was too, they were here for ages.'

Mac looked beyond the fence on the other side of the street to the shining steel tracks that lay beyond. In his mind's eye he could see the traffic lights on his hill that had annoyed him so much and the massive rail works that they were cutting into the hillside.

'So that's how he did it,' Mac intoned softly.

Tommy got a glimpse of the far away eyes again as Mac stood and gazed at the train tracks. He suddenly stirred himself.

'Come on Tommy, we've got work to do. Thanks very much Mr. Davies. Would it be okay if we drop you back at the station, Charlie?'

'Fine by me,' Charlie replied.

Mac got out at the station too and shook his colleague's hand again.

'It's been so good to see you again Charlie,' Mac said with complete sincerity.

'You too, Mac. Can you do me a favour though?'

'What's that?'

'When you get him, come and see me afterwards and I'll buy you a pint. You can tell me all about it.'

'I wish I had your confidence Charlie but yes, I'll definitely do that,' Mac replied.

Mac never said a word to Tommy as they drove down the motorway and back into Hertfordshire. He was too busy on his phone. They were just passing Stevenage when he finished talking.

Tommy looked over at him with a question in his eyes.

'Oh, I'm sorry Tommy but I needed to make those calls.'

'I guess that the first one was to Dan. Who was the second one to if you don't mind me asking?'

'An old friend and colleague of mine who works with the Transport Police. He's going to send Martin some details of the company who worked on both the Barnet and Hitchin jobs.'

'So, you think our man is someone who's employed on the rail works?' Tommy asked.

'I do,' Mac replied with some certainty. 'He's very clever too.'

'In what way?'

'Say the rail works last a year or so. While he's in the area he abducts a girl and does whatever he does to her. Just the one though. Then they move to the next job which might be over the other side of the country and again he takes just the one girl. Who'd be able to put the two crimes together? No-one because the two crimes have happened in different patches and even now we're not all that good at talking to other forces. Years ago, we were bloody terrible.'

Tommy thought about what Mac had said.

'So, you think there are more girls involved? It's not just Jessica and Natasha?'

'I'd be amazed if that was the case,' Mac replied. 'If I had to bet, I'd say that there's definitely more, perhaps a lot more. A man can do a lot in fourteen years.'

Dan and Adil were waiting for them when they returned to the incident room. Amanda was at her post by the door and Martin was glued to his laptop screen.

There was a sort of grim smile of Dan's face as he asked, 'Do you really think you've got something?'

'I do,' Mac replied, 'but it would be nice to have some hard evidence to back it up. That's what we need to work on right now.'

He went over to Martin's desk.

'Has anything come?' he asked, feeling a little flutter of nervousness.

'Yes, an email and attachment from the Transport Police,' Martin replied. 'I've printed them off for you. Here.'

He handed Mac several sheets of paper.

Mac scanned the sheets avidly. The first sheet was the covering email. Mac skipped this and looked at the other sheets. It had columns full of dates and locations. Mac picked out the ones for Barnet and Hitchin. There was a column for companies. Everyone saw Mac's face fall when he noticed that it was a totally different company that had done the Barnet works to the one currently doing the Hitchin works.

'What is it?' Tommy asked.

'Different companies,' Mac said. 'I thought that it must have been the same company that worked on both the Barnet and Hitchin works but it isn't.'

He'd been so sure.

Chapter Fourteen

Without looking up Martin said, 'Different companies, same people though.'

'What do you mean?' Mac asked a small light dawning in his head.

'The employees, they were TUPE'd. It's all in the email,' Martin replied.

Mac's relief was evident to everyone.

'I'd forgotten all about that. Thanks Martin, you really saved me there. How do you know about TUPE?'

'You'd be surprised at what I know,' Martin said with a little smile.

'What's TUPE?' asked a mystified Tommy.

'I'm not sure exactly what it stands for but it's a law that allows for whole workforces to be transferred over when a new contract is agreed. I'd guess that a lot of the jobs in a big rail project are quite specialised so you wouldn't be able to go out and get a load of new employees even if you wanted to.'

Mac quickly read the email.

'Yes, it says here that there have been three different companies running the contract in the last twenty-five years but it's probable that most of the same employees would have worked on all the projects.'

'So, what now?' Dan asked.

'Girls will have gone missing during the period of the works and we need to know who they were,' Mac replied. 'We need photos too. I've got a feeling that our man is going for a particular type, young, dark haired and striking.'

'Well, that's the theory anyway,' Dan reminded him.

Mac glanced up at Dan and nodded. He realised that Dan might be right and he might be running away with himself a bit.

Dan continued, 'I wouldn't bet against you Mac, not with your track record, but we need more evidence before we start putting any resources into it. Okay then, Martin what's the best way of getting photos and information about missing girls?'

'In theory I suppose they should all be on the national databases somewhere,' Martin said with some hesitation.

'And?' Dan asked.

'Well, I should be able to just look it all up right now and show you but, as a lot of these cases are quite old, it would be my bet that the information on the databases is going to be patchy at best. Some of the databases are text only anyway which also doesn't help. If there was proof of a serious crime, we might be a bit better off but as they've just gone missing...' Martin stopped and shrugged his shoulders.

'So, what do you suggest?' Dan asked.

'To get the best results you might be better off contacting each of the police forces which cover the areas that the girls were abducted from and get them to send us the data from their local systems,' Martin replied. 'Going that far back there's a good chance that a lot of the information will be on paper anyway. It will take a little longer but you'll probably get better results.'

Dan gave this some thought. It was obvious from his expression that he would have liked all the data right that second. However, he could see that Martin had a point.

'Okay, we'll do it your way.'

'No problem,' Martin replied as he started compiling the first email.

'I'm also going to ring someone in every force just in case they don't read their emails that frequently,' Dan said. 'A bit of belt and braces won't hurt.'

'Mind if I lend a hand? I know a few of the Detective Chief Superintendents personally,' Mac suggested.

'Absolutely, I could do with all the help I can get. Adil can you start putting all the dates and locations on the whiteboard. Leave some columns for the names and photos.'

'Sure thing,' Adil replied looking relieved to be doing something.

'What shall I do?' Tommy asked.

Dan gave it some thought.

'How many coffees?' Dan asked loudly.

All their hands went up except for Tommy's.

'Okay I'll get the coffees,' Tommy said looking a bit miffed.

'I could do with a hand when you get back. If you want to, that is?' Mac asked.

Tommy smiled.

'Sure thing, Mac.'

A little over an hour later the incident room was silent and they were all looking at each other.

'This is the bit I hate,' Dan said grumpily, 'the bloody waiting.'

'Me too,' Mac replied. 'By the way what's happening with the Hamilton case?'

'Oh yes, I was nearly forgetting about that. I had a chat with someone from the CPS and they say that the testimony given by the witnesses make a case for prosecuting Joy Ackley for at least making a false statement and wasting police time. However, they're looking at other charges too.'

Mac gave this some thought. He looked at his watch, it had just gone eleven thirty. He was surprised as he'd thought it would be much later.

'So, there's no case against Tony Hamilton then?' Mac asked.

'No, we haven't found a single shred of evidence that supported Joy Ackley's allegations,' Dan said. 'I guess that she was just trying to settle old scores, in quite a vicious, nasty way too.'

'I think the money had something to do with it too.'

'Money, what money?' Dan asked.

'She read somewhere that some of the victims of historic child abuse came in for some compensation,' Mac said. 'I could see her eyes light up at the thought.'

'Christ, she just makes it that little bit harder for the next genuine victim to come forward, as if it isn't hard enough for the poor sods. I can see that you want to do something, what is it?' Dan asked.

'I thought I might as well go and give Tony Hamilton the good news, tell him that he won't be charged.'

'That's a good idea. Take Tommy with you,' Dan said turning away. He turned back again. 'Ask him again if he's thought of anything that he hasn't told us yet. Even a tiny bit more evidence would help.'

'Will do.'

Mac breathed deeply as he walked out onto the pavement. He'd had a moment of fear in the incident room as the thought occurred to him that his little theory might just be a house of cards. The information coming in might confirm it or it might blow it all down. He knew that he'd sooner be doing something than hanging around waiting to see which one it turned out to be.

He rang Tony Hamilton who said that he'd meet Mac at Letchworth Police Station.

'That's strange,' Mac said as they drove towards Letchworth.

'What's strange?' Tommy asked.

'I said that I could meet him at his house but he said that he'd sooner come to the station.'

'Perhaps he just doesn't like the neighbours seeing the police call around so frequently,' Tommy suggested.

'Perhaps.'

Mac wasn't convinced though and he wondered if something had happened.

They were both waiting for them in an interview room when they got there. Mr. Hamilton sat still and stony faced, looking straight at the wall in front of him. He'd aged since the last time they'd met. Mrs. Hamilton just looked sad. Mac sat down.

'I've some good news for once,' Mac announced brightly.

Neither of the Hamiltons responded. They just looked at Mac with a blank expression.

'We're not going to charge you with anything,' Mac said. 'In fact, it's Miss Ackley who's going to end up being charged.'

'Oh,' they both said with no excitement whatsoever.

'I thought you'd be glad,' Mac said surprised at their reaction.

'Glad? Glad about what?' Mr. Hamilton said with some bitterness. 'Charge me, don't charge me, it really doesn't matter all that much now, does it?'

'What doesn't matter?'

Mr. Hamilton gave Mac a bleak look.

'What's happened?' Mac asked.

'This, haven't you seen it yet?' Mrs. Hamilton said as she handed him a newspaper.

It was one of the better-known tabloids. Better known for being at the scummier end of the market that is. A picture of Tony Hamilton working in his front garden dominated the page. The headline, printed in red ink, read 'Did Pervert Teacher Kill Natasha?' In the corner was a photo of Joy Ackley looking sad. It was a good photo too, Mac thought. She almost looked human.

Mac felt his heart go into his boots.

'This isn't right!' he said with some anger.

'Right or not it's done now isn't it?' Tony said. 'When I was walking to get the paper this morning an old friend of mine crossed the street when he saw me. I'd known him for twenty years. He was a real friend, or so I'd thought. It happened again with someone else on the way back. Half an hour later and there they were camped outside our house. Bloody press, some of them even followed us here.' He gave Mac a bleak look. 'I used to love living in Letchworth but I can't now. We'll be selling up as soon as we can.'

Mac couldn't think of anything to say that might help. Tony Hamilton was unfortunately right. There are some things that just can't be put back together.

'I'm sorry, I really am,' Mac said feeling absolutely helpless.

He looked again at the photo of Joy Ackley. He knew that she must have been behind this in some way. Well, it might not be much but there was one thing he could do.

'As I said we'll be charging Joy Ackley but, before you go, I just want to ask if there's anything else you can tell us that might help us to prosecute her?' Mac asked.

The husband and wife looked at each other. Mr. Hamilton shook his head.

Mac was surprised to see Mrs. Hamilton stand up and shout, 'I've had enough! You and your bloody pride, you and your 'I'm only half a man' bleating. For Christ's sake tell them. TELL THEM!'

Mr. Hamilton gave him wife a sheepish look and slowly nodded his head. She sat down again.

'It was the war,' he said. 'The Gulf War that is. I'd served nine years in the Army and I'd already started teacher training when I got called up. I was a reservist. I'd been there a couple of months when it happened. We were destroying munition dumps when one lot went off by itself. We lost three men and, at first, I thought I'd got off unscathed. Then someone saw the blood seeping out of my trousers. I'd been hit by a piece of shrapnel in the groin. I nearly died. There've been lots of times since when I wish I had.'

His wife held his hand with both of hers.

'It cut a load of nerves and damaged the blood supply, you know, down there. I had a couple of operations but they couldn't do anything, so that was that. No more sex for me.' He glanced at his wife. 'You know I wish I hadn't been away so much, I wish we'd had more time together...'

She gripped his hand more tightly.

'I know love, I know,' she said, tears filling her eyes.

Mac didn't say anything for a moment.

'Why didn't you tell this to your headmistress or the policeman who did the investigation?'

'Shame I suppose,' he replied. 'I just didn't want anyone to know about it. Carol said that I should have told them but when the girls said what they did, about Joy telling them before she made the accusations, I thought I didn't need to. So, I said nothing. That decision's come back to bloody haunt me now though, hasn't it?'

'You've got nothing to be ashamed of Mr. Hamilton,' Mac said. 'However, I do understand why you didn't want to say anything. I'd appreciate it if you could let me have your doctor's name. We'll need to confirm what you say.'

'Of course. I'll give you the name of the army doctor who treated me. I still see him once a year.'

He wrote it down. Mac was surprised that the hospital was in Birmingham and it was one that he knew well. Then he remembered that it had a military section where they treated soldiers coming back from overseas.

'Thank you both,' Mac said as he stood up to go. He glanced again at the newspaper. 'You should sue them, you know.'

'Will that give us our lives back?' Mr. Hamilton replied.

'No but it will hurt the paper, only a bit perhaps, but it would be something.'

Mr. Hamilton shrugged.

'Perhaps,' he said with no interest whatsoever.

As they were getting into the car Tommy said, 'I really felt sorry for them, Mac.'

'Yes, me too. There's not much we can do now but let's do the little we can,' Mac said. 'Can you phone Luton police and get them to arrest Joy Ackley? Tell them to take her to Letchworth station and leave her there in an interview room. I think we'll take our time charging her. I'll call Martin and ask him to get the ball rolling with regard to Mr. Hamilton's medical records.'

Once they'd finished their calls Tommy asked, 'Where to now? Back to the incident room?'

'Do you mind if we go by the Hamilton's house on the way back?' Mac asked.

'No of course not. Why though? Did you forget to ask them something?'

'It's not them I want to see.'

A small crowd of pressmen were hanging around outside the bungalow. Unbelievably there was also a camera crew from an American news station.

Before they left the car, Mac had Tommy confirm that Luton police had picked up Joy Ackley. She was already on her way to Letchworth. He looked at the by-line of the newspaper story. It was by a 'Clemency Burrows'. It had a little photo by her name.

The sharp faced young blonde with the camera that he'd seen outside the Aldis' house was there again. Mac pulled her to one side.

'Ah, the famous Mac Maguire,' she said with a big smile. 'I read up on you, you're quite a star. Have you got an exclusive for me?'

'Yes, sort of. Let's go over there,' he said, pointing to a nearby entryway between the houses.

'You don't want to be seen with me. That's wise,' she said.

144

Safely out of the gaze of the other pressmen Mac showed her the paper.

'I take it that this is your work?'

She smiled as she looked at it.

'Yes, it turned out really well. The red really makes it work, don't you think?'

'Well it will have turned out better than your career then,' Mac said looking directly into her eyes.

The smile left her face.

'What do you mean?'

'I get it alright, you're a young, thrusting journalist, making a name for herself in a male dominated world,' Mac said. 'Sometimes you have to shove a bit, cut corners a bit, don't you?'

'Yes, so what? They all do it. What are you getting at?'

'Well, if I were you, I'd make sure that I was at the next press conference we hold, you might be in for a few surprises. By the way is Bob Holderby still your editor?'

'Well yes, but I've never actually met him though.'

'No, you're too far down the food chain I suppose,' Mac said. 'Well, after what's going to come out, you'll be even further down, in fact I doubt that you'll have a job at all.'

'What do you mean?'

For the first time she looked concerned.

'You'll see. I'll be giving Bob a call myself too, just to make sure he gets the full picture. Have a good day.'

'Tell me what you mean!' she shouted but Mac was already halfway to the car.

Tommy started the car up and pulled away.

'Well you told her alright. Do you really know this editor?' Tommy asked.

'I do, we've had quite a few dealings over the years,' Mac replied. 'I'll be warning him that not only will Mr. Hamilton be suing but that I'll be testifying on his behalf.'

'So, what do you think will happen?' Tommy asked.

'Oh, it'll all be settled out of court as the paper hasn't got a legal leg to stand on. They won't care anyway as the story will have sold umpteen more copies of their rag and that will have more than covered their court costs. Then Miss Burrows will hopefully get the sack and the Hamiltons will get a shed load of money and an apology tucked away on page ten. It's not much I know but it's all we can do. Come on, let's check in on the incident room first before we visit Miss Ackley. She can stew for a while.'

The whole thing had left Mac with a bitter taste in his mouth. As they drove back towards the incident room, he said a little prayer that things were going better there.

Chapter Fifteen

As soon as he entered the incident room Mac glanced over at the white board. His heart skipped a beat when he saw two photos on the board until he realised that they were of Natasha and Jessica.

'Nothing yet?' Mac asked.

'No, I suppose it will take them some time to go through the records,' Dan replied.

He looked as anxious as Max felt.

Mac went over to the white board. The dates and locations were all there.

1996 Southampton
1998 Glasgow
2000 York
2002 Barnet – Jessica Watson 19 - Disappeared
2003 Birmingham International
2005 Peterborough
2006 Cardiff
2008 Crewe
2011 Carlisle
2013 Bristol
2016 Hitchin – Natasha Barker 18 - Disappeared

From one end of the country to the other, Mac thought. It was no wonder that we never noticed any connection.

'Anyone want a coffee?' Tommy asked.

They all put their hand up.

'Get a tray of doughnuts too please, Tommy. I'm starving,' Dan said.

'Come on, I'll give you a hand,' Amanda offered.

'Dan,' Martin said with some urgency. 'Printing off.'

Dan ran over to the printer and begrudged it the time it took to print the page out. He looked at the sheet of paper.

'Yes!' he said with a tone of triumph.

He gave the sheet to Mac. It was information on a young girl called Jackie Oldfield who had disappeared from the Peterborough area in 2005. One look at the photo was all Mac really needed.

He passed the sheet to Tommy.

'Martin, can you print off the photo?' Dan asked.

'Already done,' Martin replied.

Adil took the sheet and trimmed the photo and then stuck it on the white board. Next to Peterborough he wrote 'Jackie Oldfield 17 - Disappeared'.

Now they had three.

'Right, I'd better get those coffees,' Tommy said with a smile.

The next one came in just after Tommy had returned.

Another photo on the white board. Against 'Carlisle 2011' Adil wrote 'Monica Byrne 18 – Disappeared'.

Mac decided that he would wait for five before going to tell Joy Ackley the good news. Five would be a real pattern.

They were now getting lots of information in about missing girls but they weren't all good matches.

It took over an hour before Martin once again said, 'Printing off.'

They all watched as Adil wrote on the board against Cardiff 'Carla Menzies 16 – Disappeared'.

Mac looked closely at the five photos. The similarity in the girls was striking. He relaxed now knowing that his house of cards had survived the test.

'Come on Tommy, let's go tell Joy Ackley the good news.'

'You're not staying Mac?' Dan asked in surprise.

'No, we've got some unfinished business to attend to. I'm not so worried now, we've definitely got a pattern.'

Dan looked at the white board.

'Yes, I guess we have,' he said with a growing smile.

Joy Ackley was not at all impressed at the amount of time she'd had to wait.

'What the bloody hell is going on?' she shouted as Mac opened the door. 'They've had to take me to out to piss twice since I've been here! I've got places to be you know.'

Mac said nothing. He started recording the interview.

'I'd just like to say that this interview is being recorded. Do you have any objections to this?'

She shrugged her shoulders.

'No, why should I?'

'Good. I'd also like to say that you do not have to say anything. But it may harm your defence if you do not mention when questioned something which you later rely on in court. Anything you do say may be given in evidence.'

'What?' she asked.

Mac could see from her puzzled expression that she hadn't got a clue where this was heading.

'Please sit down, Miss Ackley,' Mac said.

She sat down, crossed her arms and glared at Mac with a sullen expression.

'I'm here to tell you about the progress we've made with your case. We've consulted fully with the Crown Prosecution Service and I can tell you that we will be pressing charges.'

A smile broke out on her face.

'Really? You're going to prosecute old Hamilton?'

'No, we're going to prosecute you for making a false statement and wasting police time. I'd guess that the CPS might also throw in a couple more charges when they see the new evidence.'

'You what!' she shouted. 'You're going to set that perve free and you're going to charge me!'

'Yes, that's exactly the situation,' Mac confirmed. 'You know you lied and now we know it too. We have lots of girls from your school who are willing to testify against you, even some of your former friends.'

'The bitches!' she said with feeling.

She thought about this for a moment. Her shoulders slumped. She'd been found out and she knew it.

'What am I looking at?' she said eventually.

'A couple of years at least, I'd say,' Mac replied.

She just sat there with her mouth open. For once he'd said something that had actually made her speechless. Mac stood up.

'Someone else will be in shortly to formally charge you.'

Mac made good his escape. He had a quick word with the desk sergeant who would be formally charging Joy Ackley. He told him to take his time about it.

'Well that's that,' Mac said as they walked to the car. 'She'll go to jail, not that it will help the Hamiltons much, I suppose.'

The question that Tony Hamilton had asked came back into his mind, 'Why do people wilfully hurt each other so?'

He still wished he knew.

'Come on Tommy, let's get back and see what's happening.'

The rain was falling heavily as they walked out into the car park. Flashes of lightning illuminated the dark clouds. Tommy had to keep the wipers on top speed all the way to Hitchin. The general gloominess somehow suited Mac's mood.

Mac looked at the board as soon as he got in the door of the incident room. Two more photos had appeared. Alongside Bristol was written 'Kate Beckworth 20 – Disappeared' and alongside Birmingham International was written 'Sheila Matthews 20 – Disappeared'.

It was only just after four and Mac was surprised to see that the incident room was full. All of the team were there except for Jo and Gerry who Mac guessed were still hunting around the undergrowth for Jonny Aldis. They were standing around talking to one another but all eyes were either on Martin or the white board. Mac could sense their excitement.

'Do we have the files for these girls yet?' Mac asked Martin.

'Only for Kate Beckworth and Monica Byrne so far. Dan and Chris are looking at those now. I've requested them all but I guess that some of the earlier ones might be paper files so they'll need to be scanned first.'

'Tell me when the Birmingham one comes in,' Mac said.

'Why are you so interested in that one?' Martin asked.

'I was born there and I know the area around the airport fairly well. I'm hoping that this might help in some way.'

'Fair enough, I'll let you know when it comes in then.'

Jo and Gerry turned up before the file did. Jo shook the rain from her raincoat.

'Took a bloody great storm to make this one stop,' she exclaimed her eyes pointing accusingly towards Gerry. 'Anyway, what's going on?'

Dan thought it might be a good time to tell the whole team.

'Jo's just asked a good question. I know that you've all drifted in as you've heard that we may have a major lead. All it takes is a look at the board there to confirm that you heard right. I'll go over what we've got so far so you'll all be up to date. This morning Mac remembered an old case, a fourteen year old case to be exact, where a young girl called Jessica Watson went missing in circumstances that were incredibly similar to Natasha's. Not only the circumstances were similar though if you have a look at the photos.'

Jo went to the white board and looked closely at Jessica's photo.

'They could be sisters,' Jo exclaimed. 'They're not related though, are they?'

'No, they're not,' Dan said. 'The thing that we think might be relevant is that there were major rail works taking place just down the road from where Jessica lived, just as there are now in Hitchin. We've asked for details of girls who went missing around the time of the works and you can see the candidates on the board here.'

'So, you're picking them on how similar they look to Natasha?' Jo asked.

'Yes,' Dan replied. 'The theory is that our man consistently goes for girls with the same looks and around the same age. We've only started getting the complete case files in but I've had a quick look at Kate Beckworth and the circumstances in which she disappeared aren't that dissimilar to Natasha's. She lived in a place called Lawrence Hill just down the road from where they were carrying out the rail works. She set out one Saturday evening to meet a friend at a bus stop. They were going into town for a night out but she never turned up. The route she'd have most likely taken involved a short cut down an entryway that ran down the back of a block of flats. That sounds a bit familiar, doesn't it? Chris, what about Monica Byrne?'

Chris stood up.

'Monica worked at a company on an industrial estate next to where they were doing rail works on a major freight site. She worked shifts in a warehouse. She left work at nine saying that she'd meet up with some colleagues at a nearby pub who'd finished work an hour earlier. This pub was also frequented at the time by rail workers as it was the nearest pub to the site. As you can guess she never made it. Around nine thirty, one of her friends went back to the warehouse. They took the same route that she'd have had to take but they found no sign of her. It was noted that this warehouse was the only business in the vicinity that ran shifts so it was highly unlikely that anyone else would have been about anyway.'

'So, I think that you can already see many similarities. The girls' looks, their age, the fact that they all went missing while the rail works were in their area and the manner of their disappearances is also similar,' Dan said. 'None of the girls gave any indication that they were going anywhere and all went missing where at least part of the route was secluded or, in Monica's case, where no-one was likely to be around. Not cast iron yet maybe but it's looking promising...'

Dan was interrupted by Martin.

'Printing off.'

Everyone went silent and looked at Dan as he waited for the printer. His smile said it all. He waited for the photograph and gave that to Adil. He then went to the white board and against Crewe wrote 'Maria Sanchez 15 – Disappeared'.

Once Adil had tacked the photo to the white board everyone crowded around. Mac had to wait a while but it was worth it. Maria could have been Natasha's younger sister.

'Fifteen?' Tommy said. 'She's the youngest yet then.'

'Yes, he likes them young, the oldest is only twenty,' Mac replied. 'The big question is who was first? Was it really Jessica Watson? We've still not had anything from Southampton, Glasgow or York. Of course, that could be just because they're the oldest cases and they might need a bit more time to dig out the files.'

Dan called everyone to order.

'Okay, we've now got eight good candidates and a high likelihood that we've got a serial killer on our hands, a killer who takes advantage of the fact that he regularly moves his locale and in a fairly random way at that. As a national police force, we've been pretty rubbish at communicating with each other about our cases so I suppose it's not surprising that he's gotten

153

away with it for this long. I've asked Martin to find out who holds the HR records for the rail workforce and then to arrange to get them sent over to us as soon as possible. It's now coming up to five and I know you might have made arrangements for this evening but I'd like you to cancel them. We're going to have a lot of work to do, not only with all the case files coming our way but hopefully all of the information about the rail workforce too. I'd like to try and make some sense of it all before we go home if that's okay.'

'Well, at least it's dry and warm,' Jo said. 'I don't suppose that there'll be a pizza in it for us, will there?'

Dan smiled.

'Yes, I'd say that pizzas are a distinct possibility.'

'Well, I'm in then,' Jo replied as she struggled to take off her wellingtons.

Everyone in the team nodded.

'Thanks,' Dan said. 'It would be a good idea if we stick to our teams and take a file or two each. Discuss it between the two of you and one of you take notes. I'd like to hold a quick session before everyone goes home so that each team can give us the crucial points about their cases. Martin, Adil and me will take a look at the rail workforce data, if it ever arrives that is.'

Dan picked up a memory stick and gave it to Jo.

'This is the Kate Beckworth file. I've already had a quick look but if you and Gerry could go through it in detail, I'd appreciate it.'

Jo took the stick gratefully.

'Well, at least it's not poking about under bushes. A spider jumped out at me today, a big one too, and all he could do was laugh,' she said as her eyes glanced contemptuously towards Gerry.

Martina joined Chris at his computer. The rest just talked amongst themselves while they waited.

'It looks as if you might have cracked it, Mac,' Andy said.

'Perhaps but I can't understand why it took me so long to remember Jessica Watson. It's been bugging me for days now.'

'It was fourteen years ago,' Leigh said. 'God, I can't remember what happened fourteen days ago.'

'It would be good if we could establish who was first though,' Mac said. 'It might help narrow down the suspects.'

'Do you think there'll be that many who would have worked on the contract for that long?' Andy asked.

Mac shrugged.

'I've absolutely no idea…'

He was interrupted by Martin.

'Mac your file's here,' Martin said holding a memory stick aloft.

'I'll see you later,' Mac said glad to get down to some proper work.

He and Tommy found an empty desk and fired up the computer.

'Do you mind taking notes?' Mac asked. 'I can't read my own writing these days.'

'No problem,' Tommy said with a smile. 'How do you want to do this?'

'How about if we read each page and then we'll discuss if there's anything we need to make a note of?'

'That sounds like a plan.'

Mac read on.

Sheila Matthews was twenty when she disappeared. She worked as a cosmetic salesperson for one of the large pharmacy chains in Solihull town centre.

'Solihull, is that another town?' Tommy reasonably asked.

'Technically I suppose it is,' Mac replied, 'but it's still part of greater Birmingham if you like, one of the posher parts too.'

Sheila lived in Sheldon with her parents and two younger brothers, only a stone's throw from the airport and the rail works at Birmingham International. She always worked a little later on Thursday nights and, as it was February, it would be dark as she made her way home. She got on the bus with one of her friends from work and they chatted on the way back. Her friend got off two stops before Sheila. Two other passengers saw Sheila get off at her usual stop on the Coventry Road. She lived in a flat at the far end of a cul-de-sac so she had a relatively short walk home.

'Can we get a look at where she lived?' Mac asked.

Tommy found the cul-de-sac on the map and then selected Street View. The short street was lined with three storied blocks of flats. They looked as if they were all built in the seventies or eighties so not too much would have changed since her disappearance. They walked down the virtual street towards a block of flats at the end of the close. This was where Sheila was heading on the evening she disappeared.

'There,' Mac said.

On the right, at ninety degrees to the street, there was a short cul-de-sac lined with garages on both sides. Their white metal doors looked freshly painted.

'What are you thinking?' Tommy asked.

'Our man's clever, there's no doubt about that. He'll have spotted that there's only one place on Sheila's walk home where he could easily abduct her and that's right there. She'd have had to walk past the entrance to the garages to get home and it doesn't look as though they're directly overlooked by any of the flats. I know that at one time they used to give each flat a garage whether they had a car or not but sometimes they'd rent them out too...'

Mac went silent for a moment.

'Let's read on,' he said eventually.

Sheila's family confirmed that she seemed very happy and she'd given them no idea that she might have wanted to leave. A number of her friends also confirmed this. All her clothes were still in her room and no money had left her account. There were reams of statements which they both diligently read through as well as lots of photographs. They learnt nothing from them. Towards the end of the file there was a statement from one of Sheila's closest friends. She said that she was sure she'd seen Sheila in Birmingham town centre some weeks afterwards. The police investigated but uncovered nothing.

'So, what have we learnt?' Mac asked.

'Another girl disappears on her way home and isn't heard of again. What about this sighting of her though?' Tommy asked.

'In all probability it's just wishful thinking on behalf of her friend. When you desperately want to see someone you sometimes do. There is one person they might have forgotten to interview though.'

'Is this still about the garages?' Tommy asked. 'They obviously thought about it as they interviewed everyone who kept a car there. Who else might know something?'

'I'd have asked the local council if anyone had called them recently to see if any of the garages were empty and available to rent,' Mac said.

Tommy gave this some thought.

'I think I see what you're getting at. All our man needs to do is find out which of the garages might be empty then he could force the door and park his own car in there. Those metal doors used to be easy to force, I remember my uncle used to open the lock on his with a small nail file if he forgot his key. If the garage was empty then he could break in a few days before so, on the night, he could just turn up and innocently park his car. Even if he were seen, no-one would give it a second thought. It was nearly nine and dark when she walked by so, if he used the same MO, he would have hit her then dragged her inside the garage and shut the door. It wouldn't have taken more than a few seconds and, once he had her inside, he could have done what he liked.'

Mac smiled at Tommy's thorough explanation of the sequence of events.

'Yes, I think that's exactly what might have happened. It definitely wasn't Sheila that her friend saw. Sheila was dead. Come on let's go through it all again, just in case.'

They'd nearly finished when Martin shouted, 'Printing off.'

Everyone stopped what they were doing and looked at Dan. He looked at the sheet and did a little fist pump. On the white board he wrote against Glasgow 'Stella Gordon 17 – Disappeared.'

Mac looked at what they had so far.

1996 Southampton –
1998 Glasgow – Stella Gordon 17 - Disappeared
2000 York –
2002 Barnet – Jessica Watson 19 - Disappeared
2003 Birmingham Int.–Sheila Matthews 20 -
Disappeared
2005 Peterborough – Jackie Oldfield 17 - Disappeared
2006 Cardiff – Carla Menzies 16 - Disappeared
2008 Crewe – Maria Sanchez 15 - Disappeared
2011 Carlisle – Monica Byrne 18 - Disappeared
2013 Bristol – Kate Beckworth 20 - Disappeared
2016 Hitchin – Natasha Barker 18 - Disappeared

Mac thought it was highly possible that Stella Gordon was the first victim and that they might get nothing from Southampton anyway. However, York puzzled him. Having taken his first victim would he really wait four years for the next. Mac had his doubts.

Mac went over to Martin.

'Have we had everything in from York yet?'

'That's what they're saying,' Martin replied. 'I've been through the data two or three times but I can't see anyone of the right age or who looks like Natasha. Here I'll show you.'

Martin showed him the photos of all the women who had gone missing in the York area in the period that the works were there.

'You're right, there's nothing even close in there,' Mac said.

There was something that wasn't right about this. Mac had the feeling that once he'd started killing nothing would stop him doing it again. Every time he took a girl though he'd know that he was putting himself at some risk. As smart as he was and, plan as he might, things can always go wrong. It would seem that two years was as long as he could go without having to do it again. So, why the four year gap between Stella Gordon and Jessica Watson?

Things can always go wrong. The phrase echoed around his head.

'Martin, can you get back on to York and ask them for the photos of any young women who were attacked in any way or who were found murdered. Can you do that?' Mac asked with some urgency.

'Will do but it might be worth trying the national databases first for the murders though,' Martin suggested

'Thanks. Shout if you find anything,' Mac said.

Dan stood up and looked at his watch.

'As it's now gone nine thirty let's have our round up of what we've learnt so far and then we can go home. Let's do them in order, the oldest first. We haven't had the file for Stella Gordon arrive yet so let's start with Jessica Watson.'

Mac stood up and went over the basic points of the case once again. He told them that Jessica at the time had been working as a barmaid at a pub not too far from where she lived. She was a very sociable girl and had lots of friends. One of these was at university in London and it was her that Jessica had been planning on going to the all-nighter with but, of course, she never turned up. He carried on with Sheila Matthews and outlined Tommy's theory about how she'd been taken using the garage as cover.

Andy stood up next and gave the high points of the Jackie Oldfield case. She'd been a sixth form student who was studying for her A levels at the time she disappeared. She was hoping to be a doctor.

Mac immediately thought of his Bridget and of the number of times she'd walked out alone when she'd been that age. He couldn't help saying a little prayer of thanks.

Jackie disappeared while on her way to a friend's house for a birthday party. She'd been there once or twice before but she wasn't a regular visitor. Part of the route included a walkway that was secluded. It was also dark as the single street light that illuminated the walkway had been smashed the night before. The investigators thought that this wasn't a coincidence. Again, there was no indication that she was thinking about leaving home and all her clothes were still in her wardrobe.

Adil stood up next. He explained that he and Dan had a look at the Carla Menzies case while they waited for the rail personnel data to arrive. It was a pretty thin file. Carla was out of work when she disappeared. She was living alone having been kicked out by her family and appeared to have few friends. She suffered from depression and was known to go walking by herself at night. No-one even noticed that she'd disappeared until some weeks afterwards. The investigators estimated that she hadn't been back to her flat for at least three weeks judging by the mail and the state of her fridge. Even though she'd left all her clothes and some

160

personal items, it was assumed by the investigators that she'd just done a runner. That was it.

Easy pickings for our man, Mac thought.

Martina stood up. She and Chris had covered Maria Sanchez too. She was a schoolgirl and the daughter of refugees who had come to this country from Chile in 1988. Maria had been born here. She disappeared on her way back home after staying late at school as she had a lead part in the school drama and was attending extra rehearsals. She'd been given a lift to the bottom of her road by the parent of one of her friends. She only had a hundred yards or so to walk but she never made it back home. The short street was a mixture of old Victorian terraced houses and some new buildings. About halfway down the street there was an entryway that led to a small car park. The investigators surmised that it was likely that this was where she was taken. However, despite having a large team that had spent many weeks looking for Maria, the police found absolutely nothing. She had disappeared into thin air.

Chris stood up and went over the Monica Byrne case again. He had nothing new to add though.

Lastly, Jo stood up and talked about the Kate Beckworth case. She'd worked as a trainee journalist for a local paper. The investigators had spent some time following a lead. A girl who looked like Kate was seen getting on a train at Temple Meads station with a man. They were being very affectionate with each other. They followed this up until Kate's girlfriend turned up demanding to know what they were doing to find her. Kate was apparently most definitely gay. This gave them another angle to investigate but that fizzled out too.

Dan took his customary place in front of the white board.

'So, it's not just the looks and the dates then. There's a definite similarity between the MO in all of the cases.

Thanks everyone, we've really gotten somewhere tonight. Now, with regard to the workforce data there's some good news and some bad news. The good news is that we now have the names and addresses of everyone who's worked on the rail contracts over the past twenty-five years. The bad news is that we've also identified that there are ninety-two employees who have been continuously employed since Stella Gordon disappeared. All men of course.'

The team groaned.

'Yes, it's not as small a group as I would have liked,' Dan said, 'but smaller than the one we had before today which was just about every man in the country. Okay let's call it quits now, go home and get some sleep. As I said before don't burn yourselves out. We've plenty to do tomorrow so we'll meet here at eight thirty...'

Dan was interrupted.

'Printing off,' Martin said looking straight at Mac. 'We've got one for York. It was on the database.'

Dan went over to the printer and waited impatiently while the paper slowly emerged. He gave it a quick look and then went over to the board and wrote against York 'Rhiannon Rees 19 – Murdered'.

He looked like he was about to say something but then stopped. Dan stood there for quite a while reading the print off.

'Here, read this,' he said giving Mac a most peculiar look.

Mac took the sheet and read the paragraph that Dan was pointing to.

It was a summary of the forensics report. The body of Rhiannon Rees had been found almost two months after she'd disappeared. From the forensic evidence, mostly through insect larva, they were certain that she'd only been dead for a month at most.

Mac read this again just to make sure.

'Christ almighty,' Mac exclaimed. 'He keeps them. The bastard keeps them! Natasha might still be alive!'

She was awake but she kept her eyes firmly shut. She pictured herself waking up in her bedroom after a particularly bad dream. However, when she finally opened her eyes, it was only blackness and silence that surrounded her. She'd been scared of the dark since she'd been a child and she was scared again now.

She had no idea how long she'd been wherever 'here' was. In the blackness time meant nothing. She tried to explore her surroundings but it seemed to be a feature-less space bounded by walls made of the same sort of pliable stuff that the floor was made off.

She went back to her corner pulled up her knees, rocked herself and cried. She eventually lay down and drifted off into a troubled sleep.

She awoke again and suddenly there was light and sound. A man came towards her. He smiled at her but his eyes did not smile, they devoured her. He carried a baseball bat in one hand.

'Welcome,' he said with a smile. 'I mean you no harm, at least not today anyway. There are some rules however that you need to know about during your short stay here and these rules must be observed.'

He smiled at her again.

'In mediaeval times they used to show the accused the instruments of torture,' he said.

When he said the word 'torture' he lengthened it and said it with some affection.

'So here they are. First the blunt instrument.'

He held the baseball bat aloft.

'Not a real one as that might be a bit too hard. This is a child's version and, as you can see, covered with rubber so the little dears won't hurt themselves too much.'

He swung the bat so near her head that she could hear the loud 'swish' as it went by.

'It will hurt but it won't bruise too much. If you don't behave then I will use it on you. You will keep quiet and *obey me instantly at all times, is that clear? If you don't then I will use this as much as is necessary.'*

The bat went 'swish' right past her ear again.

'Unfortunately, there was one girl who wouldn't behave herself,' he said. 'She broke the rules and cried and bawled so much that I lost my temper, very unusual behaviour for me. I'm afraid that I ended up breaking the bat on her but of course she was well dead by then.'

He placed the bat against the wall.

'I really hope that we won't have any recourse to use such a brutally blunt instrument as that though. It must be a very distressing way to die.'

He smiled at her again.

'Now for the real instrument, an elegant and simple one I'll think you'll find.'

He pulled a slim, silver coloured metal implement from his pocket and held it close so she could see it. She knew what it was, she had used one often enough in art classes.

'Yes, a scalpel, simple but elegant and perfect for my needs. See how sharp it is.'

He touched the blade against her right breast, just a touch, but enough for a thin stream of blood to flow. She could see him lick his lips as he avidly watched the blood trickle down her body.

He turned as if he'd heard some sound. Natasha had heard nothing.

'Okay, I'll be up in a minute,' he shouted.

He turned back to her.

'Here's how it will be. Sometime soon I'll come back to you. I'll fuck you very hard and, while I'm doing that, I'll hold this elegant little blade right here.'

He touched her throat with his finger.

'Right here where the artery is. While I'm inside you I'll keep it right there but, when I ejaculate, I'll give you a little snick.'

He smiled when he said the word 'snick'. It was a word he seemed to really like.

165

'Yes, just a snick and as I gush inside you your life force will gush out of that artery. There's a really nice symmetry there, don't you think?' He paused and smiled. 'Oh, you poor thing, you look worried but don't be. You won't feel much, perhaps the warmth of your blood as it cascades down your breasts then soon all will be blackness and you will be dead. That is how it is going to be.'

He smiled at her again and Natasha knew that every word he said was true.

'There are some energy bars in a box and some water bottles in the corner and there's a bucket for your other needs. I wish I could attend to you right away but I'm afraid that there's someone else who needs my company. Sleep well.'

Then the blackness and the silence returned and she found that she was profoundly grateful for it. She sat down in the corner, pulled up her knees and hugged herself. So long as the blackness and silence remained, she was safe.

She knew that death would come with the light.

Chapter Sixteen

'This changes everything,' Dan said with some excitement. 'And, as for what I said earlier about not burning yourselves out, forget it. Burn yourselves out as much as you like, we might just save Natasha's life by doing that.'

Dan stood thinking for quite a while.

'We all need to be very careful about this new information. Our man is likely to be one of those ninety-two on the list and if he knew that we were this close to catching him the chances are that he'd kill Natasha immediately and get rid of the evidence. So, it would be best if you don't tell anyone at all about this, not even family members. Is that clear?'

The team all nodded.

Dan looked at his watch. It was now past ten.

'Okay go home, get some sleep and I'll see you back here at six o'clock sharp. Bring a bag with enough clothes for three or four days and tell your families you're going to be away for a while but don't tell them why. There's a hotel around the corner and I'm going to book some rooms so we can grab some sleep when we need to. Go on, go!' Dan turned and said in a lower voice, 'Mac, Adil and Andy can you stay behind for a while?'

The rest of the team filed out of the room. Amanda stayed behind too.

Dan noticed her and said, 'Oh I thought you'd gone home some time ago.'

'No, no,' she said hesitantly. 'I thought as I was part of the team...well, I just wanted to know what I could do. I want to help.'

Her saying this gave Dan an idea. He looked at her quite closely.

'Yes, there might be something. Can you get a black dress, one as much like Natasha's as possible, and a black wig? Let's see how much we can make you look like her. Can you do that first thing tomorrow?'

'Yes of course,' she replied looking a bit puzzled.

'Just put it all on expenses,' Dan said.

After everyone had gone Mac asked, 'I take it that you're thinking of holding a reconstruction?'

'Yes, that's exactly what I was thinking of doing. Let's see, its Friday tomorrow so we could do it Saturday, if we haven't found her by then that is. Yes, that would be good, a week to the day since she went missing.'

'Do you really think it will help us to get more information though?' Andy asked, looking somewhat sceptical about the idea.

'No, I doubt it will do that,' Dan replied, 'but it will make the news and if I also appear and bleat on about how we've got no leads and that Natasha's disappearance is a total mystery to us...'

'Then it might just convince our man that we haven't got a clue about his existence,' Andy said enthusiastically. 'Now that's a bloody good idea.'

'I sometimes have them. Sorry for asking you all to stay but I wanted to make sure that I had the next steps in place for tomorrow.' Dan turned to Martin who was still at his laptop in the corner. 'By the way Martin when I said everyone was to go home that meant you too.'

'In a minute,' Martin replied without looking up.

'Oh, before you go can you book those rooms?'

'Will do.'

'Good idea that,' Mac said.

He'd survived a whole day mainly due to the fact that he'd been so wrapped up in what he was doing that the pain hadn't had much impact on him. He didn't feel too bad but he also knew that he'd been lucky. Knowing that a room would be available nearby if he needed to lie down would be a real bonus for him.

'Okay, so any ideas anyone?' Dan asked.

'The first thing might be to see what we have on the ninety-two, prior convictions and so on,' Andy suggested.

'What have we got Martin?' Dan asked without turning around.

'Nothing more than speeding tickets for most of them. Otherwise just an assault in a pub but there was something interesting. One of them, a Scheme Project Manager called Wayne Turnell, was investigated for sexual assault. The case was eventually dropped but I can't find out why just yet.'

'What else?' Dan asked.

'I'm looking at all of the ninety-two on social media. You can usually tell a lot from their posts and likes and so on.'

'And?'

'Not a lot so far, wrong demographic,' Martin replied.

Dan laughed.

'That's Martin-speak for them being too old,' Dan explained. 'Okay, so we'll have a look at this Mr. Turnell then. Anything else anyone?'

'We need some way to cut the group down to a reasonable size,' Mac said. 'We could do simultaneous raids on a number of premises but ninety-two at once would take some preparation.'

'And that's assuming that he's keeping her at home,' Adil added. 'He could be keeping her anywhere.'

'That's true and if he gets one sniff of what we're up to then she's as good as dead. Okay I think that we need to keep digging away at top speed for at least the next day or two and then see where we are,' Dan suggested.

'That makes sense,' Mac said.

'I'd also like to discuss any major operational decisions with you three first,' Dan said. 'I'm not saying that I'm going to go along with everything you advise but it might provide me with a sanity check. There's going to be a lot of pressure on us all over the next few days. What do you think?'

Mac looked at Dan with renewed respect. Making sure that there was some sort of control mechanism when tough decisions were going to have to be made was wise indeed.

Mac and the other two nodded their agreement.

'So, what do we do tomorrow?' Andy asked.

'I'm going to bring the chief up to speed with this once we've finished this meeting. Of course, he'll suggest that we throw a lot more manpower at it but right now I'm not so sure it will help. Mac what's your thoughts on that?' Dan asked.

'I've been in situations like this before,' Mac replied. 'You always think the safe bet is to bring in a load of new people but it rarely works in the short term. It takes a lot of time to bring them up to speed and the original members of the team who know the case well will spend most of their time answering questions rather than getting on with it. I'd advise using other detectives or uniforms for specific tasks only, unless this goes on for a lot longer of course.'

'Thanks Mac, that's exactly what I was thinking,' Dan said. 'So, to answer your question Andy, I'm going to leave Jo and Gerry looking for Jonny Aldis. I still think there's a good chance that he might know something.'

'Now that's really going to cheer Jo up!' Adil exclaimed.

'She's getting plenty of fresh air so I don't know what she's moaning about,' Dan said with mock innocence. 'As for the rest of us we need to find out as much as we can, as quickly as we can, about these disappearances. So, what I'm thinking is this, Mac can you and Tommy spend tomorrow reviewing all the cases again? I know we've looked at them already but I want to make sure we spot all the patterns there are to spot, plus there'll be the Rhiannon Rees murder file to look at.'

'No problem,' Mac replied.

It would certainly be easier on his back which Mac guessed was why Dan had suggested it.

'Thanks,' Dan said as he looked at the board. 'So, we've now got six members of the team left. I'd like to get them talking to the people who originally investigated the cases, if possible, face to face. There's always a lot found that never makes it into the file for one reason or another. I'd like to do Peterborough, Bristol, Birmingham and Barnet face to face, as we can get there and back in a day, but the rest are a bit further away and will have to be done over the phone. Does that make sense?'

They all nodded again.

'Okay, let's all go home and get some sleep.'

Dan turned around.

'That means you too Martin. Now.'

'Okay, I'm closing down now.'

'See you all at six then,' Dan said.

Tommy was waiting in the car for him when he got out.

'You should have gone home. I could have caught a taxi back,' Mac said.

'That's okay, I was just sitting here thinking about things. A meeting of the high council was it?'

Mac smiled.

'Yes, something like that. By the way I nearly forgot, how did the flat viewing go?'

'It went really well actually,' Tommy replied. 'Bridget definitely liked it. The building's a few years old but that's good as you get a lot more space than you do with some of the new builds. Some of the rooms in those are so small you hardly have the space to turn around in. There are a few other people viewing today so we should know in a couple of days if we can have it or not.'

'I'd have thought you'd be on the inside track, a doctor and a policeman. Steady professions at least.'

'We'll see. How are you feeling? It's been a long day, hasn't it?' Tommy asked.

'Yes, a long one but a good one,' Mac replied. 'I'm not too bad right at this moment but I'll find out tomorrow if I've done too much.'

Mac set his alarm for just before five and lay down in his bed. There was a spike of pain as he relaxed but thankfully it subsided quickly. He'd made sure that he'd taken all the possible medication he could. He could only hope that it wouldn't be too bad when he woke up.

Thankfully sleep soon overtook him.

Chapter Seventeen

Six days missing

He was aware of the beeping of his alarm clock but he still woke up in stages. He eventually turned it off and looked at the time. It was four fifty. Tommy said that he'd be around at quarter to six so he had just under an hour.

He performed his morning ritual of sitting up as gently as he could and then, when he'd gathered his courage, standing up and steeling himself for the expected surge of pain.

It didn't come. A lot of the time he could see a pattern, overdo it one day and then suffer for it the next three, but sometimes it didn't work like that. He could have a severe pain episode after having hardly done anything the day before. Anyway, he was really glad that it looked like today was going to be a moderate pain day.

After showering and shaving he threw some clothes and his shaving gear into a bag not forgetting to take enough patches and tablets to last him five days. He sipped at his coffee as he looked out of the window. Tommy turned up bang on time.

Mac looked at the rail works as they sped down the hill. He saw them in a totally different light now. Today a man might turn to work on that site as he had done every day for months. He would smile and say hello to his colleagues but this was no normal man. This was a man who, in all likelihood, delighted in the torture and killing of young girls. He'd look just the same as anyone else and would probably chat about football and the weather and moan about the job. Then he would go home and do whatever he was doing to Natasha.

He stopped himself thinking like this. They could only do what they could do to find her. He needed to concentrate on that.

Almost everyone else was there when they arrived. Mac helped himself to a coffee and a Danish pastry. Dan waited for Martina to arrive before he started.

'Listen up, here's today's plan of action,' Dan said. 'We've got ninety-two suspects and we have to narrow them down before we can do anything else. I've asked Mac and Tommy to review all the case files we have plus the one on Rhiannon Rees which has just arrived. We need to see if there are any more patterns that might be spotted by having a single team look across all the cases. We also need to find out as much as we can about the circumstances at the time of the disappearances. Andy, can you go to Peterborough and interview the coppers who did the original investigation? Dig around and find out as much as you can. Try and find if there were any suspects that didn't make it into the files or anyone that they came across that they had second thoughts about. Chris, I'd like you to go to Barnet, Martina to Birmingham and Adil to Bristol and do the same. Martin will give you all the contact numbers so get on the train now and arrange your interviews as you're on the way there. The rest are probably a bit too far to get there and back in a day so Leigh, Amanda and myself will cover those by phone. I'll need you all back here by eight o'clock at the latest to see what we've learnt.'

'And what do I do?' Jo asked.

'I want you and Gerry to carry on looking for Jonny Aldis. I still think it's possible that he might know something that could help us.'

Gerry seemed quite pleased with Dan's decision but Jo could be heard muttering some choice words under her breath.

'Then later, you can both help me with the reconstruction. I've arranged the press conference for just before nine thirty outside the pub.' Dan continued as he glanced over at Amanda. 'Have you got the dress and wig?'

'Yes sir,' she said pointing to some fashionable looking carrier bags. 'Shoes and tights too if that's alright.'

'That's fine. Okay let's go,' Dan said. He then went over to Mac. 'We touched on this yesterday but our man has got to be keeping her somewhere. What's your guess?'

Mac had indeed been giving this some thought.

'I'd guess that it needs to be a space he totally controls the access to and close enough so he can go and do what he does when he wants to. What's the point of keeping them otherwise?'

'So perhaps he's bought a house to fit the purpose, a house with an outhouse or a cellar perhaps?' Dan asked.

'I guess a cellar would be the ideal solution, sound proof it and no-one would ever know. I mean Fritzl kept his daughter prisoner for over twenty years that way, didn't he?'

'Okay, it's a bit of a long shot but I'll get Martin to start checking with the local estate agents to see if they've sold a house to any of the ninety-two, especially any with outhouses or cellars,' Dan said.

Mac got the case file for Rhiannon Rees from Martin who also gave him the file for Stella Gordon which had eventually arrived. He was hoping that these might hold the key to finding their murderer.

Mac and Tommy started with Rhiannon. They read each page with Tommy taking notes as he'd done before.

Rhiannon had been found in a nature reserve some twenty-five miles to the north of York. It was just pure luck that she'd been found at all. A couple of mycologists…

'What's a mycologist?' Tommy asked.

'Mushroom hunters but scientific ones,' Mac replied.

He read on. These mycologists were researchers from the university looking at the distribution of a type of a white fungus called a Stump Puffball. They thought they saw one at the bottom of a small valley in a remote part of the reserve. When they clambered down, they discovered that it wasn't a Stump Puffball or any other type of fungus but a woman's hand. The week before there had been heavy rain for days on end and it was thought that this had washed away enough soil away to make the hand visible.

They were able to positively identify her as Rhiannon Rees from her dental records. Death was caused by an incision into the jugular artery and exsanguination. The incision was clean and precise and the forensic examiner stated that it had been done by a very sharp instrument, probably a scalpel. There was evidence of some violence before death in the form of subcutaneous bruising, caused by a blunt instrument, and many small cuts, especially around the breasts. Again, the examiner thought that these were most likely done using the same sharp instrument that killed her.

She hadn't lost too much weight so it looked like she'd been fed and given enough water during her presumed spell of captivity.

As for any forensic evidence that might identify her killer there was none. The body appeared to have been carefully washed and there was no evidence of any foreign DNA. This may have been because of the time that the body had been in the ground, or because the murderer had been very careful, or both.

Perhaps most chillingly abrasions were found around her neck, abrasions that were consistent with those of a metal collar having been worn for some time. The forensic investigator suggested that this might have been used to restrain her during a period of captivity.

Rhiannon seemed to be enjoying the social whirl of student life and had disappeared while on the way to a party being given by one of her fellow students. The party was at a student house right next to the hospital, a house that Rhiannon had only visited once or twice before. Mac looked it up on Street View and was surprised to find a street full of substantial Victorian villas in obvious good repair. Rhiannon lived in a row of terraced houses the other side of the railway lines from the hospital. The only route she could have taken would be by using a pedestrian bridge over the lines and then she would have most likely taken a short cut through the hospital grounds. The investigators noted that there were lots of places on that walk that were not well used at night.

Mac glanced at the following pages which were mostly technical and conveyed nothing new until a word leaped out at him from the screen. He leant forward and read that section very carefully.

'What is it Mac?' Tommy asked noticing Mac's heightened interest.

'Look there, in the tox screen report,' Mac said as he pointed at a particular paragraph.

'It says that there were fairly high levels of Fentanyl in her system. Fentanyl? That's in those patches you take, isn't it?' Tommy asked.

'Yes, it's the only thing that keeps me sane. I'd guess that it would be relatively hard to get illegally. I've heard of it being used for recreational purposes in the USA but it's still fairly rare in this country. I think that there's a good chance that our man might be a pain sufferer himself.'

'Why would he use Fentanyl on Rhiannon though?'

Mac paused for a moment.

'After Nora, my wife died, I became...well I suppose depressed is the word. I used to forget things including changing my pain patches and sometimes I'd put on too many. A couple of patches on and everything is well, hazy and not quite real. I dropped everything I tried to hold in my hands; cups, plates, remote controls, they all got broken during that period. I didn't care though, in fact I didn't care about anything much. It was as though I wasn't really there but just looking on as a spectator in some weird sort of way.'

'So, you think that he might have used Fentanyl to sedate and control Rhiannon?' Tommy asked.

'Yes, I do and if he was using it on her I think that he might well be using it on Natasha right at this moment.'

'If that's the case then all we need to do is go through the medical records of all the ninety-two and if any are pain sufferers then we've got him!' Tommy exclaimed.

'Perhaps but I wouldn't be so sure it's going to be that simple. Martin!' Mac called out.

'What do you need?' Martin asked without turning around.

'Is there any way we can access the ninety-two's medical records without them knowing?'

Martin gave this some thought.

'I dare say that we could get the official occupational health records from the rail company easily enough. Want me to ask?'

'Please,' Mac replied.

Tommy looked quite excited.

'We could be on to something.'

Mac wasn't so sure.

'Our man is careful so he knows that there's a finite chance that one of his victims might be discovered. I'd bet that if he is using Fentanyl you won't find it on any of his work records at least.' Mac turned towards Martin again. 'Am I right in thinking that there's still no national medical record system yet?'

'Yes, you're right. They tried a few years ago but after spending ten billion pounds the whole thing collapsed,' Martin replied.

'Ten billion?' Mac said in some surprise. 'So, how could we find out what medication the ninety-two might have been prescribed by their GP?'

'Well, there's something called a Summary Care Record which only details basic health information about a patient. I'm pretty sure that also includes medication.'

'Any chance you could check the summary records for the ninety-two?' Mac asked.

Martin gave it some thought.

'I think there'll be some hurdles to jump over but I'll give it a go.'

'Thanks,' Mac said.

'But how would he get enough patches to sedate someone if he has to use them himself?' Tommy asked.

'That's a very good question. Thinking about that I suppose we have to consider the fact that he might have access to Fentanyl through being a doctor or a carer for someone. But, if he is a pain sufferer, I'd guess that it might not be that hard as he probably won't be taking Fentanyl on its own. I also regularly take an anti-inflammatory drug but there's a bit of a mismatch as the drug lasts me for twenty-eight days but the patches last for thirty. I just re-order everything at the same time so I end up having a patch over each month. So, if he did this, then over two years he'd have twenty-four patches which I'd guess would be more than enough for his purposes.'

Tommy nodded.

'So, I take it that you don't re-order the patches every now and again?'

'That's right,' Mac said.

He didn't tell Tommy about the two full packs of patches that he kept at the back of his sock drawer. Just take the plastic wings off, put them in a cup of warm water and a few minutes later Mac knew that he'd have the cure for all his ills. Knowing he had the solution at hand if things got too black had somehow helped him make it through his darkest hours.

They carried on reading through the file but found little more of interest so they started on Stella Gordon.

Stella had been just seventeen when she disappeared. She lived in a place called Bishopbriggs to the north of the city of Glasgow. In 1998 work on a new station had started and the tracks were also being renovated. She lived no more than five minutes walk from where the works were going on. They had a look at the house that she'd lived in using Street View. It was a typical two storeyed council house, grey pebble dashed with a little garden out front. It was the end of a small terrace of four houses.

Stella had started work at the local library as an assistant when she'd left school the year before. She was described as a bright girl who was hoping to make it her long-term career. She'd already become a member of a librarians' institute and had mapped out her future career path towards becoming a professional librarian.

Mac located the library on the map.

'Look,' he said pointing to map. 'She only lived a couple of hundred yards away from the rail station and she would have had to walk past the works twice a day to get to and from work.'

'Do you think that's how our man spotted her?' Tommy asked.

'Almost definitely, I also wonder if that was the reason why she was the first?'

Tommy looked puzzled.

'Murder's a very big step to take,' Mac said. 'I reckon that a lot of people might think about it, some even quite seriously, but few ever actually cross that line. I'm wondering if seeing her day in, day out, was more than he could bear and whether it eventually wore his resistance down. Once the line is crossed the next murder isn't quite so hard.'

They read on.

Stella was described as a quiet girl who only went out once or twice a week with a group of friends she'd known since primary school. There were no known romantic attachments. There was also no indication that she might have been unhappy at home or have any wish to leave, indeed it was exactly the opposite. She would have been eighteen ten days after she went missing and she'd been planning a big party. Her family had booked a restaurant in central Glasgow and she seemed to be really looking forward to the celebrations.

The night she disappeared she'd been on her way back home from a friend's house. She visited this friend's house regularly at least once a week, some-times more. The house was just on the other side of the station. She left her friend at nine fifty and only faced a five or six minute walk home. The investigators thought that the tunnel under the railway bridge was the most likely place that any abduction would have taken place.

'Let's have a look,' Mac said looking at Street View on the computer.

He could see why they might have thought that. Under the bridge, obviously dating from Victorian times, there was a long, narrow tunnel that had a pavement on the one side only. At the end of the tunnel that Stella would have walked towards there was a hedge behind which was a fair bit of space. Mac checked the report and it said that there was a hedge there at the time that Stella disappeared. Someone could have waited there without being seen by people passing by. Just beyond the hedge to the right there was a service area at the back of the shops on the main road.

Mac thought it through.

'It looks like it would be easy enough,' Mac said.

'Tell me how you think it went then,' Tommy asked.

'Okay, I think our man laid in wait in this area just behind the hedge. That way he wouldn't be seen by any-one walking towards him through the tunnel. It was nine fifty so there's still a chance that there might be someone around but I reckon that our man was patient. I'd guess that he might have waited there for quite for a few nights, just looking for that perfect opportunity. He had plenty of time after all. On the night Stella was taken it was raining so it was little wonder that there was no-one about. So, as she walked past him, he grabbed her and pulled her off the street. He then punched her, taped her up and put her in the suitcase.'

Mac stopped for a moment. Tommy didn't interrupt his thoughts.

'I'm just trying to think if such large suitcases were around back then. If not, I suppose the works team would have had storage boxes on wheels for transporting technical equipment and he could have used something like that. A man wheeling something like that certainly wouldn't have looked out of place at the back of the shops. Anyway, all he needed to do then was wheel whatever he was using to the service area where he'd have parked his car, or perhaps a van, which might have been easier. Then pop her in the back and then he'd be off.'

'Yes, it sounds familiar alright,' Tommy said.

'From what it says here they did a forensic investigation and were especially thorough in that little area near the hedge. All they found was a button that they think might have come from her coat but they couldn't be totally sure. She was using her umbrella that night but it was never found. They noted that it rained very hard for most of the night and the forensics examination was carried out the next morning. I suppose that might also be part of the reason why nothing else was found.'

The rest of the file revealed little of interest. The investigators had been thorough but they had nothing to go on. Mac noted that they'd talked to some of the rail contractors but none of the names detailed were those of the ninety-two.

'So, what now?' Tommy asked.

'I've got a feeling that we can get a bit more juice from these files. We'll need to re-read them all but let's have a think first about some common factors that we might note down as we go.'

'Like what?'

'Well, we know that they're linked by age and looks but were they also linked by their jobs, whether they were living at home or alone, hobbies, types of places they frequented and so on? It would be nice to see if there are any patterns that we can spot,' Mac said.

'Perhaps something about the routes that they might have taken too?' Tommy suggested.

'Yes, that would work,' Mac said.

In fact, he thought that it was a very good idea.

They took five files each and made notes as they read. Once they'd finished Mac drew a table on a free white board with the girls' names to the right and the questions on the top. He started filling it in.

Once completed he looked down each column.

The jobs column showed that four of the girls were students otherwise all of the others were different. Mac guessed that if you were going to abduct girls of that age range the majority might tend to be students of one type or another anyway.

The 'Abduction site' column showed that he was fond of entryways as half of the girls had probably been taken in one. He supposed that a tunnel might be classed as a sort of entryway too.

The 'Frequency route used' column, as suggested by Tommy, was even more interesting. While six of the girls had taken routes that they walked regularly, the routes that Rhiannon and Jackie had taken were ones that they had rarely used. On top of that, while Natasha's route was one that she used all the time, she'd used it that night at a very unusual time. Normally it would have been well after eleven when she used the shortcut and she would have had the company of her friend Julie.

'Hobbies' and 'Sociability' yielded nothing but 'Places visited' again gave Mac food for thought. Except for Carla Menzies they all visited local pubs and cafes.

'Your suggestion was a really good one Tommy. Looking at the 'Frequency route used' column begs the question; how did our man know that Rhiannon and Jackie were going to parties on the nights they were taken? It wasn't something they did every day so how could he know? Come to that how did he know that Natasha had gone home early?' Mac said.

'You're thinking that they were being stalked, aren't you?' Tommy asked.

'I do,' Mac replied. 'They all went to local pubs or cafes so perhaps he got close enough to hear what they were talking about.'

'In Natasha's case she announced it to the whole pub though,' Tommy pointed out.

'Which meant that he had to be in the pub in the first place to hear it.'

Mac looked at his watch. It was already twelve forty five.

'Come on let's go and get something to eat. I'm just hoping that Kelly's on duty.'

They left Dan, Leigh and Amanda to their phones and walked the short distance to the pub. Mac was glad to get a breath of fresh air. When he opened the pub door, he could see Kelly at her usual station at the end of the bar. He ordered two burgers and coffees and asked her to bring them over and sit with them for a few minutes.

He took a big bite from his burger before he asked her anything. He was hungry.

'I know we've asked this before but I need to ask you again. Who else was in the pub the night that Natasha and Julie had their argument?'

She shrugged her shoulders.

'As I said before they were mostly regulars, although there were a few in that night that I hadn't seen before.'

Mac took another bite.

'Tell me about these regulars, especially those that were drinking in the same area of the bar that Natasha and Julie were in.'

Knowing that there was a good chance that their man might have stalked Natasha for days, perhaps many weeks, Mac felt that he might well qualify as a 'regular'.

'Well, the rugby mob were in and there was a group of lads from the supermarket down the road, they sometimes come in after work.'

'Anyone else?' Mac asked.

She shook her head.

'Oh, the footballers' wives were here but then again they always are.'

'Who are the footballers' wives?' Mac asked.

'Oh, that's just what we call them,' Kelly said. 'It started out when one of the local teams had a long cup run a while back and a few of the wives were fed up being left alone. So, they thought that if the husbands could go out and enjoy themselves then they could too. I think it was Big Chrissie and Trudy who started it. Anyway, a group of them meet up regularly and, if any single women come in, they invite them to sit at the big round table. Quite a lot of them come back too.'

'Tell me more,' Mac asked.

'Well, they sit at that big table there and come in around five or six and they usually go not long after nine. Sometimes there's only three or four but a lot of nights there's quite a few more.'

'Why do they go around nine?'

'That's when the music's turned up,' Kelly replied. 'Before nine we get a bit of a mixed crowd in but after nine it's mostly younger people, shooters and cocktails and that.'

'What do you know about the rugby crowd?' Mac asked.

Kelly thought for a while and shrugged her shoulders.

'Not a lot really. The leader's called Rob, he's quite old, at least thirty-five I'd say but he's not bad looking. Then there's this guy who's sometimes with them who's an absolute giant, we call him 'The Hulk'.'

'Are they ever any trouble?' Mac asked.

'The rugby mob? No never, now the supermarket lot are totally different. Two or three pints and they're wobbling if you know what I mean. They're always arguing between themselves too.'

'Do you know the names of any of the supermarket crowd?' Mac asked.

'Yes, one of them is called Bazzer, he's a bit of a loudmouth, then there's Scott and Danny. Danny's the quiet type, good looking too,' Kelly volunteered with a smile.

'And the rugby crowd?'

'Sorry, I just know Rob by name but I did hear them call The Hulk by name once.'

'What was it?' Mac asked.

'Wayne, I think.'

Mac had a sudden thought.

'Just sit there and don't move,' Mac ordered.

He rang Martin and asked if he could get a certain photo through social media. Martin rang back a few minutes later.

'He doesn't have a Facebook page but I found a photo of him on a rugby team site. I'm sending it over.'

It arrived a minute later.

Mac showed it to Kelly.

'Is this the person you call The Hulk?' Mac asked.

'Yes, that's him,' she replied with certainty.

'And you're sure that he was here when Natasha had her row with Julie?'

'Yes, I remember that he bought a round not long before Natasha left,' Kelly said.

'Did you see him go?'

'No, I didn't. He couldn't have hung around long though, he's not exactly someone you'd overlook.'

Mac thanked her and made sure he had her address and mobile phone number.

On the way out of the pub Tommy could no longer contain himself.

'Who is it? Who's in the photo?'

Mac showed it to Tommy. It was cropped from a team photo and showed a young giant of a man. Underneath the photo it detailed his position and name.

Second row forward - Wayne Turnell.

She must have dozed off because the light woke her up. He was coming towards her. A sudden jolt of fear coursed through her causing her to gasp. She knew she was going to die soon.

He only had a dressing gown and slippers on. She could see his erect penis poking through the gap between the two sides of the gown. As before he carried the baseball bat in one hand and the scalpel in the other. She found that she couldn't take her eyes off the scalpel.

It flashed out at her. She didn't know she'd been cut until she felt the blood trickling down from her breasts.

'Yes, I think it's sharp enough. Put your hands up against the wall,' he ordered brusquely. 'Yes, that's it. Now keep your hands against the wall and take a step back.'

She did as she was ordered. She was now leaning against the wall at an angle.

'Open your legs up,' he shouted, tapping the inside of her legs with the bat.

She did as he ordered. She could hear the swish of his dressing gown hitting the floor.

'Good girl.'

His fingers gripped her hair and pulled her head back. She froze as she felt the thin steel blade against her throat.

He entered her from behind and started pumping away. He was rough and hurt her which she supposed was the point. All her attention though was focussed on the thin sliver of metal that would soon end her life. She tried to make the seconds go slower but failed. From the sounds he was making he was not far from coming.

'I've only been on this earth for eighteen years. Please God, please God let me live!' she silently prayed.

'Yes, yes!' he shouted as he came inside her. She closed her eyes as she felt the blade move across her throat. She could feel the blood gush out and the warmth of it flow down her body. The blackness would not be long in coming now, not long.

But it didn't come. She heard him laughing. She opened her eyes. There was no blood. She felt her throat. There was no cut.

'Oh, imagination is a wonderful thing isn't it? It was the blunt side of the blade this time. You're just too good to throw away so soon. The next time...perhaps.'

He walked away, his laughter echoing around her head. Then it was dark and silent again. She crawled into her corner and her body shook with the shock of the experience. She felt dirty and stained and used.

She suddenly wished that he had cut her throat.

It would have been all been over by now.

Chapter Eighteen

'Dan, we might have something,' Mac said as he entered the incident room.

'What?' Dan asked, putting down the phone.

'Wayne Turnell, he was in the pub the night Natasha had the row with Julie.'

'Now that is news. Mr. Turnell seems to be cropping up all over the place. While you were away Martina rang from Birmingham. Apparently, Sheila Matthews was a member of a local gym and guess who else was a member?'

'Mr. Turnell, I take it,' Mac said.

'It's all a bit circumstantial so far but the evidence is definitely mounting up,' Dan said thoughtfully.

'Has anything else come in?'

'No, nothing earth shattering as yet.'

Martin came in eating a hamburger.

'Found anything yet on the house search?' Dan asked.

'I've got a few back. I'll print off the list if you like.'

The printer chugged away. Dan read the list and Mac could see that there was something there that excited him.

'Look,' Dan said handing the list to Mac.

Wayne Turnell's name was on the list. He'd bought a house five months ago. It was an old house, a Victorian semi-detached. It had a cellar. The agent said that he'd been instructed by Mr. Turnell to only look for houses that had an extension or a cellar.

'Well, Mac what do you think?' Dan asked with a grim smile.

'With this much evidence you have to do it,' Mac replied.

'Okay I agree. You say that this Wayne Turnell is a big man?' Dan asked.

'A giant so I've been told.'

'Okay, we go but only as soon as I've lined up a couple of firearm officers and an entry team,' Dan said. 'We can't take any chances. I'd better get on the phone.'

While Dan was on the phone Mac had a chat with Martin.

'There's still a chance that he might not be our man so it might be best not to make too public a show of the raid. Is there any way that we could get into the house unnoticed?'

Martin had a look on Google Earth.

'Yes, see just there,' Martin said pointing with his finger.

Mac couldn't quite make it out.

'It's an entryway,' Tommy said. 'It looks like it runs along the back of the whole row of houses.'

An entryway, Mac thought, now wouldn't that be poetic justice.

Martin printed the photo and the map off.

'The two firearm officers will be here in an hour,' Dan said. His face clouded over. 'I must admit that it really worries me Mac. If he isn't our man and it becomes public knowledge that we've tied Natasha's disappearance to one of the rail workers then we might be signing her death warrant.'

'On the other hand, if Turnell is our man and we don't raid him now, we might be doing exactly the same thing,' Mac said. 'Our man won't keep her forever. Sometimes all you can do is go for the most likely suspect and hope for the best.'

Dan nodded.

'Oh, by the way it looks like there's a back way into Mr. Turnell's house,' Mac said, handing over the photo and map.

'Even better, let's keep this as low key as we can.' Dan looked at his watch. It was nearly two o'clock. 'They should be all here by three but let's go through it all first.'

Dan, Mac, Tommy and Leigh all got around a table and looked at the map and the photographs of the area. It looked like they would need to access the entryway from a side street that ran at a right angle to the road Wayne Turnell's house was on.

'The only problem,' Dan said, 'is a van and two cars pulling up and then all of us piling down the entryway is all too likely to be noticed. I wonder if there's some other way we could do it?'

Amanda had been hovering for a while.

'Sorry sir but I just wanted to say something.'

'Go ahead,' Dan said.

'I saw the map when Martin when printing it off. One of our sergeants lives just here,' she said pointing to the street that ran behind and parallel to the street where Wayne Turnell's house was situated. The sergeant's house almost backed onto it.

'Yes, I see what you mean,' Dan replied with a smile. 'They both access the same entryway. All we need to do is to go through the sergeant's house, through the back garden and into the entryway and a few yards up is the back door that leads into Turnell's garden. Well spotted Amanda, bloody well spotted!'

Amanda smiled and blushed.

'Well, that certainly makes the whole operation an easier prospect,' Mac said. 'It also means that if Wayne isn't our man then we should stand a better chance at keeping it quiet, so long as he doesn't want to tell the local papers all about it afterwards that is.'

Dan frowned.

'Yes, there's always that isn't there? Well, we can only do what we can do. Amanda, as you know him, can you contact this sergeant and ask him if we can be at his house in about an hour or so?'

'Yes sir,' she said pulling out her phone as she walked away.

'I wish that she'd lay off the 'sir' a bit', Dan said. 'It makes me feel old. Okay, it looks like we've got a plan and a better one than I could have hoped for.'

Forty minutes later and the incident room was full again. Dan briefed the four members of the entry team and the two firearm officers.

'So, there's just the one suspect, is there?' one of the firearm officers asked.

'As far as we know but I've been told he's something of a giant so that's why I want you along just in case,' Dan said as he glanced down at the very efficient looking semi-automatic rifle the officer was cradling. 'What is it you're using nowadays?'

'SIG 516, Swiss made. The best I've ever used,' the officer replied.

'Well, let's just hope that we won't need them today,' Dan looked at his watch. 'Okay, it's now ten past three. Amanda is the sergeant at home yet?'

Amanda gave him the thumbs up.

'Okay, let's get our stab vests on and get going,' Dan said. 'Best of luck everyone.'

Tommy drove with Mac in the passenger seat, Dan and Leigh sat in the back.

The door to the sergeant's house opened as they pulled up outside. The van pulled up behind them.

'Sergeant Morris?' Dan asked.

'Detective Superintendent Carter, come in. Just follow me.'

'Tell me, do you know if your house is similar to the one that we're going to visit today?' Dan asked.

'Yes, I've been inside a few houses on that street and I think they're all pretty much the same as mine.'

Dan had the sergeant show him where the door to the cellar was before he led them through the house and into the back garden. He unlatched a wooden gate at the back and let them into the entryway.

'That's Turnell's house there,' the sergeant said pointing to a green coloured gate. 'Good luck.'

'Thanks,' Dan replied. 'Hang about though, we may need to come back this way.'

Dan made sure that everyone was in the entry way. He then let the two firearm officers lead. Thankfully the gate wasn't locked and was only held shut by a latch. The garden was being worked on. A large part of it had been dug up and in one corner there were bags of cement and packs of wooden decking. The fencing on both sides was new, solid wood and around six feet high. Mac thought that it should help shield them from the gaze of the neighbours.

A firearm officer looked in the kitchen window and then signalled at the rest to come forward. He tried the kitchen door and they were in luck again, it wasn't locked. As planned the firearm officers went in first and the rest waited. One came out a minute later.

'Clear downstairs,' he said softly.

The team made their way inside as quietly as they could. Mac went in last.

The kitchen was new and well laid out. Mac thought that someone had put some real work in. The room beyond the kitchen had a sofa, a big flat screen TV on the wall and a pile of taped up boxes in one corner. By the time they got to the stairs they met a firearm officer coming down.

'Clear upstairs too,' he whispered.

Dan pointed towards the cellar door. One of the firearm officers quietly opened the door. A narrow staircase ran down to a single door, the door to the cellar. Behind the firearm officers the entry team followed on tip toe.

They stopped and listened. They could all clearly hear a man grunting and then loudly saying 'Yes, yes'. They looked at each other, the disgust showing on their faces. If Natasha was inside then it was absolutely clear what was happening to her.

One of the entry team carried a small orange coloured Enforcer. He swung the battering ram at the door and it flew open. The firearm officers went in first. A few seconds later they shouted with some urgency to the entry team to come and help.

Mac and rest of the team stood at the top of the stairs wondering what on earth was going on. Had they finally found Natasha?

Chapter Nineteen

A short while later one of the firearm officers came out and shouted up the stairs.

'All clear, you can come down now.'

Mac let the rest go first and then gingerly made his way down the steep staircase. He walked through the door and into a gym. A set of free weights was neatly arranged on a rack; dumbbells, bars and round metal discs of varying sizes. Two padded benches took up most of the space, one was raised up at a forty-five degree angle while the other one was flat. Wayne Turnell was seated on the flat one. He was holding his head with both hands and moaning.

'Christ that hurt!' he exclaimed.

'What happened?' Dan asked one of the firearm officers.

'He was lifting weights when we broke in, you know bench pressing. We surprised him and he nearly lost control of the bar. That's why I shouted for the entry team to come and help. It took all of us to get the bar back on the stand.'

Mac looked at the bar now nestled in its cradle. There was a very impressive amount of weight on it. Mac wasn't surprised that he'd nearly lost control.

'How did he get hurt then?' Dan asked.

'I sat up too quick and banged me bloody head on the bar,' Wayne helpfully explained.

He stood up and his head was only half an inch or so from the ceiling. Mac decided that he really wouldn't like to see Wayne when he was angry.

'I hope to God you lot are from the police,' he continued, looking suspiciously at the two rifles.

Dan showed him his warrant card.

Wayne handed it back.

'Mind if we talk upstairs? I could do with getting some ice on this,' he said pointing to his forehead which was already reddening.

Dan nodded to the firearm officers. One went ahead of Wayne and one behind. Again, Mac let everyone go ahead of him and took his time getting back to the ground floor. His back was starting to feel somewhat tender.

By the time he got into the kitchen Wayne had applied a bag of peas wrapped in a tea towel to his head.

'So, what's this all about?' he quite reasonably asked.

'I'm sorry but I need to have a word with my colleague first,' Dan said.

Dan glanced over at Mac and nodded at him to follow him into the living room.

'It's not him,' Dan stated.

'I think you're probably right there. As you said, just about everything we had was circumstantial. At least now we know why he wanted a cellar,' Mac replied.

'So, what now?' Dan asked. 'I think we're going to have to come clean with Mr. Turnell. At least if we explain why we needed to carry out the raid it might persuade him to keep quiet. What do you think?'

Mac could only agree. He followed Dan back into the kitchen.

'We're sorry for breaking in like this but we're investigating the disappearance of Natasha Barker,' Dan said.

Wayne's face creased with puzzlement.

'She's that girl that was in the news, about a week ago, wasn't it? Was it because I was in the pub that night that you thought I might have something to do with her disappearance? I've got an alibi you know, you could have just asked.'

'Yes, there's that plus we've also had information that links someone who is currently working on the rail

197

project in Hitchin with Natasha's disappearance,' Dan explained.

'And you really thought that someone was me!' Wayne said with some indignation.

'Yes, we did. Look, I'm being totally honest with you now, we also think that Natasha wasn't the first. When you were in Birmingham do you remember a girl called Sheila Matthews?' Dan asked.

'I'm not sure but the name sounds familiar for some reason,' Wayne replied.

'She disappeared, just like Natasha did, in 2003. You were both members of the same gym.'

Wayne gave it some deep thought.

'Yes, I think I remember now. People were talking in the gym about a girl going missing and then the police turned up showing everyone her photograph and asking if we'd ever met her.'

'And had you?' Dan asked.

Wayne shook his head.

'Not as far as I remember. I was working odd shifts those days so I wasn't usually there during the busier times. So, you think this 'someone' from where I work has abducted other girls. How many are we talking about?'

'Ten in all.'

'Ten!' Wayne exclaimed, looking somewhat shocked. 'God almighty and it's someone I might know too.'

'We also think that he keeps the girls for a time that's why we were interested when your estate agent let us know that you were interested in properties with cellars.'

'I can see now how all that might have made me a suspect,' Wayne said. 'I thought at first that it might have been to do with that charge that was made against me.'

'The sexual assault charge?' Dan asked.

'So, you did know about that then. I was told that was going to be wiped and it wouldn't be on the record.'

'Tell us about it.'

Wayne put the bag of peas down. He looked up at the clock.

'Would you mind if I let the person who made the charges against me tell you the story instead? Believe me, it'll make a lot more sense.'

Dan and Mac looked at each other in puzzlement.

'She'll be back in about ten minutes or so,' Wayne continued. 'You lads fancy a brew while we wait?' he asked with a smile while filling the kettle with water.

Seven minutes later a very pregnant young woman walked into the kitchen and froze at the sight of the crowd. She quickly noticed that two of the crowd had semi-automatic rifles.

'What the...' she said.

Her mouth opened but no sound came out.

Dan quickly showed her his warrant card. She then noticed the red mark on Wayne's forehead. She put her hands on her hips and, bump sticking out, fearlessly faced down the entire squad of policemen.

'What have you been doing to my Wayne? If you've been knocking him about then I'll make sure you lot never work again!'

'It's alright love,' Wayne said, 'calm down. I did it myself. I sat up too quick and banged me head on the bar.'

'You ninny,' she said. 'I keep telling you about that.'

Mac looked at the two of them, him six feet five and broad with it, while she was blond, slim and five feet five in high heels. Next to each other they didn't even look like they belonged to the same species.

'And you are?' Dan asked.

'Belinda Martens, I'm Wayne's partner.'

Dan explained once again why they'd all ended up in her kitchen.

'Wayne was in the pub on the night Natasha disappeared. He said he had an alibi, was that you?' Dan asked.

'Yes, I picked him up about quarter to ten outside the pub.'

'What did you do then?'

'We went for a curry, the one on Nightingale Road. We always go for a curry after he has a rugby day,' Belinda explained.

'Okay then, that's something that we can easily check. Wayne's not exactly someone who would blend into the background. Did you see anything out of the ordinary when you picked Wayne up?' Dan asked.

'No, not that I remember. Wayne was a bit the worse for drink but then he always is on rugby days.'

'We also found that Wayne had been investigated for a sexual offence and that the charges were dropped,' Dan said. 'He said that you could tell us all about it.'

'Oh that,' she said her face clearly showing that this was a subject that she really didn't want to talk about.

'I'm sorry love but they knew all about it,' Wayne said, holding her hand. 'I thought it would be better coming from you.'

She looked down at her bump and then pulled out a chair and sat down.

'It was just over four years ago. I was pregnant just like I am now. God I was so desperate for a baby, I still am,' she said giving them a sad smile. 'Seven months is all it lasted and then I had some rare complications, that's what they told us anyway. So, we lost her, we lost our little Juliet. That's what we'd decided to call her. I went mad, not angry, I mean mad, totally potty. The doctors said that it was partly down to my hormones going all over the place, that and the grief. I was having delusions that everyone was after me, even poor Wayne here. I went to the police, said that he was a total stranger and that he'd tried to rape me. They investigated and did their job but they quickly came to the conclusion that it was me that needed help. I got it eventually but only after I'd stabbed Wayne.'

'You stabbed Wayne?' Dan echoed with some disbelief.

'Yes, it's hard to believe isn't it? The poor man has got the scars to prove it too. I mean, look at him, he's massive but he's just a big jelly baby really. I suppose that's why I fell for him in the first place. Anyway, I was committed and spent three months in a hospital where they managed to sort me out. Wayne here stuck with me through it all though. He's even persuaded me to have another go, can you believe it?' she said, her hands caressing her bump. 'Another girl but we're not going to pick a name until...well you know.'

'Thanks Belinda, I know that must have been difficult. Can I ask you both to keep what's happened totally to yourselves for now? If word gets out to whoever's holding Natasha that we're closing in then he might kill her,' Dan said.

'I saw her on the news, that girl's mother,' Belinda said. 'I saw the pain in her face. I only carried my girl for seven months while she's had hers for eighteen years but I knew what she was feeling. I knew. Don't worry, no-one will hear about this from us.'

'Thank you both and the very best of luck,' Dan said. 'Oh, by the way, when you get your door fixed just send me the bill.'

'What do we say if any of the neighbours have seen you?' Wayne asked. 'They can be a nosy lot.'

Dan thought for a while.

'If anyone mentions seeing us just say that we're filming a pilot for a police TV series. It might even make them a little jealous.'

Mac smiled at Dan's quick thinking.

They made their way out as quietly as they had coming in. The sergeant was waiting for them and escorted them back through his house.

As they drove back Dan said, 'I think we just got very lucky back there.'

'Yes, it could have turned out a lot worse,' Mac said. 'So, what's next?'

'I was nearly forgetting that I've still got the press conference and this bloody reconstruction this evening,' Dan said with some exasperation. 'Tommy can you drop me and Mac at Mrs. Barker's and then pick us up in about half an hour?'

'Sure, no problem,' Tommy replied.

'I just want to explain to her that she shouldn't take any notice of what she might see on TV tonight,' Dan explained. 'I'm hoping that we'll come over as a bunch of complete idiots but I don't want her thinking that.'

'Good idea,' Mac said.

He wasn't sure that it was such a good idea when he was struggling up the stairs. He realised that he was very nearly spent but he was trying desperately not to let it show.

Dan waited for him at the top.

'What do you think we should tell her Mac?' Dan asked.

Mac leant against the wall and thought it through.

'Perhaps the truth would be best. It might get her hopes up but there is real hope, isn't there?'

Dan nodded.

'I agree. The truth it is then.'

Once again Stella opened the door and she had the same question on her face.

'We've made some progress but I need to speak to Mrs. Barker about the reconstruction tonight,' Dan said as he walked inside.

Mrs. Barker appeared at the living room door. The worry lines on her face had deepened.

'I heard voices,' she said. 'Is it....?'

'We've not found Natasha yet,' Dan said quickly, 'but we do have some news.'

Stella sat beside Mrs. Barker. Mac noticed that Mrs. Barker's hand immediately reached out and grasped Stella's. They had obviously become friends.

'It's been a week to the day since Natasha disappeared so we're going to do a reconstruction,' Dan said. 'A police officer is going to dress like your daughter and then take the same route home that she took. We're hoping that it might jog someone's memory but there's another reason why we're doing it.'

Dan paused and looked at Mac.

Mac nodded.

Dan licked his lips and took the plunge.

'We've made quite a bit of progress with the case and we think there's a good chance that your daughter might still be alive.'

He paused again, waiting for Mrs. Barker's reaction. It took quite a while to come.

She looked at Stella, then at Dan, then at Mac and back to Stella again. It was clear that she still didn't believe a word of what she was being told.

'We believe that the man who abducted Natasha has done it before, several times before in fact. We also believe that he...well, he keeps the girls for a while,' Dan said.

He didn't want to dwell on what might be happening to Natasha while she was being kept so he raced on.

'The main point of the reconstruction tonight is to make her abductor feel secure. I'm going to admit, under some very critical questioning from a friend of mine in the local press, that we have absolutely no idea what's happened to Natasha. To be honest we're going to make ourselves look a bit foolish, all in the hope that this encourages him to keep Natasha for a good while longer. The real truth is that we've got some very good leads and I'm hopeful that we'll have him before too long.'

Mrs. Barker said nothing but the tears streaming from her eyes and the half-smile on her face said it all.

Dan stood up.

'We'll be in touch if anything happens but please don't tell anyone else what we've discussed,' Dan said. 'We don't know who he is yet and we want to make sure he has no idea that we're on his trail.'

Mrs. Barker stood up and grasped Dan's right hand in both of hers.

'Thank you,' she said. 'Thank you.'

Stella saw them out.

'Is that true, that we really might be close to identifying him?' she asked.

Dan nodded.

'We're fairly certain that he's one of ninety-one suspects. The only problem we've got is figuring out which one is him.'

'Good luck with that sir,' Stella said.

'Thanks Stella, we'll need it.'

Tommy was waiting for them when they got back downstairs. Mac's back was screaming at him now. There was no point in covering it up any longer.

'Sorry Dan but would you mind if Tommy dropped me home? It's only up the road and, if I'm honest, I'm not feeling so well.'

'Sure, of course,' Dan said with some concern. 'Will you be okay?'

'If I can get some rest now then I should be fine for tomorrow,' Mac said with a lot more confidence than he actually felt.

Before he got out of the car he said, 'Best of luck tonight with the reconstruction.'

'Thanks. I'll see you tomorrow,' Dan replied.

Mac changed patches and took his other medication then made his way straight to his bedroom. He let his clothes drop to the floor and gratefully crawled between the sheets. He lay back and grunted when the expected spike of pain hit him. Sleep was what he needed and he was fairly sure it wouldn't take too long in coming.

With luck the two little blue pills he'd just taken would see to that.

Again, the light told of his coming and again he came in a dressing gown with the baseball bat in one hand and the scalpel in the other. Again, he cut her first to prove the keenness of the scalpel, not once but twice this time, and then he ordered her to lean against the wall.

'Take a step back,' he ordered.

She was so scared that she couldn't make sense of his words. She heard a swish and then felt an overwhelming surge of pain emanate from her upper back. He'd hit her with the baseball bat.

'Quicker next time,' he whispered in her ear.

He grabbed her hair and positioned the scalpel at her throat. He then took her roughly from behind.

Next time.

The words went around her head. Would there be a next time? She hoped he'd do it now. She was tired of being afraid.

Then he noisily came and the scalpel blade ran across her throat. Her eyes were tight shut but she felt the warmth of her blood flowing down her breasts. She was sure that the blackness would now take her and she welcomed it with open arms. She was disappointed when she once again heard his laughter and opened her eyes to find that he had used the blunt side again.

She hadn't had to fake her fear, it was real enough, but somehow, sitting alone in the darkness, she'd found some steel inside herself. She decided that there must be a way out and, if there was, she'd only have a brief time to find it.

She quickly scanned the room while the light was still on as he made his way out. It was featureless with the walls, ceiling and floor being made up of plasterboard panels. Featureless, that is, with the exception of two ancient wooden ceiling beams that ran across the width of the room.

It was there that she spotted it. Her way out. The light went off but she'd memorised its location. There was only one thing she needed now.

The courage to do it.

Chapter Twenty

Seven days missing

When he awoke the room was dark. For a while he had no idea where he was or what day it was. His memory returned in instalments. He eventually turned on the bedside lamp and looked at the clock. It was four thirty. He'd been asleep for well over ten hours but he still felt exhausted.

He turned off the light and lay back hoping that sleep might overtake him again but his brain had gotten into gear and the memories of the abortive raid and the interview with Mrs. Barker paraded through his head. He sighed and turned the light back on.

He went through his morning ritual of first sitting up and then standing up to see what the pain was like. The pain wasn't that bad so he decided to have a shower and a shave and see how he felt afterwards. The shower, followed by a cup of strong coffee, helped to make him feel a little more alert. It was still only five fifteen. Not knowing what else to do he decided that he might as well drive into Hitchin and see if there was anything he could do in the incident room.

The sun was just beginning to rise over the town as he drove down the hill through a thin morning mist. He ignored the speed limit but still stopped at the red light even though he could clearly see that the gates to the site were locked. It was Sunday and Mac wondered if anyone would be working today.

When he pulled up outside the incident room, he was mildly surprised to see a light on inside. The door was unlocked. There was no-one inside except for Martin who was clicking away at his laptop in the corner. The smell of freshly made coffee welcomed him in.

'You're early today,' Martin said without turning around.

'So are you,' Mac replied.

Martin turned and gave Mac a disappointed look.

'I couldn't sleep and I was hoping that someone might have reported something overnight, you know from the reconstruction.'

'And I take it from your face that they haven't?'

Martin shook his head.

'Did you go?' Mac asked.

'No, I stayed here just in case anyone called through but I heard all about it from Dan afterwards.'

'How did Amanda do?'

'Really well, so Dan said. I saw her on the news afterwards, she looked quite confident even when all the photographers were taking pictures of her.'

'Did anything interesting happen?' Mac asked.

'No, not really,' Martin said. 'Oh, apart from Jo catching a glimpse of Jonny Aldis in the crowd that is.'

'What happened there?'

'Well, Jo had this idea that Jonny might be curious enough to turn up to see what was going on. So, she, Gerry and a couple of uniforms spent the whole time scanning the crowd watching the reconstruction and they got lucky. They saw him looking at Amanda as she walked towards Purwell Lane. They tried to follow him but unfortunately they lost sight of him near the Millhouse pub.'

'That was really good thinking on Jo's part. It's a pity that they lost him though.' Mac said.

'Well, it seems to have given Gerry an idea. He thinks he knows where Jonny's been hiding out.'

'Any idea where exactly?'

Martin shook his head.

'No, but Jo and Gerry are meeting up here in around thirty minutes so you can ask them yourselves.'

'Thanks, I'll do just that.'

Mac helped himself to a cup of coffee.

'By the way did you ever get anywhere with the medical records of the ninety-two? No sorry, it's the ninety-one now, isn't it?'

'I did get some information but I'm afraid that it's a bit patchy,' Martin replied. 'Only forty-six had Summary Care Records and none of them mentioned Fentanyl.'

'So how come the other forty-five don't have records then?'

'Well apparently you can opt out of the system if you want and I believe some doctors never bought into the idea in the first place. It's a bit of a mess really,' Martin explained.

'I see and I suppose that we can't really rule out any of those who have records in case they're carers and getting Fentanyl that way.' Mac sighed. 'We desperately need something to whittle down the number a bit, any ideas?'

Martin gave the question some thought.

'I've been thinking and thinking but I've not come up with anything that might help. I thought the house idea might work but there's only Wayne Turnell who bought a house locally as far as we can tell. There are around twenty or so who bought flats while the rest seem to have either rented flats or are commuting from London. We need a completely new angle. What about using a criminal profiler?' Martin suggested. 'You see them on TV all the time.'

'Yes, you see a lot of things of the TV but they don't always get things right, do they?'

'Have you worked with profilers before then?'

'Just the once,' Mac replied. 'He was foisted on me by one of my more gullible bosses and it turned out to be a total waste of time. He came up with some ideas but in the end they all proved to be way off the mark, so it was just as well that none of us took any notice of him. A friend of mine, a professor of criminology, did a study not long ago and he challenged anyone to come up with a case where profiling had led directly to an arrest. Unsurprisingly no-one did.'

Martin looked surprised.

'So, it's all just rubbish then?'

'No, not totally,' Mac replied. 'It's not profiling really but I think it can help if you think about the man behind the crime. On a case by case basis you can learn a lot about someone but I guess where profiling in general falls down is trying to force all criminals into particular categories. People can be very different to each other and murderers are no exception.'

'So, what do you think our man's like?' Martin asked.

'The old cliché about being a loner, living alone and not being good with people always stands a good chance of applying,' Mac replied.

'It looks like a good proportion of the ninety-one are single or divorced anyway,' Martin said.

"I suppose it's all that working away from home, so not much help there then. Even so you can't even rule out the married ones. Think of Fred West whose wife was a willing accomplice and Gacy who was married and quite sociable, so with serial killers you can never ...'

Mac didn't finish the sentence. He had an idea.

'Are you alright Mac?' Martin asked worried by his sudden silence.

The door opened and Jo walked in. She looked tired and grumpy.

'Morning,' she said. 'I thought that Bear Grylls would be here by now. We need to start looking at first light he said. So where is he then? Has anyone had any breakfast yet?'

Mac and Martin shook their heads.

'I've got some nice spicy beef patties if anyone's interested. Best patties in the world, my mum dropped them around last night. I'll need one to keep my strength up if I'm going to be poking around in the undergrowth all day again.'

211

She produced a big plastic tub that was stuffed full of yellow half-moon shaped pastries. Mac loved Caribbean food and the patties especially.

'I'll have one,' he quickly piped up.

'Yes, me too,' Martin said.

'I'll heat them up then,' Jo said with a smile.

While she was at the microwave Gerry walked in.

'Morning all,' he said cheerily. 'Morning Jo, looking forward to another day in the great outdoors?'

'No, I am not!' she snapped. 'I'll be glad when I can start wearing my heels to work again. Mud and bloody spiders, how can anyone like that? Want a pattie?'

'Oh God yes, they smell fantastic!' Gerry replied. 'Okay if we eat them on the way? The uniforms are going to meet us in the Millhouse car park in fifteen minutes or so.'

'No problem, I brought some napkins along as well,' Jo replied.

'I believe that you've got an idea as to where Jonny Aldis might be holing up?' Mac asked as Jo gave him and Martin a piping hot pattie each.

'Yes, it looks like he went into the Millhouse car park which puzzled me until I had a look at Google Earth,' Gerry replied. 'We searched Walsworth Common but there's a little neck of land that somewhat hidden away when you look at it from the common and I've been wondering if it might be easier to get to from the back of the pub. There seems to be a lot of trees and bushes there so plenty of cover for him to hide in. It will be well worth a look anyway.'

Mac took a bite out of the peppery pattie. It was wonderful, the pastry was flaky and the chunks of steak and brightly coloured vegetables coated his mouth with spices. His face must have shown it because Jo gave him a wide smile.

'So, you think that he's been hiding behind the pub all this time?' he asked once he'd swallowed his first bite.

212

His mouth was tingling in the nicest possible way.

'Yes, and it would make sense,' Gerry replied. 'It's not too far from home and, close as it is to the pub, you wouldn't know this bit of land was there if you didn't look at an aerial view.'

Jo handed Gerry a pattie wrapped in a napkin.

'Come on, let's not keep the spiders waiting,' she said as she headed for the door.

'See you,' Gerry said with a smile as he left.

'It's a wonder that those two haven't killed each other by now,' Mac said once they'd gone.

He then returned to the serious business of putting away his pattie.

'I know what you mean,' Martin replied. 'I'd bet that Jo will ask for another partner as soon as this case is over.'

'Yes, it does appear as if Gerry actually enjoys annoying her.'

The door opened and Dan walked in.

'What is that wonderful smell?' he said.

'Patties,' Martin replied in between bites, 'in the box over there. Absolutely fantastic.'

Dan went and helped himself to one and put it in the microwave.

'I take it that Jo and Gerry have been in then?'

'Yes, you just missed them. They're still hoping to track down Jonny Aldis,' Mac replied.

'Let's hope Gerry's right, we could do with some good luck. What's the betting that, even if they do find him, he won't be able to tell us anything new anyway?'

Dan's grumpy expression returned.

'Ninety-one suspects and I haven't got a clue where we go next. What about the Fentanyl, anything there?' Dan asked hopefully.

'We were just talking about that before you came in,' Mac replied. 'Apparently not all of the ninety-one's medical records are available and, even if they were, our man might be a carer so not much help there I'm afraid.'

Dan's face got a notch grumpier.

The microwave signalled that it had finished. Dan wrapped the pastry in a napkin and took a bite.

'God, these are bloody good! Did Jo do them herself?'

'Her mum,' Martin replied.

'I wouldn't mind inviting myself around for dinner when she's next cooking then,' Dan said.

'How did the press conference go?' Mac asked. 'Sorry but I never got to see it. I was asleep not long after you dropped me home.'

'It went better than I expected if I'm honest,' Dan replied. 'I had a look at it later on the news and my reporter friend made me look a right idiot which, of course, was the plan. I even got him to ask a question about Tony Hamilton so everyone would know that the newspaper story about him was just a pack of lies.'

'Thanks for that but, unfortunately, I think the horse has already bolted on that one,' Mac said sadly.

'So, we got nothing new from the reconstruction, not that I was expecting much, and here we are,' Dan said glumly. 'We've whittled it down from millions of suspects to ninety-one and now we're stuck. If I'm honest, I just haven't got a clue where we go next. I'm beginning to think we should just raid them all at the same time.'

'It would be a hell of a gamble and quite difficult logistically but I agree that it's something we might need to think about before long,' Mac said. 'We stand a chance of being able to hush up a single raid, like we did with the Turnells, but the cat would be well and truly out of the bag if we raided them all. We'd have one shot at it and if that went wrong then...'

'I know, it'll be Natasha's body that we'll be looking for,' Dan said with a frown.

'For now, I think that it might be best to just keep patient and see what we can turn up. Based on what we know, he might keep Natasha for at least another couple of weeks so we've still got a real chance,' Mac said, hoping his words might cheer Dan up a bit.

'God, I hate being patient though!' Dan said with some exasperation. 'I just want to get going and knock some heads together but I know you're right.'

He took another bite from his pattie.

'Oh well, we'll just have to wait until everyone gets in and hope that someone's had a brainwave overnight.'

'There was something that just occurred to me, a bit of a long shot perhaps, but it might be worth a try,' Mac said.

Dan's face lit up.

'Go on, right now I'd settle for any type of shot at getting our man, long or otherwise.'

'Just before you came in, we were talking about John Wayne Gacy and it gave me an idea. Most serial killers I've been involved with or that I've read about have had quite traumatic childhoods in one way or another. It would take a lot of digging but if we've got nothing else...'

Dan's face turned thoughtful.

'Gacy, yes he killed a lot of young men, didn't he? What happened to him then?'

'He had an alcoholic father who beat him from the age of four and belittled him constantly. Even when he was ill and in hospital his father accused him of faking it. I'm not saying that everyone who has killed has an obviously traumatic childhood but I'd bet that a very high proportion have. It's just an idea,' Mac said.

'Martin how could we get information on the early years of the ninety-one?' Dan asked.

Martin thought for a moment.

'Well, the obvious sources would be schools, hospitals, social services and the local papers, I'd guess. We know where each of them was born and went to school from their work records so that could be our starting point.

The only problem is that some of the data might be thirty or forty years old so it might not be easily available, if it's available at all, that is.'

'Okay, but still worth having a go at perhaps?' Dan asked.

'Absolutely, especially as we've nothing else worth following up at the moment,' Martin replied.

'Yes, we need to keep the team working away at something. Okay then, start thinking about how we'll need to organise it. Bloody hell, it's Sunday, that's not going to help much is it?' Dan exclaimed.

'The schools and social services probably won't be available until tomorrow but we could try the hospitals and local papers in the meantime. They might have someone around who could get us the information,' Martin suggested.

'Okay then, that's what we'll do for now.'

Dan looked much happier now.

The rest of the team dribbled in over the next forty-five minutes or so. They all looked more than a little disheartened when they heard the news that the reconstruction hadn't provided any further clues.

'However, Mac's come up with an idea and it will give us something to have a go at for the next couple of days unless anyone's come up with something else?' Dan asked with more hope than expectation.

No-one had.

'Okay, so what we're going to be doing is seeing what we can find out about our ninety-one suspects' child-hoods. If we assume that something traumatic might have happened to our man to turn him into a killer then that information might still be out there.'

Dan looked at the team's faces.

'I can see that one or two of you aren't quite sold on this idea but I want you to give it your best shot. Even if it doesn't give us a killer clue, we'll end up knowing more about the suspects and that can't be bad. Are we all okay with that?'

Apparently, the team were.

Dan continued, 'Okay then Martin's going to give you a sheet of paper with a suspect's name on. It will also give you the location where the suspect was born and brought up. As it's Sunday, concentrate on local hospitals and newspapers as they might have someone on duty. Oh, and warn anyone you speak to that they should keep the fact that we've called to themselves. Our man might still have friends and relatives in the area and if they go blabbing around it might stand a chance of getting back to him. If we've gotten nowhere by tomorrow then we'll start contacting schools and social service departments. When you've finished, go back to Martin and he'll give you another suspect to look at. If you find anything, no matter how insignificant it might seem, note it on the sheet of paper and return it to Martin. He'll be collating everything we find and, hopefully, by the end of the exercise we might know a bit more than we do now.'

'What about Jo and Gerry?' Martina asked.

'They're still out looking for Jonny Aldis,' Dan replied. 'Gerry had an idea about where he might be hiding so keep your fingers crossed that they find him and that he knows something. Until then let's get cracking.'

Mac and Tommy were given a sheet of paper by Martin. It was headed 'John Hasington' who was born in Lincoln in 1969 and attended a local primary school called St. Peters. They looked up the local hospital and newspapers on the internet and got started. They started with the local newspaper, The Lincolnshire Echo. There was only a junior reporter on duty. She said she'd do her best to see what she could find and call back. Mac gave her his mobile number.

'We'll probably get a lot of this, so it might be best if we call out on your phone and use mine for call-backs,' Mac suggested.

They got another sheet of paper with another name and ploughed on. Bits of information dribbled back over the next few hours. In the case of John Hasington, they found out that he was admitted into hospital for a badly sprained ankle when he was eight and two years later was named Cub Scout of the Year for the Lincoln area. Mac duly noted this on the sheet of paper and returned it to Martin.

Some three hours and nine suspects later they still had little to report and Mac was beginning to wonder if it had been such a good idea. He stood up to stretch his back when the door to the incident room opened and Jo and Gerry walked in. In between them was a tall young man with had long bedraggled hair and a look of total exhaustion on his face.

They'd found Jonny Aldis at last!

Chapter Twenty One

Jo sat Jonny down at a vacant desk. He slumped down into the seat and closed his eyes.

'Bloody good work you two. How did you find him?' Dan asked with some excitement.

'He more or less walked into us when we were searching that bit of land I told you about,' Gerry replied.

'Did you have any trouble?'

'No, none at all. I rather got the feeling that he was quite relieved that we'd found him to be honest.'

'Look at him, the poor lad's totally done in,' Jo added sympathetically.

Jonny's head was now on the desk, his arms hanging straight down and almost touching the floor. He was fast asleep.

'It's a pity to wake him but we need to find out if he knows anything,' Dan said.

He shook Jonny gently and then a little harder when he didn't wake up. Eventually he opened his eyes.

'What, what?' he said clearly confused as to where he was.

'I'm Detective Superintendent Carter and I'm in charge of the team that are looking for Natasha. Please don't go back to sleep, we need to ask you some questions.'

Jonny shook his head. Jo produced a wet wipe which Jonny used to wipe his face. The room fell silent as the rest of the team stopped work and watched the interview avidly.

'I couldn't find her,' Jonny said. 'I looked and looked everywhere. I must have walked for miles but I couldn't find her.'

He looked dejected and on the verge of tears.

'Is that what you were doing, looking for Natasha? Is that why you hid yourself away all this time?' Dan asked.

'When I heard that you were asking about me, I was afraid that you might have thought that I did it. I know I'm a bit different so I thought I'd be the main suspect. I couldn't have you lock me up, I just couldn't. I needed to be out there looking for her.'

'Did you find anything while you were looking for her?' Dan asked.

Jonny shook his head.

'Nothing at all?' Dan asked again clearly getting a bit desperate.

Jonny thought for a moment.

'I thought I saw her yesterday.'

'Tell me about it,' Dan asked gently.

'I saw someone walking on the other side of the street. She was a few yards ahead of me and, from behind, I really thought it was Nat. I ran ahead to get a better look but it turned out to be some old woman. I've failed her, haven't I?'

'No Jonny, not if you did your best,' Dan said. 'But tell me, what made you think that this woman was Natasha?'

'I suppose it was the dress really,' Jonny replied, 'it was just like the dress that Nat was designing. She showed me the sketches not long before she disappeared. It was so like it but it wasn't her.'

Mac noticed a hint of excitement on Dan's face.

'Where did you see her Jonny?'

'On the Ickleford Road somewhere, I think, but I can't be sure.'

'You're good at drawing, aren't you?' Dan asked. 'I've heard you've got a really good memory too. Could you draw this woman for me?'

Jonny thought about this for a moment and then nodded.

'I'd need my sketch pad and pencils, they're at home.'

'Tommy go around to Jonny's house and get his pad and pencils,' Dan ordered. 'Tell his parents that he's safe

220

and helping us with a line of enquiry. Tell them we're not going to be keeping him for more than a couple of hours and that we'll drop him home when we're finished.'

Tommy shot off.

Dan turned back to Jonny who was now nodding off again.

'Jonny please try to keep awake. We'll have your pad and pencils in a few minutes but while we're waiting is there anything else you can tell us that might help?'

Jonny told them what had happened the last time he and Natasha had met. They'd talked mostly about the project she'd been working on but, before he left her, she'd promised to try and meet him in the Millhouse on the night she disappeared. They now understood why he'd been looking out for her all night.

'So, you didn't see Natasha at all that night then?' Mac asked.

'No, I was outside most of the evening looking out for her but I never saw her.'

'Did you know that Natasha was dropped off near the pub at around quarter to ten by a taxi?'

'Really?' Jonny looked surprised. 'Quarter to ten?'

He gave it some thought and it was obviously hard work.

'I was outside with Matty around that time. Oh, I remember now, a police car drove by and he pulled me around the side of the pub. He was...'

Jonny didn't finish the sentence.

'Yes, we know what Matty was doing,' Mac said. 'He was smoking something that he shouldn't have been smoking. Don't worry you haven't got him into any trouble.'

'Well, I wasn't really expecting Nat until after ten so I kept him company until he finished.'

A sudden thought hit Jonny. His face went even whiter.

'God, oh God, if I hadn't gone with Matty then I might have seen Nat, I might have been able to save her.'

'It wouldn't have made any difference,' Dan said reassuringly. 'We believe that Natasha was being stalked and, if she hadn't been abducted that Saturday, then our man would just have waited for another opportunity. All that you would have achieved would be to just delay it a bit.'

Thankfully the door opened and Tommy arrived with the drawing equipment. A rugged weather-beaten man in his early forties followed him in.

'It's Jonny's dad. He insisted,' Tommy explained with a shrug of the shoulders.

Jonny and his dad hugged each other fiercely.

'Are you okay?' he asked his son.

Jonny nodded. Both father and son were on the brink of tears.

'We've asked your son to help us by drawing someone he saw yesterday,' Dan explained.

'A suspect?' Jonny's father asked.

'Yes, a suspect.'

'Well, you'd better get to work then son,' he said.

Jonny did just that.

Mac watched Jonny closely as he drew. He was totally transformed; his eyes were bright and alert as his hand flew over the surface of the paper. Out of a mass of grey pencil lines a picture slowly emerged. Detail on detail was added until something not far off the quality of a photograph emerged.

Jonny put his pencil down.

'Will this do?' he asked.

'I should think so. It's bloody brilliant!' Dan exclaimed.

Jonny's dad looked quite proud of his son.

The drawing showed a slim woman of around forty or so. She had medium length dark hair and wore glasses. She had a shopping bag in one hand and a small handbag was slung over a shoulder. She had shoes with a medium heel and she walked very erect.

'That dress, what do you think?' Dan asked.

'Martin, where's that sample of lace I gave you?' Mac asked.

Martin dug out the plastic bag. Mac compared the lace to the detailed drawing.

'Yes, it could be the same but I think that we need an expert. Could we get Julie Waddington in?'

'Good idea,' Dan said. 'Tommy can you drop Jonny and his dad back home and get Julie Waddington up here as quickly as possible. She'll probably be with Mrs. Barker.'

His father helped Jonny towards the door. He was nearly out on his feet.

'Well, there's someone who'll sleep well tonight,' Dan said after they'd gone.

He only noticed then that the room had gone quiet and no-one was working.

'Back to work everyone,' he ordered. 'This might be something or nothing and we still need as much information as we can possibly get.'

Dan looked at the drawing closely.

'What do you think Mac? Could it be that we're looking for a couple and not a lone killer?'

'Well, if it is a couple then perhaps that might explain a lot,' Mac replied. 'Our man must have been stalking the girls and perhaps over quite some time. Maybe that's why we've never been able to identify anyone showing an interest in the girls, I mean no-one would be looking for a woman, would they?'

'That's true and I suppose being in a couple is good camouflage. I mean we always seem to be looking for unsociable loners for crimes like this.'

'If that is the case then I'm also wondering if a woman could have been used during the abduction,' Mac said.

'The girls would have been a lot less wary of a woman, wouldn't they?'

'I wonder where this is exactly?' Dan asked himself. 'It looks like that's a shop in the background. We'd better get Martin to scan this, he might be able to tell us.'

Martin scanned the drawing and zoomed into the background.

'Where did he say that he saw the suspect?' Martin asked.

'Somewhere on the Ickleford Road he thinks but he's not sure exactly where,' Dan replied.

'Okay, let's have a look then.'

Martin opened up the map and then selected one end of Ickleford Road and selected Street View. He took them slowly down the road virtually. He had to go right to the other end of the road before he saw it. He adjusted the view so that they were looking directly at the shop. On the left of the shop there was a red post box. The post box was also there in the drawing.

'Yes, that's it!' Dan exclaimed. 'Well done, Martin. Now, if we can identify the woman then we might really be getting somewhere.'

Tommy turned up with Julie Waddington in tow. She looked almost as tired as Jonny Aldis had.

'Julie, thanks for coming in,' Dan said. 'Jonny Aldis thinks he saw someone wearing a dress similar to the one that Natasha was wearing the night she disappeared. He's drawn the dress and the woman wearing it. We'd just like you to have a look and tell us what you think.'

He showed her the drawing. She studied it carefully and then looked up at Dan.

'Well?' Dan prompted her.

'It looks very like Nat's dress. See just here,' Julie pointed to the bottom of the dress, 'she undid the seams and re-stitched them so that it would be tighter around the legs. It was based on a design from the fifties, a 'pencil skirt' she called it.'

'What about the lace?' Mac asked.

'Yes, she followed the shape of the dress with the lace just like this one does.'

'So, do you think this could be Natasha's dress?' Dan asked while mentally crossing his fingers.

'Yes, yes it could be but, if it is, what I'd like to know is why on earth would *she* be wearing it?' Julie asked with a puzzled expression on her face.

'She? You know this woman?' Dan asked with growing excitement.

'I wouldn't say that, I mean I don't know her name or anything but I've seen her around.'

'Where have you seen her?'

'At the pub, the Hen and Chickens, she's one of the footballer's wives.'

He sat in church hearing but not listening to the priest's sermon. He was looking at the man nailed to the cross. He was looking at the blood on his hands where the nails had ripped into his palms and his torso where the spear had cut him deeply. He had made a blood sacrifice and everyone here seemed to love the fact. The carpenter must have bled a lot.

He would also be making his own blood sacrifice soon too but not with his own blood of course. He thought of how it would be and he felt his pulse starting to race as he pictured the snick of the scalpel on her throat and the gush of red that would be such a release for them both.

It was the right thing to do and he knew that God knew that too. He'd heard God speaking to him many times. He knew who it was, that voice could belong to no-one else. He looked at the stained-glass window, Jesus was looking straight at him and smiling.

'Today,' a voice said in his head.

He had hoped to keep the girl a little longer but he knew that he could never go against God's word so today it would be. He'd take her one more time and then release her spirit. He smiled at the thought.

People started standing up around him. It was time for the communion. He shuffled towards the priest and accepted the round wafer of bread with little excitement. Well, bread was just bread, wasn't it? It gave life but it was boring. No, it was the next part of the ritual he was really looking forward to. When he didn't have a girl, it was the high point of his week.

He moved to the side of the church where a parishioner held a gold cup, a cup full of God's own blood. He slowly raised it to his lips and sipped. The blood made him tingle with excitement. God had spoken to him and he knew how it had to be.

The next blood he would drink would be warm and full of life.

Chapter Twenty Two

Mac turned to Tommy, 'Can you quickly run up to the pub and see if Kelly's on duty? If not bring the landlord.'

Tommy dashed out of the door.

'If anyone can identify her it's probably going to be Kelly. She's a barmaid at the pub,' Mac explained to Dan.

Mac waited with impatience until Tommy returned with a once again breathless Kelly.

Kelly nodded at Julie as she tried to regain her composure.

'Kelly, we believe that you might know this woman,' Dan said as he showed her the drawing.

'Yes, that's Nicky,' she replied.

'Do you know her second name?'

Kelly shook her head.

'No, I just know her as Nicky.'

'Is there anything that you can tell us about her?' Dan persisted.

'Well, she's usually in once or twice a week and she's always alone which I suppose is why she started sitting with the footballer's wives.'

'Anything else?' Dan asked hopefully.

'I remember once when I was collecting glasses and they were all talking about their husbands. She said that hers was in IT. That's all I know really.'

'Was she ever there when Natasha was in the pub?' Dan asked.

Kelly gave it some thought.

'Yes, now you mention it. She was always there on a Saturday, as was Nat, but I remember her being there on Tuesdays too. That's the only other night that Nat came in.'

'Thanks Kelly,' Dan said. 'Tommy, if I get Martin to print off a copy of the drawing can you go back with

Kelly and show it to the rest of the staff just in case they can add anything?'

He went over to Martin.

'Printing off,' Martin said before Dan could say anything.

Dan noticed a very thoughtful expression on Martin's face while he waited for the drawing to print. After he gave it to Tommy he went back.

'Come on Martin, spit it out. You've thought of something haven't you?' Dan said.

'I might have...can you give me five minutes? I just want to check something.'

Dan poured himself and Mac a coffee while he waited. He never took his eyes off Martin's hands as they skimmed over the keyboard. Three minutes later Martin's hand went up.

'What have you got?' Dan asked.

'I might have a name. It's a bit tenuous but...'

'Forgets the 'buts', tenuous is better than nothing, so tell me.'

'Okay, something's been stuck in my head ever since I started doing research on the properties bought by the ninety-two. I thought that I might be on to something, so I checked it out with the estate agent to make sure it wasn't a typo. He confirmed it, he'd actually dealt with the sale himself, so in the end I put it down to coincidence and thought no more about it.'

'Go on, cut to the chase,' Dan implored.

'A house was bought by a Ms. Nicola Moncrieff a couple of months before the rail works started, a Victorian house with a cellar. She paid cash. Now there's also a Nicholas Moncrieff who works on the project but he has a home address in London and I couldn't find anything to link the two of them at the time.'

'What's his job?' Mac asked.

'He's the Head of IT for the project,' Martin replied.

'Yes!' Dan said excitedly.

228

Martin continued, 'The best of all, the house I mentioned is also on the Ickleford Road and is no more than two hundred yards from the shop where Jonny saw the woman.'

'I've got a feeling that it's all coming together Mac,' Dan said.

Mac had exactly the same feeling.

Dan turned to face the team.

'Has anyone gotten any information on a Nicholas Moncrieff yet?' he asked.

Chris put his hand up.

'We just got this five minutes ago from a local newspaper in Scotland, the Edinburgh Evening News. An elderly reporter there remembered it because it was the first story that he'd been involved in.'

He handed a tablet to Dan who held it so Mac could read it at the same time. It was a copy of an article from just over forty-two years before.

Boy found with dead mother

Six year old Nicholas Moncrieff was found in a flat in Leith three days after his mother, 20 year old Jennie Moncrieff, had killed herself. She was a single mother and she hanged herself after suffering from depression for some years. Police found the boy cowering in a cupboard in the kitchen. They initially thought that Nicholas was a girl as he was dressed in girl's clothing, however, it was discovered he was a boy when he was later bathed at the children's home....'

'Here look at the photo,' Dan said excitedly as he handed the article to Mac.

It featured a picture of the dead mother. Jennie Moncrieff was the dead spit of Natasha and all the other girls.

'That settles it, we're going in,' Dan said. 'We don't need a warrant as we have good reason to believe that Natasha's life is at risk.'

'What about an entry team?' Mac asked.

'Well, we've got Adil's size twelve boots and I hope you've got your lock picks?'

Mac produced them for Dan.

'Then we've got our entry team.' He turned to the team and raised his voice. 'We've now got a good suspect. His name is Nicholas Moncrieff and he lives on the Ickleford Road. We have no idea how long he's likely to keep Natasha so we're going in right now. Martin, what can you tell us about the property?'

'It's a Victorian detached house, one of three that look the same. It has a side entrance and a large back garden. There's quite a good sized shed or outhouse in the garden so that might be worth having a look at. I'm afraid that there's no way you'll be able to disguise the raid like you did for the Turnells. The only way you can get to the property is from the street.'

'I'm not worried about that, Moncrieff is our man, I'm sure of it,' Dan said with conviction. 'Okay, I want everyone except Martin and Amanda in on this. Once we get access Andy, Adil and myself will go in first and detain Moncrieff and whoever else might be there. The rest will guard the other entrances. If you have to go inside the property try not to disturb anything as hopefully there'll be something from forensics to look at. Is that understood?'

'I see that the men are getting all the fun again,' Jo said as she pulled a face at Leigh.

Dan ignored her.

'I'll get some uniforms to attend the scene but they might take a little time to arrive so we're not going to wait for them. Get your stab vests on and let's get going.'

Tommy came back just as they were about to leave. He'd not found out any more about the mysterious Nicky.

Mac got a lift with Dan, Tommy and Adil. It took less than two minutes for them to reach the house on the Ickleford Road.

So close, Mac thought.

The house itself was strange, being one of three detached properties, whereas most of the street was made up of terraced or semi-detached buildings. They were all rendered a grey colour and Mac couldn't help thinking that they looked like giant tombstones. The Moncrieff house was the middle one of the three. The tarmac in the parking area in the front of the house looked like it had been re-laid fairly recently.

'Tommy, Chris and Martina guard the back door just in case he's in and he decides to make a run for it,' Dan said. 'And keep it as quiet as you can. If he knows we're here then he might decide to kill Natasha anyway.'

The side gate was locked so Tommy quietly clambered over and unlocked it from the other side.

While this was going on Mac had a look at the front door. It was new, a security door with multiple locking points.

'Any chance you can open it?' Dan asked softly.

Mac shook his head.

'I'm afraid that it will take even more than Adil's size twelves to open that,' Mac said. 'Shall we try the back door? We might have more luck there.'

'Come on Jo, slight change of plans. You can come with us,' Dan said.

Jo smiled broadly, 'Yes, that's one for the sisters!'

Dan walked quickly around to the back of the house and asked Tommy, Chris and Martina to join Leigh in guarding the front door.

The brick-built garden shed immediately caught Mac's attention as he walked into the back garden. It had a big padlock holding the door shut but Mac was confident he could open it.

'Shall we have a look in here first?' he suggested.

The lock was fairly new and so was relatively easy to open. The team held their breath while Mac opened the door but all the shed contained was various bits of gardening equipment. Mac then turned his attention to the back door.

He smiled. It was an older wooden door with a single standard five lever mortice deadlock. Mac was sure that it wouldn't pose any problem. It took him less than two minutes to unlock. The door still wouldn't open though. Mac pushed on the top of the door, which went in quite a bit, and then on the bottom which went in a lot less.

'There's a bolt holding the door shut. It's just about here I'd guess,' Mac said pointing to an area of the door about two inches below the deadlock.

Dan turned to Adil, 'It looks like you'll be needed after all.' He then turned to Mac. 'Mac can you wait here with Jo? If there's any rough stuff Adil can handle it, he's used to it being a rugby player.'

'Sure,' he replied looking slightly disappointed.

Adil set himself and then kicked out hard with the sole of his right foot flat against the door. It sprang open with such force that it rebounded almost all the way back.

Adil led the charge inside followed by Dan and Andy.

'And here was me thinking that I was going to be part of an entry team after all these years,' Jo said looking just as disappointed as Mac had been.

They looked at each other and laughed.

In less than two minutes Dan returned.

'It's clear, there's no-one in there. There's no Natasha either unfortunately,' he told them with obvious disappointment. 'Want to have a look around?'

'Sure, but Dan you go ahead, I'll follow if you don't mind,' Mac replied.

'Is the back playing you up?' Dan asked with some concern.

'It's fine, I'm just feeling a bit slow today that's all.'

Dan took him at his word and went ahead. Mac slowly followed. In truth he always preferred to be alone when he was examining a potential crime scene. He found he could concentrate better that way.

The sink was just under the kitchen window. On the draining board there was a single cup and a single plate. In the cutlery holder there was a single knife and a teaspoon. He took a tissue out of his pocket and looked in the wall cupboards, most of them were empty. One cupboard had a few cans of beans and peas and a single package of corn flakes on one side and on the other it held just a single large plate and a cereal bowl. The small fridge had some butter, an opened packet of sliced cheese, a half-used pint bottle of milk and a carton of orange juice. The even smaller freezer was chock full of frozen ready meals and bread. The bread was in several sandwich bags that contained just two slices each.

Mac was immediately puzzled. From what he'd just seen it was obvious that it was a single person who lived here and not a couple. He moved on into the living room.

A fairly new two-seater sofa faced a large flat screen TV. In front of the sofa on the right-hand side there was a small foldable table. Whoever lived here must eat their meals watching the TV, Mac guessed. He looked closely at the sofa. It looked like the seat cushions had only been used on the side where the table was. Again, it pointed to the house only having a single occupant.

He looked around the room and felt its strangeness seep into him. There was something very, very wrong here, Mac thought, but he wasn't quite sure why. The only piece of furniture besides the sofa was a single cabinet that was against the wall in the far corner of the room. Why there? Mac immediately thought. It would surely be more convenient in the other corner.

The décor puzzled him too. Three walls of the room were a cream colour while the fourth, the one on the left of the room as he walked in, was painted black. The floor was also covered in large square black carpet tiles. The impression of something being way off kilter hit him even harder.

He let Adil, Andy and Dan come down the stairs before he went up.

'Anything?' he asked hopefully as they passed by.

Dan shook his head. He didn't look happy.

Mac slowly went up the steps. He looked into the room on the right first. Inside there was a single bed, a small chest of drawers, a side table and a wardrobe. He opened the wardrobe. It contained men's clothes and, from the style, he guessed the owner was in his forties. He looked at the size labels. A thirty-two waist with a thirty-two inch leg. So, he wasn't all that tall then but definitely a lot slimmer than he was himself. Mac guessed that the last time he'd worn a thirty-two waist was when he'd been a teenager.

He looked in the bathroom but this did nothing to reduce his puzzlement. It was a couple's bathroom, men's aftershave and shaving foam, a pink woman's razor, scented shower gel and a bottle of handwash with little flowers on. There was only one toothbrush though.

The second bedroom was the strangest of all. It held a single bed, a new single bed. Mac knew it was new because the mattress was still in the plastic wrapping. There were no pillows, duvet or sheets in evidence. Obviously, no-one slept in this room. He opened the wardrobe. It was full of women's clothes, neatly arranged in sets. On the floor of the wardrobe were several sets of medium heeled court shoes in different colours.

Mac sat on the bed and tried to think it through. He quickly came to the conclusion that this house was schizophrenic, some things implying a couple lived here while other evidence clearly showed single occupancy.

For some reason the living room was the one that he found most disquieting. But why?

Mac sat there for a few minutes before making his way carefully back down the stairs. The door to the living room was open and he stepped inside. The blackness of the wall was trying to tell him something but what?

He stood there and tried not to think at all.

She heard some muffled noises from upstairs and she knew that it had to be now or never. It had taken her a while to summon up the courage but, as she went about arranging her escape, she now felt icy cold inside.

She smiled at the thought that she might be taking his little toy away from him. She would have loved to see his face when he found that she was gone.

She located the bucket and emptied it into the corner where she normally sat. She then turned it upside down and stood on it. Her hand raised up as she felt along the ceiling beam.

There it was!

She held the chain taut and then placed a link over the head of the nail. It was only sticking out a quarter of an inch or so but she felt that would be enough to securely hold the chain. She stood teetering on the bucket.

I love you mum, she thought, and then kicked the bucket away.

Her feet hit the floor. She had allowed too much slack in the chain and she'd have to try again. She felt around and located the bucket and located the nail once again. She measured the chain more carefully this time and placed a link over the nail. She didn't pray or think this time but kicked the bucket immediately away.

Her feet dangled in mid-air and she could feel the collar biting into her windpipe.

It won't be long now, she thought.

She managed to picture her mother in her mind before the blackness descended.

Chapter Twenty Three

Dan stood outside looking at the house. He'd ordered a forensics team but, in truth, he was worried. Had they got it wrong again?

Adil knew that expression well and he knew it was highly likely that his boss would explode at any minute.

Dan looked around for something to kick and, seeing nothing nearby, let off a loud volley of expletives instead. He felt better when he'd finished and, after he'd calmed down a bit, a thought occurred to him.

'Where's this bloody cellar then? Martin said there was a cellar but there's no sign of it in there.' He turned to Andy and Chris. 'Go and interview the neighbour on that side and ask if they know anything about Moncrieff and check to see if they've got a cellar. Adil and I will take the neighbour on the other side.'

Dan walked towards the house next door noting that it had a grating in front of the bow window. Where there's a coal-hole there's a cellar, he thought.

The neighbour proved to be a man in his mid-seventies named Albert Halsall who had lived there all his life. He showed them where the door to the cellar was and confirmed that all three houses had a cellar as they'd been built to the same plans.

'What can you tell us about Mr. Moncrieff?' Dan asked.

Mr. Halsall shrugged.

'Not much, I only ever see them as they walk by. They only ever say hello, they never seem to have a minute spare to pass the time of day with you.'

'They? Who are they?' Dan asked.

'Why, Mr. Moncrieff and his sister. I see him in the morning going to work but I've only ever seen her at night when she goes out. She's always by herself too.'

'Do you have any idea where he might be now?'

'At church I'd guess,' Mr. Halsall replied. 'He always goes out every Sunday morning at ten thirty and comes back a couple of hours later. A friend of mine said she's seen him at the Catholic Church in Nightingale Road. She's seen him at the sung mass at five in the evening too, very religious man apparently. Obviously, his sister doesn't take after him though.'

After thanking Mr. Halsall Dan compared notes with Andy and Chris. The neighbours on the other side, a young couple with two kids, knew even less than Mr. Halsall, in fact they didn't even know their neighbour's name. They too had a cellar but they'd had it blocked off as they were never going to use it.

'Okay, so we know there's a cellar but has Moncrieff blocked it off too or has he done something else?' Dan looked around. 'Where's Mac?' he asked.

'He's still inside I think,' Andy replied.

Dan gave it some thought.

'Okay, the cat's well and truly out of the bag now. Andy take Adil and Chris and get up to the Catholic Church on Nightingale Road. Pick up Moncrieff and we'll see what he knows. I'll wait here for forensics to turn up.'

Dan stood there just looking at the house. If only there was something he could do…

Mac stood looking at the black wall in the living room. Think logically, he said to himself. Why is it black? Of course, Moncrieff might just like the colour but Mac doubted it. So why black?

The only reason he could think of was that it would easily disguise any marks. Then it came to him!

The reason for using the carpet tiles became clear too. Mac used the end of his crutch to try and move the tiles that ran next to the black wall but he had no success until he came to the last tile, the tile in the corner. It only moved a fraction of an inch but it moved. It was stiff, the carpet appeared to be glued to a thin piece of wood. Mac

238

got down on his knees and tried to manipulate the piece of wood, eventually managing to slide it and the tile out of place. Below the tile he could see the floorboards. He could also see a line where five of the floorboards had been cut across. He put his fingers into a gap and pulled the boards out in one piece, they had been glued together. Below he could see a metal ladder strapped to the cellar wall and a light switch on the right-hand side.

He was about to go and let Dan know what he'd found when he heard a sound, a sound he'd only heard once before in his life. He knew instantly what it was and he reacted as quickly as he could. He leant against the black wall, black so that no hand marks would show, and stepped down onto the ladder. Once he was down far enough, he switched on the light and, putting his feet either side of the ladder, slid down the rest of the way into the cellar. The jolt at the end sent a wave of pain radiating outwards from the base of his spine but Mac ignored it. His whole mind was concentrated on one thing only.

Natasha.

She was dangling from a ceiling beam with her feet no more than six inches off the floor. Her legs were still twitching so Mac prayed that he wasn't too late. He ran over and grabbed her legs and sat her on one shoulder. He then stood up so that the chain was slack. The only problem was that he found it hard to keep her erect as she kept flopping over and he had to keep changing position.

'Natasha, Natasha wake up!' he shouted.

She didn't respond. Mac knew that she was either unconscious or dead. He prayed that it was the first.

The extra weight and the sudden movements caused an intense grinding pain in his lower back. He somehow managed to keep any thought of it at bay and shouted as loud as he could.

'Dan, help, help! Someone please help!'

Natasha nearly slipped from his shoulder and he had to quickly readjust again. The sudden movement made it feel as though his spine was collapsing and he knew he would only be able to keep her in this position for a few seconds longer. She flopped to one side again and Mac had to change position once more. Unbearable pain flared up but he somehow managed to stop himself from blacking out.

'Help, help!' he shouted desperately.

He was nearly spent. His head was buzzing and he could feel the blackness hovering but he pushed it away and got the best grip he could on Natasha.

'I won't let you die, I bloody well won't!' he shouted.

He said a little prayer. If God would let her live then he could give Mac all the pain in the world, if he would just let her live.

Dan stood looking at the house and finally decided that he might as well see what Mac was doing. He went and looked at where the door to the cellar should be. There was just a blank wall. He didn't hear anything until he opened up the living room door. Then he heard it clearly enough and at the same time saw the gap in the floorboards.

'Dan, help, help!'

Mac sounded desperate. Dan swarmed down the ladder and saw a white-faced Mac trying to hold a naked girl on one shoulder. It was Natasha!

'The chain,' Mac managed to get out.

His bulging eyes pointed beseechingly towards the ceiling beam.

Dan ran around and saw that the chain had been looped over a nail. He looked around and picked up the bucket. He positioned it below the nail and stood on it. He couldn't release the chain though, it was too taut.

'Come a little closer, Mac,' Dan pleaded.

He did his best but it took the last of his strength.

As soon as he had enough slack Dan released the chain.

'It's free Mac, it's free!' he shouted.

Mac quickly checked which wall the chain was attached to then let Natasha slide down so that he held her under both arms. There was nothing left he could do. He fell in the direction of the wall so that the chain wouldn't jerk Natasha's neck. It seemed to take an age before he felt the impact. He fell so that Natasha was on top of him and so his body would cushion her fall.

He tried to hit the floor keeping his body as flat as possible but even so a tsunami of pain immediately followed the impact. He somehow kept it at arm's length. He rolled Natasha gently onto the floor, lay back and waited.

Dan bent over Natasha and felt for a pulse.

'She's alive Mac, she's alive!'

He could do no more. The pain suddenly hit him like an eighty-ton truck and he heard someone screaming in the distance. A pool of blackness appeared and he gratefully dived in. He let himself fall deep into its inky depths, falling further and further away from the storm of pain that raged on the surface. He fell so far into the blackness that he didn't know who or what he was.

Here in the blackness there was no remembrance and therefore no pain.

Chapter Twenty Four

There was nothing but the blackness. No thoughts, no feelings, nothing.

Yet eventually, there was something. The blackness overhead wasn't as black as it had been and very gradually it turned to a dark grey. It felt as though he was bobbing upwards and then falling back again but never falling back quite as far as he'd gone upwards. And so very gradually the dark grey became a lighter grey and then it got lighter still.

He got so close that he was sure he was going to break through into the light when he fell back again. The next time he knew he would do it. He went upwards and upwards and then...

There was light of a sort. It was reddish and indistinct. It took him a while to realise that he was looking at the inside of his own eyelids. He struggled to open them but they seemed to be gummed together. At last they flew open and there was light, real light. Light so bright that he had to immediately shut his eyes again. When he opened them again the light had been dimmed. Someone had...had what? He had no words for it.

Shapes moved around but they were blurred and he had no idea what he was looking at. They moved in complete silence and then it was as if someone had suddenly turned the sound up on a remote control.

'Dad? Dad are you okay?' a shape asked.

He couldn't answer. He didn't know if he was okay or not. He squinted and the shape came into focus. He knew that this shape had a name. What was it? Then it came to him.

'Bridget?' he said weakly.

'Oh dad!' his daughter exclaimed.

He could see tears on her cheeks. Another shape moved behind her.

'Tim,' he said.

'Old friend, you've been away for quite a while.'

He could see the concern etched on both their faces.

'How long?' he croaked.

'Five days,' Bridget replied. 'You've been under sedation for five days.'

He was surprised. It felt as though it he'd been away a lot longer. A memory came back to him, a girl hanging from a chain. He couldn't remember her name.

'How is she?' he asked.

'She's okay dad, Natasha's okay. She's hurt her neck but it's nothing serious.'

'She's okay.'

He let the words sink in and then sleep overtook him again.

It was real sleep this time and, when Mac woke up, he found he didn't have to search for the words any more.

He was in a hospital room and the curtains were drawn. There was some light outside so it must either be evening or early in the morning. As he could see Tim fast asleep in a chair, he guessed that it was morning. The door opened and Bridget walked in clutching two cups of coffee. Mac was suddenly aware that he was thirsty, thirstier than he could ever remember being.

'Water,' he croaked.

'Oh, dad you're awake at last. Here,' she said picking up a plastic container that had a lid and a spout.

Mac thought that it looked like something that you'd use for a baby but he didn't care. He gratefully sucked the water down and it was like rain on a parched desert.

'How are you feeling?' she asked after he'd emptied half the container.

'I'm not sure, a bit strange,' he said.

'How's the pain?'

Mac hadn't noticed the pain. He looked for it and it was there but it didn't seem too bad. Then he tried to move into a more comfortable position and it suddenly flared up. He groaned out loud.

'Oh dad, I'm so sorry,' Bridget said.

The sound woke Tim up.

'Are you okay, Mac?' he asked in a worried voice.

He couldn't answer for a moment and he had to wait for a moment for the pain to subside.

'I'm sorry I wasn't expecting that,' he said. 'Could I have some more water?'

After another drink his throat felt lubricated enough for him to be able to talk.

'Is Natasha still okay?' he asked.

'Yes, she's fine, well at least physically,' Bridget replied. 'She's in a room downstairs. They want to keep her in for a while to make sure she's okay.'

'Did he hurt her much?' Mac asked.

'Yes, I think he did,' Bridget replied with a frown. 'I'd guess it'll take a while for her to get over it.'

'Did they get him, Moncrieff?'

'They arrested him in the church,' Tim replied. 'He's confessed to all the murders.'

'And his sister?' Mac asked.

'His sister?' Tim gave Bridget a strange look before replying. 'I'll let Dan Carter tell you all about her. He asked us to ring him as soon as you woke up. Oh here, I've saved something for you.'

Tim rummaged around in a plastic bag and pulled out a tabloid newspaper. He held it so Mac could see the front page.

'What do you think of this then?' he said with a wide grin.

The paper had a picture of Natasha and one of a much younger Mac. The headline shouted 'Hero Ex-Cop Saves Kidnap Girl'.

Mac shook his head. He never liked the 'hero cop' tag. On the TV the main character is usually a loner who solves the case without any help from anyone. That was never the way it happened in his experience. He thought over what had happened and how every member of the team had contributed something towards saving Natasha.

'I'm no hero,' Mac stated.

'You're my hero,' Bridget said as she held his hand.

This made Mac smile. He suddenly felt tired and sleep overtook him again.

When he awoke the light was brighter. A man in a white doctor's coat was taking his pulse.

'Ah, awake at last. I'm Dr. Patel. How are you feeling?'

Mac tried to sit up and the pain hit him again. His answer was a loud groan.

'I'm afraid that your pain levels will be very high for a while. Fortunately, you've not done too much damage to your spine, which is a bit of a miracle considering what you've been up to, but there are a lot of soft tissue injuries.'

'What does that mean?' Mac asked.

'Well, with soft tissue damage there are some well-defined phases,' the doctor replied. 'You've more or less gone through the inflammatory phase which is the most painful. That's why we took the decision to keep you sedated, that plus the fact that we needed to get you into an MRI scanner just to be sure. The next phase, the repair phase if you like, will take around six weeks or so. I'd like to keep you fairly immobile for this time so we'll be keeping you in, not that you'd be able to do much anyway.'

Six weeks in hospital! Even the thought of it instantly depressed Mac. The longest he'd ever spent in hospital was three days while they were doing tests and that nearly sent him mad.

'So, after six weeks I'll be okay?' he asked hopefully looking for a silver lining.

The doctor and Bridget exchanged looks. Mac knew from the looks that he wouldn't be okay.

'What is it?' he asked.

'Well, there's a third phase, the remodelling phase, which will probably last about a year or so. Pain levels should return to normal after that time,' the doctor said with a sympathetic look.

It took a few seconds for what he said to sink in. Back to normal after a year?

'You mean that I'll be in even more pain that I was and for a whole year?'

'I'm afraid that's exactly the case,' the doctor said.

Mac suddenly felt even more depressed. He then remembered when he was holding up Natasha and asking God for his help. He said that God could give him all the pain in the world if he would just let Natasha live. He hadn't expected God to take it so literally. The thought of the Fentanyl patches he'd squirrelled away in his sock drawer popped into his head. It had been a struggle managing his pain as it was, he just didn't know if he could cope with even more.

'Don't worry Mr. Maguire, there are things we can do to help you,' the doctor said before he took his leave.

Mac didn't ask what. He knew from experience that 'the things' usually involved more drugs. He'd be able manage the pain alright but he'd also lose the ability to think rationally. He'd always tried to avoid going down that route. The thought of losing the only thing he really valued about himself was truly scary.

'There's someone who's waiting to see you,' Bridget said. 'Is it okay if they come in?'

Mac nodded. He expected it would be Dan.

It wasn't Dan. It was Natasha.

She was in a hospital wheelchair and Jonny Aldis was doing the pushing. She looked pale and had a neck support on. She noticed Mac looking at the wheel chair.

'It's okay, I can walk it's just that they prefer me using the wheel chair when I move around the hospital. How are you, Mr. Maguire?'

'Seeing you has made me feel much better,' he replied with a smile.

And it was only the truth.

'More importantly, how are you?' he asked.

She hesitated before answering which was an answer in itself.

'I'm... okay I suppose.'

'I'm afraid that it might take you some time to get over this but you will get over this.'

'Will I?' Natasha asked obviously unconvinced.

Jonny moved to her side and took her hand in his. She looked up at him and tried to smile. It was clear that they had become very close.

'It may seem hard to believe right now but you will,' Mac said. 'It may never go away but you will learn to live with it.'

'How can you be so sure?' Natasha asked.

It was a good question and one that made Mac think.

'Yes, it's an easy thing to say, isn't it? What you need to do is talk to someone who's been through something as traumatic as you've been through. And I know just the person.'

'You do?' she asked with a hopeful look.

'She was involved in a case of mine many years ago and she went through some terrible things,' Mac said. 'She'll tell you all about it herself but believe me she has been there and bought the T shirt.'

'And how is she now?' Natasha said.

She leant forward, waiting with obvious trepidation for what Mac was going to say.

'She's married with two wonderful children. She and her husband run their own business and they're making a great success of their lives.'

'She's happy?'

'Yes, she has her bad times too but yes, I think she's happy.'

Natasha smiled a real smile and her body relaxed a little.

'Bridget can you get me my phone?' Mac asked.

He looked up the number and gave it to Natasha.

'Her name's Pauline Dempsey and she's a trained counsellor too. I know that she'll be glad to hear from you.'

'Thank you, Mr. Maguire, you've really helped,' Natasha said. 'I hope you get better soon and thanks, thanks for everything.'

'Oh, and don't forget to thank this young man here too,' Mac said as he pointed at Jonny. 'If it hadn't been for him being so persistent, we'd have never found you at all.'

She looked up at Jonny with a look of real love on her face.

'Don't worry Mr. Maguire, I'll be thanking him for quite some time to come I hope.'

Jonny returned the look with interest.

He watched them as they left. Natasha and Jonny looked so right together. They would have a life together now, one that seemed very improbable not too long ago. They would make a mark on the world by creating designs and drawings and perhaps even children too. All of a sudden, the price of a year's worth of extra pain didn't seem so high.

Mac smiled. He'd just discovered how he was going to cope with the pain.

Chapter Twenty Five

Dan and Tommy showed up a couple of hours later.

'Well, you're looking better than the last time I saw you,' Dan said.

'I don't suppose that would be very hard though, would it?' Mac replied. 'I vaguely remember someone screaming. Was that me?'

'Yes, you went unconscious pretty much straight away afterwards which, from the sounds you were making, was probably the best thing.'

'What happened after I blacked out?'

'Well, it was a bit of a challenge,' Dan replied, 'but the paramedics finally got you and Natasha out by strapping you to stretchers and pulling you out on ropes.'

'We had to give them a hand,' Tommy said.

'And Moncrieff?' Mac asked.

'Luckily, I sent Andy, Chris and Adil to pick him up at the church just before you found Natasha.'

'No problems?' Mac asked.

'No, none at all,' Dan replied. 'He came peacefully but, then again, he wasn't going to run away. He uses a crutch just like you do, spinal damage from when he was a kid the doctors say. He has trouble walking.'

'So that's why he had the Fentanyl then. I heard that he confessed. Is that true?'

'Yes, he's confessed to killing all the girls. He said that God told him to do it and then blamed his sister saying that he would never have hurt anyone if she hadn't brought him the girls. In other words, everyone was really to blame except himself.'

'His sister? Just where does she fit in?' Mac asked.

'Now we're getting to the seriously weird bit,' Dan said. 'Here you might understand better if I show you this first.'

Dan produced a tablet and started up a video.

'It's part of an interview with Moncrieff and the forensic psychologist,' Dan explained.

The camera was focussed on Moncreiff who was sitting at a table. He was a slim man with fine thinning fair hair. His face was bland and featureless and he wore glasses. The psychologist was a disembodied voice.

'So, you're saying that it was all really Nicola's fault?' the psychologist asked.

Moncrieff nodded.

'I would never have done anything if she hadn't brought the girls home in the first place. I never asked her to and I honestly had nothing to do with it, she did that totally by herself. However, once they were there, I just couldn't help myself. She knew what would happen too.'

He spoke softly and with just a touch of a Scottish accent.

'So, why do you think she brought them home then?'

Moncrieff shrugged.

'I don't know, as I said I never asked her to.'

'Why don't we ask her then?' the psychologist said. 'Nicola, what have you got to say?'

Moncreiff stood up and looked down at the seat he'd just been occupying with a hurt expression. Something had happened to him, it was subtle but very real. He held his body very erect, his chest a little outwards. His face actually changed shape, became harder and more defined.

'He's blaming me now and that's not fair. He never said it in words but I could feel his need,' he said in a woman's voice. It was deep but definitely a woman's voice. 'After a couple of years, he would get twitchy and I knew that it would take a girl to calm him down. I rely totally on him, he's the only one earning and he's got a job that needs all his concentration. So, I'd get him a girl every now and then, it was easy and there are lots of them around. You'd honestly think that no-one would miss the odd one here or there. Anyway, he killed them not me. All I did was bring them in, what he did with them was his business. I never asked.'

'And did you take away the bodies?' the psychologist asked.

Nicola took a few steps away and then back again while she thought. She walked easily and with an erect posture.

'Of course, but only at first. After that girl was found we had to come up with something else.'

'Two years is a long time. What did your brother do for sex in between the girls?'

Nicola looked down with some love at the vacant chair.

'He always had me and I knew just what he liked. It kept him going but of course I knew it would never be enough and then I'd have to go and get another girl for him to play with. But that's just the way it is I suppose,' she said with a small smile.

Dan stopped the video.

'Good God! Was Moncrieff really both the brother and the sister then?' Mac asked.

'That's what the psychologist is saying. Barmy as they come. Gender confusion on a massive scale he called it. His mother had always wanted a girl, so being a fruitcake herself, when she had a boy, she just dressed him up as a girl and called him Nicola. Then, when he started to be treated as a boy in the children's home, Nicola became his imaginary friend, one who unfort-unately never went away.'

'And one who gave him permission to do terrible things,' Mac said.

'That's exactly how the psychologist put it,' Dan said. 'He said that Moncrieff as himself would never have been able, either physically or psychologically, to kidnap the girls. His back wouldn't have allowed it and the psychologist felt that he wouldn't have had the nerve anyway. His sister on the other hand certainly did. So, she contributed by, not only kidnapping the girls, but consenting to what was to happen to them afterwards.'

'That explains so much. How he could get so close to the girls, watch their every move without any suspicion. It explains the house too.'

Mac suddenly remembered the shoes in the wardrobe. They only had medium heels but Mac couldn't even imagine himself wearing anything like that. It would throw his back out straight away.

'But how could he do it with his back being the way it is? You know wear heels and walk without a crutch? And how did he manage to get all that work done in the cellar? He couldn't have done it himself.'

'Well, the psychologist said that the answer was simple, Nicola doesn't have a bad back,' Dan replied. 'While he was Nicola, he simply didn't feel any pain. He thought that Moncrieff might also have been using Nicola as a sort of pain relief.'

'A very extreme way of doing it though,' Mac said.

Mac wondered if he would dress up as a woman if it would relieve all his pain. He decided that he probably wouldn't but he had to admit that he'd definitely think about it for a while first.

'I'd have to agree there,' Dan said. 'As for the house Nicola got one lot of builders up from Kent to sound-proof the cellar. She said that her husband wanted to use it for a recording studio. Then she got another lot of builders from Peterborough to block off access to the cellar and re-lay the drive so the entrance to the coal-hole would disappear. All they had to do then was saw through the floorboards so they could access the cellar.'

'That's very clever. So, I take it from what you've said that that he's most likely to end up in a secure hospital?'

'Odds on the psychologist said,' Dan replied. 'He's rubbing his hands together though. He reckons that there's a book in this for him.'

'It's such a strange case that I wouldn't be at all surprised,' Mac said. 'By the way what was the 'other way' that they found to get rid of the bodies?'

Mac was surprised that he'd actually said 'they'.

'Well, he just had a big truck come along and fill up the cellar with a couple of feet of cement. Damp proofing or so he claimed.'

'So, I take it that they're already tearing up the cellar floors at his previous addresses?'

Dan nodded.

'They've found two bodies already and they've been able to identify them from their DNA. The families are really grateful, they can hold a proper funeral at last.'

Mac had been involved in returning bodies before and he knew how important it was to the victims' families. It gave real closure.

'Talking of bodies, we also found out about that body we found in the field,' Dan said.

'Was it a murder?' Mac asked.

'No far from it, more like a very cheap funeral really. The team we passed it over to found out who was behind it quite quickly when they started interviewing people in the houses overlooking the burial site. A man in his mid-twenties told them it was the body of his old next-door neighbour. She'd had a heart problem and made her husband promise that, when she died, he'd bury her in the field opposite their house. So, she could keep an eye on him, she said.'

'How did the neighbour know all that?'

'Apparently, he helped the husband to bury the body,' Dan replied. 'He was only fourteen at the time and was apparently very close to the old couple. He also said he was glad that we'd found the body as her husband had died just a few months ago and he'd been buried at Icknield Way Cemetery. Now they could be together again.'

Mac shook his head.

'No matter how many times you've been around the block the things people do will always surprise you.'

'I heard that you saw Natasha, is that right?' Dan asked.

'Yes, and Jonny Aldis was in attendance too. They look a real couple now.'

'How was she?'

'Worried about how she was feeling I think,' Mac replied, 'but I put her in contact with someone who should be able to help her with that.'

He suddenly felt a little sleepy and yawned. Dan stood up.

'Well, I can see you're tired so I won't keep you. I'll pop in later on this week and see how you're doing. Thanks again,' Dan said as he offered Mac his hand. 'We couldn't have done it without you.'

'And you couldn't have done it without Jo and Gerry who found Jonny Aldis and Martin who remembered that crucial fact about the house sale and yourself for getting Jonny to do the drawing and then acting so quickly on it. Even those on the team who were only able to rule out possible leads did a vital job. It was a real team effort, Dan,' Mac said with some feeling. 'The team is the reason that Natasha's alive today.'

'Thankfully that's what my bosses seem to think too, although I believe that not all of them were in favour of the team in the first place.'

'Well I'll bet they are now. Anyway, don't forget me if you anything else comes up. I know I'm an old crock now but I'll be better before long,' Mac said hopefully.

'Don't you worry about that,' Dan replied.

They shook hands firmly.

Tommy waited behind after Dan had left.

'How are you doing Tommy?'

'Great, well really great actually. I was just wondering if Bridget's told you yet?'

'Told me what?' Mac asked.

'The flat, we've got it!' he said with a big smile.

'Now that's good news indeed.'

Mac and Tommy shook hands. It was great news indeed to Mac. Knowing that his daughter would be living only a short distance away cheered him up even more.

Tommy was about to go when Bridget joined them.

'I told him about the flat,' Tommy said.

'God, I'd almost forgotten all about that. It'll be a few weeks before we can move in though. I can't wait,' she said as she smiled in Tommy's direction. 'Plus, I've got some other good news.'

'What's that?'

'You won't need to stay in hospital for six weeks.'

'Really? How did you wangle that?' Mac asked.

'Us doctors stick together you know. Anyway, Dr. Patel has agreed to you going home in a couple of days so long as you promise to strictly follow his orders and so long as I get a qualified nurse to look after you. I've got a good one lined up too. Nurse Amrit used to be a senior nurse on one of the wards where I did my training. She's recently retired but she's willing to help out until you're back on your feet. Not only that but she's been trained as a specialist pain nurse as well. She could really help you dad.'

Mac smiled broadly. The thought of escaping six weeks in hospital felt like being acquitted from a long prison sentence.

Suddenly life didn't look so bad after all.

Chapter Twenty Six

A couple of days afterwards two very nice paramedics transported Mac back home and deposited him gently in his bed. It was a real comfort to him to be back in his own house and with his own things all around him.

His nurse was a woman in her mid-fifties with jet black hair who was wearing a brightly coloured sari and sandals. She had a kind face, a face that Mac immediately warmed to.

The thing that really scared Mac wasn't the pain as such but how he was going to fill the yawning six week stretch that lay before him. Boredom was the enemy now and he'd decided to attack it all fronts.

Bridget had bought him some books that he'd wanted to read for a while but had somehow never found the time. She'd also bought him a special tray that would hold a book at forty-five degrees so he could read it easily while lying down. She said it would also be good for holding his laptop if he wanted to use it. She'd hinted that now was perhaps a good time to start writing down some of his experiences as a policeman. He also had his tablet to hand so that he could access the internet and keep up with all the latest news and sport.

So why was it then that less than two hours later he found himself staring up at the ceiling and feeling bored rigid? He picked up his tablet and looked at the news again. It hadn't changed in the last three minutes.

In desperation he picked up his phone and called Dan Carter.

'Mac, how's it going now that you're home?' Dan asked.

'It's better than the hospital that's for sure but I'm still bored stiff and on the edge of going doolally. You've got to help me Dan,' Mac pleaded.

'You must have been reading my mind. My bosses, as they now recognise that we're such a superior team, have just lumped a ton of cold cases on us just in case we run out of things to do. I was thinking of putting Jo and Leigh on them as we're a bit quiet at the moment but I haven't asked them as yet. Do you want to have a shot at them yourself?'

'Absolutely! When can you get them over to me?'

'I'll send someone over with them now,' Dan replied. 'Take care of yourself Mac and let me know when you're up and about. Oh, and if you do think of any new leads for any of the cases let me know straight away and I'll get Jo and Leigh to follow them up.'

Half an hour later a uniformed policeman delivered a memory stick. Nurse Amrit brought it to Mac who gratefully took it from her and inserted it into his laptop.

He counted the files, there were twenty-three in all. Mac looked over the titles and almost salivated. For him it was like opening the most sumptuous box of chocolates and being unable to make up your mind which of the wonderful treats inside you should try first.

The binman who was run over? The university lecturer who was robbed and presumed murdered? The young girl murdered in what looked like an 'honour' killing?

He smiled broadly and dived in.

Nurse Amrit didn't want to interrupt but she began to get a little worried when she hadn't heard anything for well over an hour and a half. She gently opened the door a couple of inches and peeped inside. She could see that her patient was fine and obviously deeply engrossed in whatever was on the memory stick.

Bridget had warned her that her father might be a bit difficult and grumpy at being confined to his own bed but now the nurse wondered about that.

He was absolutely no trouble at all.

THE END

I hope you enjoyed this story. If you have then
please leave a review and let me know what you think.
PCW

Also in the Mac Maguire series

The Body in the Boot

The Dead Squirrel

The Weeping Women

23 Cold Cases

Two Dogs

The Match of the Day Murders

The Chancer

The Tiger's Back

The Eight Bench Walk

You can find out more about me and my books by
visiting my website –
https://patrickcwalshauthor.wordpress.com/

Made in the USA
Monee, IL
15 October 2020

45248335R00156